PRAISE FOR

For

"Sick, depraved, and heartbreaking—in other words, a great read, a great book. *Suicide Casanova* is erotic noir and Nersesian's hard-boiled prose comes at you like a jailhouse confession."
—Jonathan Ames, author of *Wake Up, Sir!*

"Nersesian has written a scathingly original page-turner, hilarious, tragic, and shocking—this may be his most brilliant novel yet."
—Kate Christensen, author of *In the Drink*

". . . tight, gripping, erotic thriller . . ." —*Philadelphia City Paper*

"Sleek, funny, and sometimes sickening . . . a porn nostalgia novel, if you will, a weepy nod to the sleaze pond that Times Square once was."
—*Memphis Flyer*

"A vivid, compelling psychothriller, *Suicide Casanova* confirms Nersesian's place as one of New York City's most important chroniclers. His unique psychological vision of the city rates with those of Paul Auster and Madison Smartt Bell." —Blake Nelson, author of *Girl* and *User*

"Every budding author should read this book. Stop your creative writing class on the technique of Hemingway and study the elegant gritty prose of Nersesian. Stop your literary theory class on Faulkner and read the next generation of literary genius." —*Cherry Bleeds*

"This is no traditional Romeo & Juliet love story. It is like no love story I've ever read, which is why it reads fast, deep, and intense . . . A great story by a talented writer." —*New Mystery Reviews*

For *The Fuck-Up*

"The charm and grit of Nersesian's voice is immediately enveloping, as the down-and-out but oddly up narrator of his terrific novel, *The Fuck-Up*, slinks through Alphabet City and guttural utterances of love."
—*Village Voice*

"Nersesian creates a charming everyman whose candor and sure-footed description of his physical surroundings and emotional framework help his tale flow naturally and therefore believably." —*Paper*

"For those who remember that the eighties were as much about destitute grit as they were about the decadent glitz described in the novels of Bret Easton Ellis and Jay McInerney, this book will come as a fast-paced reminder." —*Time Out New York*

"*The Fuck-Up* is *Trainspotting* without drugs, New York style."
—Hal Sirowitz, author of *Mother Said*

"Fantastically alluring! I cannot recommend this book highly enough!"
—*Flipside*

"Combining moments of brilliant black humor with flashes of devastating pain, it reads like a roller coaster ride . . . A wonderful book."
—*Alternative Press*

"Touted as the bottled essence of early eighties East Village living, *The Fuck-Up* is, refreshingly, nothing nearly so limited . . . A cult favorite since its first, obscure printing in 1991, I'd say it's ready to become a legitimate religion." —*Smug Magazine*

"Not since *The Catcher in the Rye,* or John Knowles's *A Separate Peace,* have I read such a beautifully written book . . . Nersesian's powerful, sure-footed narrative alone is so believably human in its poignancy . . . I couldn't put this book down." —*Grid Magazine*

For *Manhattan Loverboy*

"Best Book for the Beach, Summer 2000." —*Jane Magazine*

"Best Indie Novel of 2000." —*Montreal Mirror*

"Part Lewis Carroll, part Franz Kafka, Nersesian leads us down a maze of false leads and dead ends . . . told with wit and compassion, drawing the reader into a world of paranoia and coincidence while illuminating questions of free will and destiny. Highly recommended."
—*Library Journal*

"A tawdry and fantastic tale . . . Nersesian renders Gotham's unique cocktail of wealth, poverty, crime, glamour, and brutality spectacularly. This book is full of lies, and the author makes deception seem like the subtext of modern life, or at least America's real pastime . . . Love, hate, and falsehood commingle. But in the end, it is [protagonist] Joey's search for his own identity that makes this book a winner." —*Rain Taxi Review of Books*

"Funny and darkly surreal." —*New York Press*

"... a hilarious and warped passion play, *Manhattan Loverboy* ... the dense story surges with survivalist instinct, capturing everyman's quest for a sense of individuality." —*Smug Magazine*

"MLB sits somewhere between Kafka, DeLillo, and Lovecraft—a terribly frightening, funny, and all too possible place." —*Literary Review of Canada*

"Nersesian's literary progress between *The Fuck-Up* and *Manhattan Loverboy* is like Beckett's between *Happy Days* and *Not I* ... MLB is about how distance from power and decision-making can skew our reality, can leave us feeling like pawns in an incomprehensible game." —*Toronto Star*

For Chinese Takeout

"Not since Henry Miller has a writer so successfully captured the ... tribulations of a struggling artist ... A masterly image."
—*Library Journal* (starred review)

"One of the best books I've read about the artist's life. Nersesian captures the obsession one needs to keep going under tough odds ... trying to stay true to himself, and his struggle against the odds makes for a compelling read."
—*Village Voice*

"... a heartfelt, tragicomic bohemian romance with echoes of the myth of Orpheus and Eurydice ... Infused with the symbolism of Greek legend, the hip squalor of this milieu takes on a mythic charge that energizes Nersesian's lyrical celebration of an evanescent moment in the life of the city."
—*Publishers Weekly*

"Capturing in words the energy, dynamism, and exhaustion of creating visual art is a definite achievement. Setting the act of creation amidst Lower East Side filth, degradation, and hope, and making that environment a palpable, organic character in a novel confirms Nersesian's literary artistry. His edgy exploration of the love of art and of life, and of the creative act and the sweat and toil inherent to it, is hard to put down."
—*Booklist*

"Thoroughly validates Nersesian's rep as one of the wittiest and most perceptive chroniclers of downtown life." —*Time Out New York*

"Nersesian has a talent for dark comedy and witty dialogue ... Woven throughout ... are gems of observational brilliance ... A vivid tour."
—*American Book Review*

"A witty tour through the lowest depths of high art . . . A fast paced portrait of the joys and venalities of *la vie bohème.*" —*Kirkus Reviews*

For *Unlubricated*

"Reading *Unlubricated* can make you feel like a commuter catapulting herself down the stairs to squeeze onto the A train before the doors close . . . In his paean to the perplexities of dislocation and discovery—both in bohemian life and in life at large—Nersesian makes us eager to see what happens when the curtain finally rises."
—*New York Times Book Review*

"Nersesian's raw, smutty sensibility is perfect for capturing the gritty city artistic life, but this novel has as much substance as style . . . Nersesian continuously ratchets up the suspense, always keeping the fate of the production uncertain—and at the last minute he throws a curveball that makes the previous chaos calm by comparison. Nersesian is a first-rate observer of his native New York . . ."
—*Publishers Weekly*

"Nersesian knows his territory intimately and paces the escalating chaos with a precision that would do Wodehouse proud."
—*Time Out New York*

"A real delight—fast and funny and pure New York. *Unlubricated* has only one flaw: It ends." —Steve Kluger, author of *Last Days of Summer*

For *dogrun,*

"Darkly comic . . . It's Nersesian's love affair with lower Manhattan that sets these pages afire." —*Entertainment Weekly*

"A rich parody of the all-girl punk band." —*New York Times Book Review*

"Nersesian's blackly comic urban coming-of-angst tale offers a laugh in every paragraph." —*Glamour*

EAST VILLAGE TETRALOGY

EAST VILLAGE TETRALOGY

FOUR PLAYS

BY ARTHUR NERSESIAN

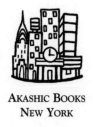

AKASHIC BOOKS
NEW YORK

This book is comprised of four works of fiction. All names, characters, places, and incidents are the product of the author's imagination. Any resemblance to real events or persons, living or dead, is entirely coincidental.

Published by Akashic Books
©2006 Arthur Nersesian

ISBN-13: 978-1-888451-85-6
ISBN-10: 1-888451-85-8
Library of Congress Control Number: 2005925464

First printing
Printed in Canada

All inquiries concerning performing rights should be addressed to:
ArthurNersesian@yahoo.com

Akashic Books
PO Box 1456
New York, NY 10009
Akashic7@aol.com
www.akashicbooks.com

ACKNOWLEDGMENTS

Among countless friends who helped in developing these works were Michael Luciano, Mark Farnsworth, Aaron Beale, Delphi Basilacato, Michael Granville, Hal Sirowitz, Samantha Maietta, Jennifer Holmes, Lauren Wilkinson, Paul Rickert, Alfredo Villanueva, and Uncles: Rich, Tom, and Mike—thanks.

CONTENTS

RENT CONTROL

In memory of Ross Alexander,
a playwright and a generous mentor

Rent Control was first produced at Nada, on 166 Ludlow Street in New York City, on October 16, 1992.

Cameron	Bonnie Burgess
Ted	Mark Farnsworth
Ossip	Steve Roberts
Jake	Alex Cobo
Officer Gallo	Mary Kowalski
Director	Mark Farnsworth
Carpenter	Michael Granville
Stage Manager	David Rosenthal

Production Note: If the stage has a trap door, a frame of wood that appears to be the floor can be fitted over it for the floor demolition. Otherwise the demolition can appear to take place behind a sofa so that the floor scenes are obscured from audience view. A small section of plasterboard should be framed over some part of the wall so that it can be stripped away. Lastly, a large abstract painting—one that should require no talent to paint—should be composed of colors that are reflective of the clothes Ted, Cameron, and Ossip are wearing.

The Taser gun can be simply made by gluing wires to a rubber-tipped toy dart gun. In order to assure the adhesion of the dart, Ted should press the gun against Ossip so he can hold the wired dart when Ted pulls the trigger.

ACT ONE

The entire play takes place on the single set of a bachelor's attractive living room. There's an expensive collection of cigarette lighters prominently displayed. Ted is wearing his business suit after a day's work. The play begins as he opens the front door. When he flicks on a switch, bright lights glare and loud music blares. He lowers the volume and helps Cameron take off her coat.

CAMERON Wow! What a place. Are you sure your parents don't live here?

TED If they do, I don't know anything about it.

CAMERON So this is Westminster Abbey or— What's the name of this building again? The Buckingham Palace?

TED Windsor Castle.

CAMERON *(Gazing at the view out an imaginary window downstage)* Oh, I can actually see the river—it's so sensual. *(Ted sits down casually)* Now, you said you were just going to get another jacket and we were out of here.

TED But look! *(Pointing out the window)* It's definitely going to rain.

CAMERON Even if it's raining, let's go back to the bar. I want to get drunk as a skunk and not remember a thing of what I'm going to do.

TED *(Going to his bar)* What d'you drink?

CAMERON Ummm—Diet Coke with a twist of citrus skin.

TED I thought you wanted to get skunk drunk.

CAMERON You know what I could really go for now?

TED Tell me.

CAMERON A bite, I'm ravished.

TED Fine. How about some Chinese food?

CAMERON That would be perfect.

TED I know a good place that delivers.

CAMERON Actually, Chinese is so ordinary, isn't it? Let's go out for something exotic, like, I don't know, Croation.

TED (*Picking up a phone book*) Restaurants—where did you come up with that idea?

CAMERON There was a place in Marseilles I would go to when I was studying.

TED (*Flips through the phone book*) Studying what?

CAMERON Acting. I'm an actress.

TED Why does anyone become an actress? It seems more an insecurity than a profession.

CAMERON Please, let's not go into it.

TED (*Finally finding a restaurant listed*) Croatian. One that delivers. Bingo! I love New York.

CAMERON (*Abruptly*) I'm not hungry anymore.

TED You certainly are an impulse slave.

CAMERON Know what I'd really like?

TED Just say it.

CAMERON I'd like to bring you back to *my* apartment so I can get some sexy lingerie.

TED Sexy lingerie? Wow!

CAMERON Why *wow*?

TED I don't know, I just met you. You're going a bit fast for me.

CAMERON Well, you said it yourself, I'm impulsive.

TED What size are you?

CAMERON Eight, why?

Ted leaves the room. She slips one of his antique cigarette lighters in her purse. He returns with a suitcase filled with sexy lingerie, which he opens before her.

TED *Voilà!* All in size eight.

CAMERON *(Holding them up, one at a time)* Where the hell did you get this?! What kind of person are you?

TED It's not what you think. A friend of mine from Winnipeg sells them retail. This is his sample case.

CAMERON Oh. Well, what *don't* you have?

TED A beautiful woman who loves me.

CAMERON That's not really what you want, is it?

TED It's central.

CAMERON *(Sarcastic)* Sex is a wonderful gesture of love.

TED I suppose it can be.

CAMERON A big handsome brute like you, a showy place like this— you must win over a lot of the ladies.

TED Just you, I've been waiting for you.

CAMERON *(Antagonistically)* Where'd you read that, *The Cinderella Complex?* You don't have to make me feel special.

TED Why do I have this strange feeling that something's off?

CAMERON What's off? You're the guy.

TED What does that mean?

CAMERON Well, you're kind of the one in control. I haven't read about any recent cases of female rapists or murderers. Ted Bundy wasn't a woman. And your name's Ted.

TED *(Sighs)* What was your original question? Have I had a lot of ladies up here? I've had my share.

CAMERON How many is your share?

TED A harem load.

CAMERON Any boys in that harem?

TED What's the matter?

CAMERON Nothing.

TED Why do I sense hostility?

CAMERON Hostility? *(Smiles)* I have no reason to be hostile. You've never impregnated me, or screwed and then dumped me, or harassed me on the street.

TED And I'd be disgusted with any guy that would.

CAMERON Asking if you've ever slept with guys during these plague years is a fair question.

TED I suppose it is.

CAMERON Maybe I did feel a bit insecure, though. I mean, I approached you and picked you up. That puts me at a disadvantage.

TED Oh, don't—

CAMERON Then, soon as I came in, I ran around like a chicken with my head cut off—

TED Oh, don't—

CAMERON —and looked at the place all excited, like I was the first, last, and only girl you brought here. And maybe you thought that I thought that maybe if I can please you, all this can be mine—

TED Oh no I didn't. I mean, that really didn't occur to me.

CAMERON In New York, an attractive apartment is very thrilling.

TED I know.

CAMERON I just feel uncomfortable being in your place and all. Do you have a car?

TED No.

CAMERON If you take me by cab to the Brooklyn Bridge right now— I'm not sure why, but if you take me there right this instant— (*Gives him a gentle kiss on his lips*)

TED I've got a balcony.

CAMERON This is different. When you climax it's like being in heaven.

TED Climax? I'd probably fall into the river.

CAMERON Come on. It'll be one of those nights that you'll remember all your life. But we have to hurry. (*Checks her watch*) It'll be something to remember when you're in your office sweating like a pig.

TED (*Starts carressing her*) I really don't want to go out.

CAMERON Why not?

TED I don't know. I can just see something weird happening, like getting mugged with my pants down. Something awful.

CAMERON I'll protect you. Let's go. (*She rushes out the door; when he doesn't follow, she returns a moment later*) Teddy, have you ever made love in public?

TED No. That's another thing. I don't think I could be nude outside.

CAMERON Well, you can still be dressed. All you got to do is unzip. (*Unzips his zipper and kisses him again*) You'll be in complete control.

TED How do you mean?

CAMERON The more dressed person is always in control.

TED What's this control thing?

CAMERON (*Starts walking toward the door again*) Let's go.

TED (*Makes a motion to go, but stops*) But you know, when we first left the bar, you pretty strongly inferred that we'd do it.

CAMERON Yeah, outside. I expressly said *outside.*

TED Look, this really isn't fair.

CAMERON (*Sarcastically*) 'Course not, you should be able to have sex with me. I should lie down submissively—

TED Hold it. *You* approached me. *You* bought me a beer. *You* flirted with me, and *you* suggested leaving the bar and going somewhere romantic.

CAMERON I didn't think *you'd* try to fuck me in *your* apartment.

TED They've been doing it that way for years. (*Angrily*) Now I don't want to anymore.

CAMERON Calm down. You're taking all this too seriously. (*She chuckles, then leans over, hugs and kisses his neck; he turns and tries to kiss her back*) Whoa, cowboy! (*Pulls away, and he sighs*) Look, I feel bad about all this. It's just that—how can I say it? Nowadays, one has to be—

TED It's AIDS, isn't it?

CAMERON Oh, right! AIDS!

TED Here. (*Locates and holds up a framed document and a cigar box*)

I just got it back from the laminator. *(She reads)* Test negative. Also— *(Opens the cigar box filled with condoms of all types)* the Havana cigars of latex condoms. You won't find a lambskin in there. Even though lambskin are more expensive, they're semi-permeable. Also read that. *(Points to the back of a condom)*

CAMERON Spermicide additive?

TED State of the art. Nothing but the best. But just in case, I also have— *(Pulls out a tube)* Nonoxynol-9. The Dom Perignon of spermicides. *(Slowly starts undoing his tie)* I never had a gay experience. *(Starts unbuttoning his shirt)* Never had sex with an IV user—

CAMERON But you said we'd go— *(There is a banging on the wall, it sounds as if it's from a neighboring apartment)* All I want— *(Banging intensifies)* is to go for a walk. What is that?

TED Neighbors. It's dangerous out there. *(She starts getting worried, he gets closer and more comforting)* You're not from the city, are you?

CAMERON No. Let's get out of here—

TED *(Starts unbuttoning her blouse)* After the rain stops.

The banging grows louder, then we hear a muffled voice.

OSSIP *(Offstage)* Keep it down!

TED Dare they be referring to us?

CAMERON *(Sighs, resigned)* Who knows? This is New York.

TED I came from Oregon in 1983. Portland. But I'm originally from California.

CAMERON My parents moved out here in the 1960s from Lowell, Mass.

OSSIP *(Offstage)* Stop the damned noise! I'm trying to sleep!

TED They're talking about us! I can't believe it. I paid a quarter-million for this place, only to have some asshole move next door—

CAMERON Take it easy. I don't think it's coming from next door.

They both listen in suspense.

OSSIP *(Offstage)* Keep down that damned racket! I'm trying to sleep!

TED SO GO TO SLEEP, ASSHOLE!

OSSIP *(Offstage)* I can't!

TED SO IT AIN'T MY FAULT!

OSSIP *(Offstage)* You're keeping me up!

TED TRY SLEEPING PILLS!

OSSIP *(Offstage)* I don't take pills!

TED Do you hear this guy?

CAMERON DRINK WARM MILK AND MAKE THE FIGURE EIGHT WITH YOUR PUPILS!

OSSIP *(Distant, hollering)* I DON'T HAVE PUPILS!

CAMERON Just ignore him.

TED I can't.

CAMERON Let's go out.

TED I'm not going to be chased out of my own apartment.

OSSIP *(Banging on the door)* Open this door!

TED *(Panicky)* Oh shit!

CAMERON Where's the back door?! I'm getting out of here.

TED *(Nervously zipping up his pants and buttoning his shirt)* Take it easy. This is a civilized building. *(Grabs a tennis racket and throws open the door; a fiery orthodox Jewish man is standing there in a bathrobe, holding a white tool bag)* Who are you?

OSSIP *(Steps in and drops the tool bag)* I am your downstairs neighbor trying to get some sleep.

TED You live in this building?

OSSIP And why not?

TED I just thought of this as a young person's building.

OSSIP Great, you insult me twice in a row, and you'll probably live directly above me until I die. There goes the golden peace of my old age. *(Enters, inspecting the living room until he comes to Cameron)* Who are you, the wife?

CAMERON No.

OSSIP Well, account for yourself!

TED Look, what's the problem?

CAMERON You're from that fanatical sect that has all those sexist prayers like, "Thank God I'm not a woman."

Ossip ignores them both. He walks around the living room, continuing to inspect it.

TED Was the music too loud?

OSSIP Calm down.

TED What was keeping you awake?

OSSIP I was awake from the word go, I never go to sleep anymore. The last good night's sleep I got was in 1967. *(Heads to the window)* My God, you can't even see Broadway from here anymore. Downstairs I can see right to the El on the Bowery.

CAMERON The what?

OSSIP I mean, I can see the Bowery.

While Ossip looks out the window, Cameron steals another lighter and slips it into her purse. Surreptitiously, throughout the play, she continues to steal small objects and bric-a-brac from Ted's apartment.

TED The Bowery, you mean the avenue?

OSSIP Sure.

TED Wait a second. *(Points out the window)* That building is blocking your view.

OSSIP No it isn't.

TED It blocks the view for me, and you live below me. Explain that!

CAMERON *(With coat in hand)* We were just about to go for a walk. So you can go back downstairs and sleep.

TED No we weren't.

Cameron tosses her coat on the sofa.

OSSIP *(To Cameron)* You had your chance. It's too late now.

TED Too late!? Look, I'm sorry. What's your name?

OSSIP Ossip Bergman.

CAMERON You sure you're not related to the director Ingmar Bergman?

OSSIP I said no.

TED She never asked you that.

CAMERON Yeah, I never asked you that.

OSSIP Everybody asks me. I'm sorry, dear, you didn't ask me, but please. Please don't ask me again. *(Sighs)* I'm sorry, but I have sensitivity. See, my family changed their name from Bergofsky to Bergman because German Jews were regarded more highly than Russian Jews when they got here and— *(Notices the sofa)* You want some unsolicited advice, maybe?

TED Not right now—

OSSIP Move this couch over there. A key improvement. You help me.

Cameron grabs one side of the sofa and shoves it with him. At the same time, someone begins banging from downstairs.

TED Hey, what is this?

OSSIP It's okay. That's just my wife, Irma. *(Screams)* I LOVE YOU TOO, IRM! *(The banging stops)*

CAMERON Shouldn't the coffee table be moved if you're going to move that? *(She moves it)*

TED *(Muttering)* I don't believe this.

OSSIP And that lamp table.

CAMERON Just try it. It'll look a lot better.

TED Stop it! You must go now.

CAMERON Okay. *(Rises to go)*

TED Not you, *him!*

OSSIP Me?

TED *(Grabs Ossip and escorts him to the door)* I'll keep quieter, and see you at the next tenant's meeting.

OSSIP Oh, you think the noise was keeping me up? No, it wasn't that. It was the leak.

TED The leak?

OSSIP Yes, *drip drop, drip drop,* right on my bed.

TED Where's the leak?

OSSIP On my head.

TED Look, show me where in this apartment there's a leak!

OSSIP I don't know, let me see. Can it be in here? *(Walks into the bedroom, offstage)*

TED What's the idea, helping him push my furniture around?

CAMERON If we amuse him maybe he'll leave.

OSSIP *(Offstage)* You know, this bed would look a lot better against that wall.

We hear furniture being moved in the bedroom and a vase shatters.

TED Shit! Call the police. This guy's loony.

CAMERON They'd just laugh. He's a lonely old man. Talk to him.

OSSIP *(Offstage)* No leak in here. *(Reentering, he taps on the floor with his shoe like a prospector)*

TED So, where is it?

OSSIP I'm trying to remember. *(The pounding from below resumes)* YES, IT'S OKAY, IRMA! I'M THINKING ABOUT YOU, DEAR! I'm trying to remember what my apartment used to look like.

TED This isn't your apartment. You live downstairs. That's why you don't recognize it.

OSSIP I know that, you nitwit! My apartment is completely different from yours. It's half the size. And *(Points to Ted's living room)* this gas jet over here—

CAMERON This *what* jet?

OSSIP It's capped now, but this was the kitchen. And the bathtub was in the hall.

CAMERON In your hall?

OSSIP I mean, it is there.

TED Your bathtub is in the hallway?

OSSIP Yes. *(Looking confused)* We shared it with the Morris family. We'd boil the water—the girl's hour was always longer. It was very uncomfortable for us.

CAMERON The girl's hour?

TED How many of you are there?

OSSIP Well, there's Ira, Sarah, Moishe, Abe. Abe was born here, and Lydia—

CAMERON *(Whispering)* He's senile.

OSSIP Fifteen, including Mom, Dad, and Grandpa.

TED What?

CAMERON Your parents are *dead*.

TED How do you know?

OSSIP That's right, Miss Know-it-all. Jehovah doesn't bless everyone with death.

CAMERON *(Under her breath)* Shame you're not among the blessed.

TED Look, whatever-your-name-is—

OSSIP Ossip. Call me Ozzie. *(Shakes Ted's hand)*

TED Ossip, it's late. I've got to go to sleep.

OSSIP Oh fine, fine. And I'm supposed to just go home.

TED Irma obviously wants you back. Now come on.

OSSIP And what about the waterfall coming down on my head? Am I supposed to grow gills and ignore it?

TED What?

CAMERON So you've got a leak. You didn't make that clear.

OSSIP Yes I did. I said that. I got cats and dogs is what I've got. I got the urge to collect animals in pairs. Now, I don't want to hurt your floor. *(Pulls a claw hammer out of a tool bag)*

TED You're damned right! That's a five-thousand-dollar floor.

OSSIP I swear I won't hurt your floor. *(Hands Ted a business card)* I was an A-one contractor/carpenter/plumber for fifty-odd years. I can rip up a floor, repair a pipe, and put the floor back as if it's never been disturbed.

TED Well, I'm sorry, but—

OSSIP *(Suddenly begins tapping the floorboards with the claw of the hammer)* It's somewhere around here.

TED *(Rushes forward, pulling Ossip's arms behind his back)* WHAT ARE YOU DOING?!

CAMERON *(Pushing Ted off Ossip)* My God! He's an old man! Be gentle with him.

TED Look what he did to my floor. *(Gently rubs the floor)*

OSSIP All right, all right, get off me. I'll stop.

There is a knock at the door.

CAMERON I'll get it.

TED It's my home! I'll get it. Get your things and get out. Both of you.

CAMERON But honeee—

TED This whole evening has been a little disorienting. Another night, please. *(Ossip and Cameron collect their respective belongings and exchange odd glances; Ted opens his door and sees a stranger in a bathrobe similar to Ossip's)* Now who are you, the son?

JAKE *(Extends his hand)* My name's Jake. I'm your downstairs neighbor. I have to go to work in a couple hours, and—

CAMERON *(Cringing)* Oh God, Ozzie!

TED Wait just a goddamned second! *(Turns just as Ossip is charging them with the hammer)*

OSSIP *(Screaming)* AHHHHHHH! I'LL SMITE YOU BOTH!

TED Watch it!

Ted and Jake jump into the hall. Cameron slams the door and locks it. Ted bangs on the door, demanding to be let back in.

CAMERON Quick! Rip open the floor.

OSSIP Oh, what's the point? They're right out there.

CAMERON Half a million dollars, asshole. My budget! (*Grabs the hammer and begins whacking at the floor*)

OSSIP Hey! Look what you're doing to the poor boy's floor. Stop it! (*Grabs the hammer from her*)

CAMERON Look, asshole, you don't seem to understand. He's calling the police.

OSSIP That might be so. But that's not the right place.

CAMERON Where is it? We don't have all night.

OSSIP Okay, push the furniture this way (*Points upstage*) so's I can remember what it used to look like. And clear that garbage off the walls.

They pile everything in the corner so that Ossip might remember his home of years gone by. At some point they inadvertently pull the phone wire out of the wall.

CAMERON I can't believe you said that thing about Ingmar Bergman.

OSSIP I was sick of you needling me. (*Mimicking her*) Are you related to Bergman? Are you sure you don't know the amazing Bergman?

CAMERON The girl's hour was longer. Oh! And then you can see the Third Avenue El from your window. That was a classic. The El was torn down in the '20s or something.

OSSIP (*Focusing on the layout of the space*) Shusssh! I'm not even sure this is the right apartment.

CAMERON You're kidding, right? You're just saying that to aggravate me.

OSSIP No. I'm just not sure. It's been over two of your lifetimes since I've been here. They reconfigured the place several times. (*Points downstage*) Over here used to be the neighbor's dwelling. Our place used to be narrower, and then that wall wasn't there. And that was a small closet in the room where my grandparents lived. Thick velvet drapes with gilded tassels framing the entrance. It was like entering a sacred shrine. We weren't permitted in there.

CAMERON Great, you'll get off for insanity. I'll end up at the women's correctional facility.

OSSIP Oh, tell me you've never been there before, why don't you.

CAMERON You had me pick this guy up at the bar, and you weren't even sure this is the right apartment?

OSSIP I'm fallible. So strike me down. It's over half a century. Wars, famine, pestilence have swept the earth since I've been here. Please.

CAMERON I can't believe I got suckered into this.

OSSIP (*Tapping a plasterboard wall*) Is there brick behind this wall or is it another apartment? 'Cause we lived against an exposed brick wall.

CAMERON How the hell should I know?

OSSIP Open my bag and plug that extension cord in the wall.

She pulls an extension cord out of his bag and plugs it in, as he pulls out a stud finder and checks carefully for what might be behind the wall. After a moment, he takes a small jackhammer out of the bag and plugs it into the extension cord. Whenever she talks, he turns the jackhammer on, so she has to shout, and whenever he talks, he turns it off. Carefully he rips open a small square in the wall.

CAMERON (*Hammer on, she yells*) You can't do a thing right!

OSSIP Me?! You were supposed to keep him out of the house. Not bring him back. A simpler task can't be requested.

CAMERON (*Hammer on*) He wanted to change his jacket! It was about to rain. You weren't supposed to come here yet.

OSSIP You were supposed to be the sexy one—the great seductress. Experienced! Ha. I'll tell you what I think. I think you lost your sex.

CAMERON (*Hammer on*) If that's an insult, I'm not crying! Pig-males chewing on me isn't my idea of something to strive for.

OSSIP So if you couldn't interest him in you womanliness, what were you doing with him for the past hour, playing mahjong?!

CAMERON (*Hammer on*) At least I'm not so insecure that I have to spend my time praying. (*Mimics his accent*) Thank you, God, I'm not a woman.

OSSIP I'm no—

CAMERON I know all about your customs: the sheet with the glory hole in it.

There's now a big opening in the wall with raw red brick behind it. Ossip puts down the jackhammer.

OSSIP Bingo! This is the apartment. And by the way, I'm not Hasidic. If you leave the Hasids alone, I promise they will leave you alone.

CAMERON You're still a nasty bastard.

OSSIP Sewer mouth.

CAMERON (*Suddenly notices*) He stopped banging.

OSSIP I don't think he exactly gave up. He's probably dialing the police.

CAMERON Come on. We've trashed his place. Tell me this is it.

OSSIP (*Sniffing the hole in the wall deeply*) Come here, quick. Do you smell that?

CAMERON (*Smelling the hole*) Yeah, is it behind there?

OSSIP No, that's old brick dust. I haven't smelled that in years.

CAMERON Oh, thanks. (*Blows her nose into a tissue*)

OSSIP (*Taking another deep sniff*) That dust used to give me such asthma attacks as a child.

CAMERON If you hit any nostalgic asbestos, keep it to yourself.

OSSIP It was like living in a cave. The landlord violated the 1901 building codes! There were supposed to be interior windows. No sunlight here. I remember each May praying we'd move to a new place—

CAMERON Spare me the reminiscences. Where'd he hide the jewels?

OSSIP I can't remember. *(Points downward)* Here somewhere.

CAMERON Just rip up the fucking floors!

OSSIP But they might be in the walls.

She grabs the jackhammer and tries to break a hole through the wall. Ossip takes it from her and carefully starts chopping into a single floorboard. She rolls up the rug, shoving everything into one big pile.

OSSIP We'd feel the floor rumble beneath our feet—

CAMERON And savor the brick dust, I know.

OSSIP —and hop up onto chairs. The reason we'd feel the floor rumble were the rats.

CAMERON Rats?

OSSIP Rats the size of dachshunds. With teeth. *(Demonstrates with a snarl)* Oy got!

CAMERON I should've brought my cat.

OSSIP I'm sure it's okay now. Rats don't like living around the rich.

CAMERON Okay, okay, keep cutting. *(He resumes, and then stops again)*

OSSIP Shame. *(Rubbing the floor)* Was a beautiful apartment. Poor man, whoever he is. *(Removes several pieces of floorboard)* Look at this hard wood—maple. You know what this goes for a foot?

CAMERON *(Ignoring him)* It's open enough.

A glass shatters offstage.

OSSIP What's that?

CAMERON He's on the balcony! *(She jumps as Ted enters from upstage)*

TED What did you do to my apartment?! *(Cameron dashes for the crowbar)* Freeze!

Ted aims what appears to be a toy gun. Ossip and Cameron freeze, but after a moment they inspect it curiously.

CAMERON What the hell is that?

TED A Taser gun. It shoots wires on you and zaps you with 10,000 volts.

OSSIP A laser gun?

CAMERON He's lying. Jump him!

OSSIP You jump him.

TED It's called a Taser gun, with a T. Here's the instructions.

Ted tosses a brochure, which they both inspect. Cameron slowly puts her hands back up, and then Ossip does too.

OSSIP How much did you pay for this?

CAMERON Where'd you get it, F.A.O. Schwarz?

TED Shut up, the both of you!

OSSIP *(Puts his hands down)* This is no joke, young man. You're not going to electrocute two hapless people.

TED Try leaving and watch me.

OSSIP What do you want?

TED I want to know why you threw me out of my house and what the fuck you've done to the place. *(Pauses)* Talk!

OSSIP *(Slowly rising)* Look, young man, what's your name?

CAMERON His name's Teddy.

OSSIP Theodore, calm down. Put the weapons down and—

TED Stop right there. You think I'm fucking clowning around or something?

OSSIP I think no such thing.

TED You think I'm some fucking yuppie and can't be as insane as any psycho?!

OSSIP *(Repressing a smirk)* I can see you're a regular wild man from Borneo.

Cameron starts laughing. Ted grabs her by the arm and twists it behind her back while pointing the Taser at Ossip.

TED Laugh now!

CAMERON Hey! That hurts! OW!

OSSIP Now this is uncalled for!

TED Tell me what's going on or I'll break your arm, I swear.

CAMERON *(In pain)* Fuck you! *(Ted bends her arm back further and she screams)*

OSSIP There's a treasure worth a million bucks buried somewhere here. Let the girl alone.

TED A million bucks?

OSSIP That's a ballpark figure.

CAMERON You told him!

TED Where?

OSSIP *(Makes a broad sweeping gesture)* Well, in this general vicinity.

Ted lets Cameron go, pushing her toward Ossip.

CAMERON Big mouth.

OSSIP I was worried for you.

TED Shut up! You're both insane. We'll wait till the police get here.

CAMERON Did you ever here of the *Bloody Sunday Revolution* of Russia in 1905? It was a film.

TED Maybe.

CAMERON Well, gems were stolen by his uncle, who hid them down there over seventy years ago. Under the joints—

OSSIP The *joists.*

TED That's the stupidest story I ever heard.

OSSIP *(Muttering)* I can tell you a bunch of them.

TED Where exactly was your uncle born?

OSSIP Pinsk.

TED *(To her)* That's nowhere near Leningrad.

OSSIP Which reminds me of a joke—

CAMERON (*Speaking to both*) Look, there's a simple way of solving this. Just stick your head down there and grab.

TED (*Looking silently into the hole*) I don't see squat.

CAMERON Well, one of us has to go down there.

TED This is crazy.

CAMERON I'm not leaving without my budget.

TED The police will be taking you both away in a minute.

OSSIP I'll make you a deal.

TED I don't think you're in any position to make a deal.

OSSIP Fine. The Russian govenrment has a legitimate claim to whatever's down there. Fine. We *want* to see the police! We'll tell them how you knowingly tried to keep all that for yourself.

CAMERON That's at least ten years in the slammer.

TED Yeah, right. What do you suggest?

OSSIP My offer is we just forget all this ever happened. We'll pack up, straighten things out, and leave.

TED Straighten things out?!

CAMERON Hold on here!

TED Look what you did to my apartment. You two are going to jail.
(*Points the Taser at them*)

CAMERON (*To Ossip*) Just hold it a second, captain. (*To Ted*) Put your hand down there. You'll be able to buy every river view in this city.

TED What do you think, I'm crazy?

CAMERON If you make twenty thousand in four months, sixty thousand a year, that's at least sixteen years of your life down there.

OSSIP (*Astonished*) I had no idea you were so sharp in math.

TED I don't put my hand somewhere I can't see. For all I know, there's some kind of spring trap down there.

OSSIP Please let us go. We'll be good.

CAMERON (*To Ossip*) We got *this* close! Don't you want to know if it's down there after all these years?

OSSIP *You* reach down there. I just want to leave.

CAMERON It's your treasure.

TED He knows there's nothing down there.

OSSIP I resent that! All right, I'll reach down there. But then I'm keeping whatever I find. *(Slowly rolls up his sleeve)*

CAMERON Hold it!

TED You'll do no such thing.

OSSIP Just watch me.

CAMERON We have a deal.

OSSIP *(Sitting over the hole and looking into it)* Deal's off. You couldn't even get him out of the house.

TED *(Pointing the Taser sternly)* Freeze, I swear it!

CAMERON Fry the bastard

Ossip ignores them, bending over the hole.

TED Stop where you are!

As Ossip's about to reach into the hole, Ted shoots the Taser at him, giving him a quick electrical jolt. Ossip collapses into spasms.

OSSIP Oy vey ist mir!

CAMERON *(Pulling Ossip's head in her lap and rocking him)* Hey! Look at the big hero! A regular Bernie Goetz, aren't you? Are you okay, baby? *(Ossip quivers)*

TED Just back off. The both of you! Think I'm some yuppie stoolie?! Well, I warned you!

OSSIP *(On the ground)* May I go home now?

CAMERON *(To Ossip)* In a minute. *(Angrily, to Ted)* So *you* reach down there, big man.

TED Let me get this straight: If I put my hand down there, I'm going to grab a diamond tiara or a pearl necklace or something? Is that right?

CAMERON Yes, that's right.

OSSIP I just want to go to bed.

CAMERON Now you reach down there, or I will.

TED And his uncle hid them down there years ago?

CAMERON I'll reach down there.

TED I'm doing it. (*About to, but suddenly stops*) Why wouldn't he reclaim it? How do you explain that?

CAMERON Maybe he died suddenly. Who knows?

TED And why the hell would he hide it in my apartment?

OSSIP He didn't know some asshole with a Flash Gordon–type ray gun would be living here, is why.

CAMERON (*Stepping forward*) I'm going to do it! This coward is fucking around. Shoot me. Go ahead.

TED Stay away from that hole. (*Points the gun at her, oblivious to the fact that its wire is still attached to Ossip*)

CAMERON Either you reach into that hole or I will.

TED You can't force me.

CAMERON Then I will.

TED Do it and I'll shoot. I swear I'll shoot. I'm convinced you're both monsters.

OSSIP Be careful. He will!

CAMERON Big man when you want to fuck. But when it comes to doing something with a little balls, look at you.

She reaches into the hole. Ted shoots, causing Ossip to writhe in shock. She grabs Ossip again.

OSSIP Oy! Mein got!

CAMERON Are you okay?

OSSIP (*Crying*) No. My heart is in intense pain.

CAMERON Call an ambulance!

Ted tries to make a call, but amidst all the demolition, he finds his phone line has been yanked out of the wall.

TED I can't! You pulled the phone out!

OSSIP *(Labored breathing)* I'm finding it very difficult to breath.

CAMERON *(To Ossip)* I'm sorry for being rude, but—

OSSIP *(Reaching out before him)* Lydia, are you out there? *(His breathing becomes even more labored and raspy)*

TED Can I get you water or something?

With some difficulty, Ossip shakes his head no. Cameron, who is growing increasingly agitated, suddenly thumps on Ossip's chest. He yelps in pain.

TED Hey!

OSSIP *(Gasping)* Oh my! What the hell did you do that for?

CAMERON I thought it'd help. I saw it on TV.

OSSIP Please don't *ever* do that again. *(Cameron gently holds Ossip's head in her lap as he struggles to breathe)* In a way, it's right.

TED What is?

OSSIP *(Mumbling)* The circa—

CAMERON What circus?

TED He said *circle.* What circle?

OSSIP The circle of life. Being born here, dying here.

CAMERON *(Frenzied)* You got to get an ambulance. What have you done? I'm getting out of here.

TED Just relax. Shit!

Ossip gestures for Ted to come close. Ted puts his ear to the older man's mouth to listen. Cameron starts crying softly.

TED No, I can't, I'm not going to. Do you hear me?

CAMERON What? *(Ossip appears to die)* DO SOMETHING!

Ted remains impassive. Cameron starts giving Ossip mouth-to-mouth resuscitation.

TED Stop it!! *(Pauses)* STOP! *(Pulls Cameron off Ossip)*

CAMERON I'm trying to save him!

TED He had two requests before he died. The first was that we let him die here, peacefully. *(Cameron cries while Ted stares at Ossip's body)* Is there some kind of Jewish prayer or something?

CAMERON *(Pauses)* Shalom. *(Pauses)* What was the other thing he wanted?

TED I can't fucking believe this. I'm shaking. An old man has come to die in my living room.

CAMERON I'm sorry about the whole mess.

TED Everything is just going bust. I'm turning thirty this year, and—

CAMERON It's okay.

TED I never had someone die in my arms. I mean—

CAMERON *(Pouring him a drink)* What else did he say?

TED I killed him.

CAMERON He said you killed him?

TED No, I killed him!

CAMERON I think maybe he wanted it this way. *(Pauses)* What was the second thing he wanted?

TED He wanted us to get the loot out of the floor before calling the police. He wanted us to have the stuff. But to hell with that.

CAMERON Wait a sec, now. I don't want to sound like a—

TED A greedy bitch?

CAMERON But—

TED You want to be stinking rich?

CAMERON No. I'm saying, if we don't get that money, he died for nothing.

TED Oh that's a good one. He sacrificed his life so we can be filthy rich.

CAMERON Look, you're the one who shot him.

TED I was trying to shoot *you*.

CAMERON You are one pathetic human being. You tried to shoot a female and killed an old man instead.

TED It was an accident!

CAMERON Bullshit! You killed him because he's not scared to stick his hand down there. And you are. Coward!

TED (*Looking into the hole*) Maybe I am. (*Retrieves a flashlight, then removes his shoes*)

CAMERON What are you doing?

TED This is a five-hundred-dollar suit.

He takes off his pants and shirt, which he folds neatly on the sofa. He now wears only underwear, a wristwatch, and eyeglasses.

CAMERON (*Inspecting Ted's body*) Now I know why you're embarrassed to be nude in public.

TED (*Breathing deeply*) I'm going to do it. I'm going to do it!

CAMERON DO IT!

Ted leaps into the hole, disappearing completely. Blackout.

ACT TWO

When the lights come up, it is a short time later. Ted is under the floor and Cameron is in the next room offstage. Ossip is lying on the floor "dead."

TED *(Offstage)* God! This is filthy, I've got to have the maid hit down here. So, under the joists?

Ossip opens one eye.

CAMERON *(Offstage)* Yes, under the joints.

Ossip opens the other eye. Then, seeing the coast is clear, he gets up and quietly collects his tools.

TED Owww!

CAMERON Did it look like a dachshund?

TED No, a nail. I don't see squat down here.

CAMERON *(Becoming increasingly anxious)* How can you miss it? It's a damned treasure trove.

TED I'm telling you, there's nothing down here, and I'm lost.

CAMERON *(Enters just as Ossip is dashing out, she grabs the Taser)* Freeze, you old fart! You lying sack of shit.

TED I'm doing my best.

OSSIP Now just relax!

CAMERON *(Yelling)* He's alive! And there is no treasure, is there?

TED I can't hear you!

OSSIP Now wait a second. (*Suddenly pointing with inspiration*) It's possible that it's behind *that* wall.

CAMERON Oh, now we're supposed to climb behind the wall? What next, the ceiling?

TED (*Screaming*) I found something! I found something!

OSSIP Hallelujah! I'm a wealthy man.

CAMERON What is it?

OSSIP Is it a string of pearls, maybe?

TED (*Still offstage*) No.

CAMERON Is it a golden scepter with a double-headed eagle?

TED No.

CAMERON (*Excited*) What is it?

TED It's spherical.

CAMERON Oh my God, it's a missing Fabergé egg!

TED No, it's—this. (*Emerges covered in dust and holds up a little rubber ball*) Hey, you're alive!!

CAMERON What?!

OSSIP My ball! (*Kisses the dusty ball and bounces it*) My little ball!

TED What is this?

OSSIP Me and this ball were inseparable. I remember when it fell down there. Over sixty years ago. I cried so hard I had a fever. My little bouncy ball!

TED What the hell are you doing alive? (*Sees Cameron holding the Taser on Ossip*) And why are you holding that?

CAMERON The prick pulled a fast one. The old feign-dead-and-dash trick.

TED That is so low.

OSSIP Look, I went through enough.

TED You know, I suffered when you died. I mean, that is so . . . so cheap.

OSSIP I'm sorry. If it makes any difference, I was deeply moved. It was difficult not to cry. And by the way, you didn't really pay five hundred for that suit, did you?

TED Shit! *(Takes the Taser from her)*

CAMERON Do you know what I think?

TED FUCK!!

CAMERON I think he had us going all along.

OSSIP Huh?

CAMERON I don't think there were ever any hidden jewels.

OSSIP I beg your pardon?

CAMERON Since I met him, he spoke about visiting the site of his boyhood home. Just seeing it once before he dies, like a salmon returning to some goddamned stream.

OSSIP You think I'd go through all this just for nostalgia?

CAMERON You never talked about what you would do with the money, or any of that. *(To Ted)* All he talked about when we planned this was coming back to this apartment and his damned childhood.

OSSIP It's true, but I, I'm old, and—

TED Was all this just for—

OSSIP No!

CAMERON Admit it! I'll get the truth out of him. *(Reaching for the Taser)*

OSSIP *(Scrambling to escape)* Oh shit, hold her!

TED *(Grabs Cameron)* Wait a second. That's absurd. He could've just knocked on my door. I'd have let him in.

CAMERON Oh.

OSSIP That's not true—

TED Huh?

OSSIP Lies!

TED Huh?

OSSIP I *did* knock on your door, and you wouldn't even let me in!

TED When?

OSSIP I offered to give this man free installation! I was going to pay out of my own pocket. He could've had free cable TV with a movie channel. All free! And the only thing I wanted was to come inside.

TED I remember you!

OSSIP You couldn't slam the door fast enough, admit it.

TED I DIDN'T WANT GODDAMNED CABLE TV!

CAMERON So there never was any treasure. It was a lie all along.

OSSIP No, there might have been.

CAMERON Might've been?!

OSSIP My uncle swore. I'd lie in bed at night, in this hovel here, and he'd say, "Don't worry, Ossipala, there're gems and rubies under this filthy floor, and—"

CAMERON You jeopardized our life on BEDTIME STORIES! *(Trying to attack him)* Arghh!

TED *(Grabbing her again)* Cut it out! You're the dope for listening to him.

CAMERON How dare you. How dare you!

OSSIP When you're young, it's all in front of you. No death. You got hope, promise, even rapture. The older you get, the more things get reversed. Things are taken away. Removed one by one. Soon no hopes, death as big as the sun. Aches, poor circulation—

TED But look at my apartment!

CAMERON Fucking bedtime stories!

OSSIP Every day I'd walk by this place. Well, not every day, but I swear, I don't think a week went by in the last fifty years when I didn't walk by this building and think, that's where all my memories are locked, my real pleasures and joys.

TED Well, you finally got inside.

OSSIP I finally got my wish answered, only to find another renovated building.

CAMERON I don't believe this.

TED All you had to do was knock.

OSSIP *(To her)* Well I tried, and you know what? *(To Ted)* I don't believe you. *(To Cameron)* I just don't believe this man. People aren't that nice. They can't afford to be in this city.

TED Look, I wouldn't've been delighted. I would've been suspicious—

OSSIP See!

TED But I had a childhood home also, outside Redding, California. It was a dairy farm, a lot better than this dump, with cows and chickens and a stream that ran over it, and we'd swim and fish—

CAMERON Norman Rockwell Jr. here.

TED Didn't you have a childhood home in Lowell, Mass.?

CAMERON Piscataway, New Jersey.

TED But you said—

CAMERON I lied.

OSSIP I once bought a truss in Piscataway *(Makes a pained expression)*

TED I'm sorry, but I remember it like yesterday, and when we moved, it—it was like losing a good friend. So I would've let you in.

OSSIP Well, I thank you. And I'm sorry I had to bring this into your life.

CAMERON Me! You, you old fart.

OSSIP A fart! YOU painted slut!

TED Hey! Both of you!

CAMERON *(Muttering)* Take a hike.

OSSIP A kike? You called me a kike?! You dyke!

TED Will you two stop it?

OSSIP She was slanging my faith.

CAMERON I was not. I said, "Take a hike!"

TED Shut up! The both of you. *(To Ossip)* Now, if you show me some ID and promise to pay compensation for the damages—

CAMERON Well that doesn't include me! I plan to—

TED No, that doesn't include you. You, I intend to press charges against.

CAMERON WHAT?

TED You were just in this for the money. For some goddamned diamond tiara and necklaces and crap.

CAMERON But—but so were you.

TED This is my place!

CAMERON It wasn't *his* place. Arrest *him*!

TED He used to live here. But you were in it just for the cash.

CAMERON What? I'm the only real innocent person here. I'm a victim of male bonding. Fuck this. I'm leaving. *(She turns to go, Ted points the Taser at her)*

TED Freeze or I'll give you the biggest rush of your life.

CAMERON You bastards. Are you going to let him do this to me?

OSSIP Sure. Go ahead and fry her one.

TED I really liked you. I mean, I could see that something was off. You don't know how to apply cosmetics. Your apparel, your accessories are completely wrong for an office environment, but—

CAMERON So you're going to sizzle me 'cause I'm not sexy enough?

TED I felt personally hurt by you, and I feel entitled to a response for that.

CAMERON It's hard to talk when I'm threatened by a hand-held electric chair.

TED *(Puts the Taser down)* You must be one crappy actress, 'cause— *(There's a knock on the open door, an off-duty officer enters)* May I help you?

COP *(Shows his badge)* Officer Gallo. What the hell's going on?

OSSIP I thought you people came in pairs.

COP I'm off-duty. Some guy is out front screaming.

TED Officer, there's no problem here—

OSSIP We were waiting for you. Here she is, and I might add that if you need to persuade a confession out of her with one of those cattle prods—

COP Hold on here.

CAMERON Fuck you, you male bonders! Fuck you both, and you're not taking me anywhere, cop!

COP Calm down, miss. *(Surveying all the damage)* What the hell happened here?

TED Nothing.

OSSIP She broke in and did this to this nice man's apartment.

CAMERON He did!

COP Shut up. *(To Ted)* This is your apartment?

OSSIP Isn't it awful? This chippy—

CAMERON You son of a bitch!

COP & TED Shut up!

TED I did this, officer.

Cameron and Ossip look at Ted dubiously.

COP Why are you undressed and covered with dirt?

TED I dropped some money into the hole, so I went down there looking for it.

COP All right. Why is there a hole in the middle of your living room?

TED It's under renovation.

JAKE *(Dashes in)* There they are, officer. Look what they did to this place! I'm Jacob West, I live one floor below—

TED Officer, this is my apartment and I'm telling you, I did this.

JAKE No you didn't. You told me—

COP Okay, shut up. *(To Jake, regarding Ted)* Is this man the owner of this apartment?

JAKE Yes. *(Cameron and Ossip also nod)*

COP We're in agreement, okay. *(To Ted)* Who did this?

TED I did.

JAKE That's not what you told me!

TED I lied.

COP Everyone break out some ID.

OSSIP I don't have any.

CAMERON Me neither.

TED They're old friends.

JAKE That's not what you told me. *(To the cop)* That's not what he told me. He picked up this tramp in a bar, brings her back here, then this old guy shows up and pretends he's me—

OSSIP That's ridiculous! I don't look nothing like you.

JAKE *(To Ossip)* You know what I mean. *(To the cop)* He told him that he was the downstairs neighbor.

OSSIP Officer, this man is clearly out of his mind and should be restrained with unnecessary force—

COP You stand in that corner and shut up!

TED Everything's okay, officer. If you could all just leave now, I'd like to be alone.

COP It's not that simple.

JAKE Why are you defending them? Look what they did to your place. Unless you have them arrested, you won't see a cent of the insurance money. (*Behind the cop's back, Ted is gesticulating to Jake, trying to call off the entire situation*) Look, officer! He's making hand signals.

COP (*Turning quickly*) Were you making hand signals?

TED Of course not.

OSSIP This man has extensive psychiatric history.

TED Officer, if I may speak a minute. First of all, why would they do this to my apartment? And second, if they did it, why would I let them get away with it?

JAKE (*Rooting around, locates the Taser*) Ah ha! Officer, this is my Taser.

CAMERON That figures.

JAKE I can prove it. I've got the sales receipt. I lent it to this gentleman here to regain control of the situation. Now I ask you, why else would he have my gun? And why would it be out and exposed like this?

OSSIP Officer, two things. I have a very bad heart condition and ex-Mayor Ed Koch is a close personal friend of mine—

COP Shut up! I'm chasing my tail here. Everyone is going down to the station house. We'll settle everything there.

TED Officer, may I have a word with you?

Ted and the cop go to one side of the apartment, while Ossip and Jake keep arguing, first quietly and then loudly.

OSSIP (*To Jake*) Do you know what a yenta is?

TED Officer, this is my home. I own it, and if I don't press charges, there are no charges.

JAKE Do you know what a psychotic is?

COP *(To Ossip and Jake)* Hey! *(To Ted)* That's true, but it's still my job to investigate as to whether a crime has been committed.

OSSIP Do you know what a putz is?

TED But I've known these people for years.

JAKE Do you know what a schizophrenic is?

COP *(To Ossip and Jake)* Shut up! *(To Ted)* Look, it's for your own sake. For all I know, they could be holding you hostage.

OSSIP You know what a punch in the face is?

TED Look at them. Do you really think they could hurt anyone but themselves?

JAKE Do you know what criminal court is?

COP *(To Ossip and Jake)* If you two don't shut up, I'm taking you both in. *(To Ted)* What about this Taser? And the downstairs neighbor claims you gave him a whole different picture.

OSSIP *(Whispering)* Do you know what the appeasement of vengeance exceeding the penalty of justice is?

TED Ossip, shut up! Look, this is embarrassing. But I did go downstairs and borrow his Taser. And I gave him the appearance that something odd was going on. You see, frankly, we played a prank on *him*, and I'm trying to keep him from realizing that.

COP I'd consider letting them off if either of them had ID.

TED They're both dear friends of mine.

COP I want to believe you. I swear to God. But I'm responsible if I leave here and something actually did occur. Do you even have a photo of them to show me that you knew them before today?

TED Maybe. *(Checks through his pants pockets)* Shit, I'm kind of in flux at the moment— *(Looking at the abstract painting on the wall)* Officer, I do have a piece of evidence—but it might seem a little far-fetched.

COP I'll be the judge.

TED That picture, that's us.

Ted rushes over and grabs Ossip and Cameron. He positions them in relationship to their color schemes in the painting.

CAMERON What the hell are you—
TED Trust me.

They pose. Ted grabs a feather to make the picture seem complete.

JAKE What the hell is going on here?
TED *(To the cop)* See the resemblance?
COP Yeah. *(Pauses)* To the biggest crock I've ever seen.
TED Officer, I swear—
COP Shush up. I believe that this is your apartment. I also believe they had something to do with wrecking it. If you're not pressing charges, fine. But spare me bullshit like this. *(To Jake)* Let's go.
JAKE There's a gross miscarriage of justice happening here, I'm telling you.
COP Forget it, Jake, it's the East Village.

Jake and the cop exit, closing the door behind them.

OSSIP We fooled them! Isn't that wonderful? *(Grabs Ted and Cameron happily)*
CAMERON Don't touch me, pig.
TED *(Pulling away)* We didn't fool anyone. And I don't like what you did.
OSSIP Me? What did I do?
TED Well, aside from everything else, you tried to turn her in.
OSSIP It all worked out fine.
TED I want a check for this by tomorrow, or so help me, I'll get that cop back here and swear that you had a pistol in your pocket pointed at me the whole time.

OSSIP Take it easy. Here. *(Hands Ted a business card)* I didn't want to give it to the cop, but I do own a construction firm. I'll have the repairs done myself.

TED Right, and then you'll have a real heart attack in my living room.

OSSIP 'Course, not me. I'll send some of my boys. *(Collecting his tools)* They'll make it better than it was before.

TED How do I know you're not just going to run off now?

CAMERON I'll take you to his house if he tries to back out.

OSSIP *(Smiling)* I'm just so happy to see my old place. Can I stay a minute longer?

TED I suppose.

OSSIP This place was unsanitary, overcrowded, dim, dreadful— I'm convinced it started my heart condition. On this space here was a splintery floor, rats underneath, where I would race back and forth, playing for hours with my brother Abe—

TED He was the one you said was born here?

OSSIP Right in a bed over there. *(Points upstage)* We all had to stay with the neighbors that night. He died in '52.

CAMERON *(Playing an imaginary violin)* Oh God!

OSSIP *(Referring to Cameron)* This one always egging me on. She reminds me of my sister. She'd always tease me, we'd fight for hours, my beautiful sister Lydia—

CAMERON Who's now teaching geriatric aerobics in Miami Beach.

OSSIP No, she went back to the old country before the war and couldn't get out in time.

CAMERON For the record, I didn't call you a kike.

OSSIP *Kike* was a slang the German Jews invented against us newly immigrating Russian Jews whose names ended in "ki". So for me, when I was a kid, it was doubly hurtful. 'Course, the joke is that now it's used against all Jews.

TED *(To Cameron)* You should contribute to some of the repairs.

OSSIP It's okay. Money really means nothing to me. I do thank you.

You're a fine man and I'll take care of everything tomorrow. *(To Cameron)* And you—I'm giving you two hundred dollars, take it or leave it.

CAMERON I earned it.

OSSIP *(Opening the door, he kisses his forefingers, then gently touches a spot on the doorframe and turns to look for one last time)* The mezuzah was here. *(Exits, long pause)*

TED If I ever did bond with another male, it wouldn't be Ossip. How did you get entangled with him anyway?

CAMERON I answered an ad in the *Voice*.

TED For what?

CAMERON Someone with experience.

TED You were supposed to get me out of the house, and he was supposed to loot the place, right?

CAMERON Yeah.

TED What were you going to do with me if we did go out? I mean, you weren't really going to make love with me against the Manhattan skyline, were you? *(She responds with a doubtful expression)* You would've led me on, dumped me, then met him tomorrow to learn that he found a little rubber ball. You wouldn't've gotten a thing.

CAMERON Two hundred bucks. That was the base fee.

TED Are you even an actress?

CAMERON I'm a filmmaker. I went to NYU film school.

TED I should've figured.

CAMERON I was hoping to get a budget for a film.

TED A film about what?

CAMERON A documentary about how torturous and humiliating it is for an intelligent, attractive woman to live in this stinkhole city. About how all guys are slime who will do absolutely anything to get their cocks sucked. And how a girl gets called a bitch or a dyke if she asks for equal treatment.

TED Doesn't sound like a comedy. What's your last name, Cameron?

CAMERON My name isn't Cameron, it's Peggy.

TED I knew something was off here. You seemed more intelligent than you were coming off, even more attractive.

CAMERON (*Laughs in disgust*) You're still trying to pick me up, after all this.

TED You think I'm some yuppie.

CAMERON Aren't you?

TED Not anymore—I lost two million dollars in the last two years. My house is about to go under. This month I missed another payment. Hell, I was praying that there *was* money down there. Things get any worse, I'll have to move back in with the parents. I'll become a Middle-Aged Rural Unemployed Nobody. M-A-R-U-N, a moron!

CAMERON You'll get back on your feet.

TED It's more than just the money. I used to get a real thrill out of putting on a crisp suit. Studying market trends, making investments. Thirty looks so far away. Tonight I saw a man die right here, before my eyes.

CAMERON He didn't die. And I don't feel sorry for you, so quit looking for sympathy.

TED If you can't take anything from this entire evening—

CAMERON Yeah, two hundred bucks.

TED A million dollars in Russian heirlooms would've been nice, but—

Cameron abruptly takes out the purloined lighter and other objects she had taken from Ted's apartment and places them on the night table. Then she exits. Ted notices something in the hole. Sticking his arm in, he pulls out a small safety box hooked just under the floorboards. Opening it up, he removes a collection of jewels—the missing treasure. As the lights slowly fade to black, he displays no emotion.

WRITER'S BLOC

To Patricia Gough
—eternal thanks

Writer's Bloc (formerly entitled *East Village Writer's Bloc*) was produced at Nada in New York City on May 6, 1993.

Reggie	Michael Giannini
Miles	Thomas Boykin
Waldo	Robert Tierney
Lenny	John Patrick Clerkin
Samantha	Cynthia Newman
Lucy	Rachel Jolley
Director	Mark Farnsworth
Stage Manager	James West

The author would like to thank Patricia Gough for her kind permission in revising her short story, "Muscle Test," into Lucy's story.

ACT ONE

ACT TWO

Reggie's living room—present

ACT ONE

SCENE 1

Reggie's living room—an old couch, a coffee table, some chairs, a desk off to one side with a computer on it. The apartment is littered with dirty clothes and garbage on the floor. Everything is casually arranged. An old shotgun is leaning against a wall. A varied display of books, beer bottles, and other junk are scattered around, including some still-unopened bottles of hard alcohol. Just offstage is Reggie's bathroom and kitchenette. When the play begins, Lucy is sleeping in the bed upstage. Reggie and Lenny are in the middle of reading a play on the computer screen.

REGGIE I've been made a liar by my craft.

LENNY Pray tell, why, good Euripides?

REGGIE Because that's what writing is.

LENNY Ah yes, the great manipulation. Feel thy loss. Woe! Or—

REGGIE Come on, Lenny, read it with more feeling.

LENNY *(Overdoing it)* —Feel thy loss. Woe! Or, tickle and strum them like a lyre.

LUCY I got to go to work in three hours! *(They stop reading)*

LENNY Despite the misconception that ancient Greeks spoke in Old English, I am happy you've finally finished something.

REGGIE Let's finish reading it.

LENNY Lucy's right, it's late. How does it end?

REGGIE Do you know what happened to Euripides in real life?

LENNY A surprise sex change?

REGGIE He was torn apart by hunting dogs. I used actual historical material to shape the drama.

LENNY It seems to build toward something. But—

REGGIE But what?

LENNY Well, this is a one-act historical drama.

REGGIE So?

LENNY So, for the past six years you've been describing *Message from a Bottle.*

REGGIE You mean *A Messenger from Valhalla?*

LENNY Yeah. For the past six years you've been telling everyone what scene you're on, and what you're doing with certain characters—

REGGIE Yeah, so?

LENNY Yeah, well, you got me excited. You've made it sound like *Long Day's Journey into Angels in a Hot Tin Salesman*—

REGGIE And the messenger shall arrive.

LENNY When? The last time we spoke, you said you'd show me some of it.

REGGIE Hey, I'm showing *this* to you.

LENNY Look, I've been waiting for this messenger since the '80s. How much of it have you done?

REGGIE Most, but I'm not ready to show it.

LENNY Well, for your sake, I hope you're not showing this thing at the next workshop. I mean, expectations are running high.

REGGIE *(Pauses)* Shit, you're right. Do me a favor and consider this thing our secret, okay?

LENNY It's nothing to be ashamed of, get rid of some the *thous* and *thines*, but we're all waiting for, what did you call it, your "fuck-you-to-Frederick-of-Hollywood" play?

REGGIE *(Frustrated)* Okay, okay, even though it's not ready, I'll show some of the messenger play this week. Happy?!

LENNY Yes. Look at this. Not a word from you in years and *bang*, all this new stuff—

LUCY (*Grumbling from the bed*) Goddamn, Reggie, I got to go to work soon!

LENNY (*Looking at Lucy, he mutters*) Did I tell you Herbie dumped me?

REGGIE Oh, Len, I'm sorry.

LENNY Said he didn't want to see me anymore. Well, I don't either, but I can't break up with me.

REGGIE *That's* why you're here this late. And I made you read my awful play, I'm sorry. So what happened?

LENNY I don't know. I mean, we went out for a nice dinner, I gave him his present, and—

REGGIE You gave him that Valentine's Day card, didn't you? That poem.

LENNY He gave it back. (*Hands Reggie the card*)

REGGIE (*Reads the poetic inscription aloud*) I know you're beautiful and younger/but you're also geeky and dumber./It's still better to be always hard/and never come./Then after three strokes blurt,/"Sorry, Lenny, I'm done." (*Turns card over*) And look, a pretty picture of a limp penis. Putting his premature ejaculation problems in a card probably had nothing to do with his suddenly leaving you.

LENNY (*Ignoring him*) You sure you can't let me read just a little of your messenger play now? It'll really raise my spirits.

REGGIE Oh sure, maybe you can turn my inadequacies as a writer into a funny poem.

LENNY (*Takes back the card*) Whose house are we meeting at this week?

REGGIE Here.

LUCY (*Grumbles*) I have to go to work in three fucking hours!

LENNY (*Whispers*) So when is Sleeping Beauty gracing us with her presence again?

REGGIE Lucy decided to call it quits.

LENNY Really? Wow. And unlike the rest of us, she really was talented. Samantha the witch probably scared her off. Is Waldo going to be here?

REGGIE I don't know. He hasn't called. I think he's still in Washington, seeing the Wall.

LENNY The Vietnam memorial?! That's not like him. I hope he's okay.

REGGIE Like you care. You just want to nail him. But you never will because he's not gay.

LENNY *(Putting on his coat)* Then the only thing I have to look forward to is your great play. See you next week. *(Exits, blackout)*

SCENE 2

Reggie's living room, a week later. Reggie is watching a portable TV. He is wearing a dirty T-shirt and boxers and drinking beer. After a moment he hears voices in the outer hall. Quickly, he turns off the TV, and stowing it, he rushes to toss around articles of Lucy's clothes. Hiding the beer he's drinking, he pulls out an old coffee mug, which he places next to the computer and begins frantically typing.

MILES *(Opening the door, but remaining outside)* Hey, super, when do we get some heat?

REGGIE *(Still typing)* Hey, look who's harmonizing in my hall. Get in here. What are you two, together again?

SAM *(As she and Miles enter)* None of your goddamned business.

REGGIE Yeah, stick up for your rights. Show people where you stand.

SAM *(Sniffs)* Don't clean this apartment and people will know where you stand.

REGGIE *(Pointing to her knapsack)* So, did you bring your O'Henry Prize–winning story?

SAM Yup. *(Opens it, takes out a box of 5" floppy diskettes)* And Lenny tells us we're finally going to get a preview of this season's *Waiting for Godot.*

REGGIE *(Fumbling through his own box of diskettes)* It's on one of these.

SAM *(Continues searching through her bag)* Shit!

MILES So you finally woke up and bought a computer.

SAM No, Waldo woke up and bought one. *(Pulls out a separate box of diskettes)* These are his.

MILES *(Examining them)* Is he writing?

REGGIE Sure, Waldo writes and Lenny is into chicks. Is Waldo on drugs or something?

MILES No, why?

REGGIE He calls me up a couple nights ago at 4 a.m. for a cup of coffee at the Kiev.

MILES Classic shell-shock case.

SAM Leave the boy alone.

MILES It's no longer any of my business, but what are you doing with Waldo's diskettes? *(Sam sighs)*

REGGIE Uh oh. Last year's melodrama. *(Exits to the bathroom upstage)*

SAM You're right. It isn't any of your business.

MILES *(Whispers)* You can have sex with Great Danes, for all I care, but under the circumstances I feel a little sensitive about him.

SAM He left his knapsack at my house last week after the workshop. He asked me to bring it tonight. I stuck my story in here, or thought I did. *(She intensifies her search through his knapsack)* Shit! And I must've left my story home.

MILES Read it next week. We've got enough here.

SAM I live three blocks away. I'll be back in a moment. *(She exits, blackout)*

❦

SCENE 3

Reggie's bedroom, flashback. Lucy and Reggie are in bed under the blankets. Reggie is on top of Lucy, reading over her shoulder, occasionally fondling her, subtly trying to distract her for sex.

LUCY *(Reading)* This is what Reggie said to me—
REGGIE *(Muttering)* Oh great, more of the Reggie story.
LUCY —"You have to shape your life. Make it your own, or else the tides of circumstance take you where they want. You'll be cast out to the farthest seas, and believe me, it's hard to swim back, sharks and all." He liked larger-than-life metaphor. The more grandstanding, the better. "Wrest control of the Wheel of Life from those who would tell you where to go. Just break stride and don't look back."

He was Poet, Seer, Man, Lover, Svengali-in-Training. She was The Girlfriend, Poet-When-She-Felt-Like-It, Muse-in-Training. They had only been together six months. Quickly they acquired full-blown roles, clearly delineated, no questions, ifs, ands, buts. "You must take control! Do it for yourself. No one else does it for you."

He looked terrible, face aged lumpily by nights writing until 3 or 4 a.m., bad Polish coffee shop food, and a strenuous life philosophy. She, on the other hand, looked dewily youthful, eyes bright, possibly dazed by all the art, she saw going a mile a minute, flying out of mouths, manuscripts, Manhattan.

"Fail to plan, plan to fail," he said. "I don't like to expound a cliché, but it's true. You have to look at your life as if it matters, as if you have a plan. It's pretending to the throne, really. Can you pretend?" I pretend that I'm not hearing this all the time, she thought, but didn't say it. Instead she shrugged her thin, slightly stooped shoulders—a perpetually bad back made shrugging her preferred form of exercise. *Green to you might mean red to me*, she wanted to say, but the words settled in comfortable territory—they remained right where they were.

"I just want you to be happy. I'm most critical of people I care about. You can learn from me. I've been in your position before. I know what it's like to watch from the grandstands, rooting for the team. Believe me, I get it."

REGGIE If that guy is supposed to be me—

LUCY Let me finish!

REGGIE By all means.

LUCY "Yes, but do you love me?" she asked. That was the issue, as all inquiring female minds need to know. (*Reggie groans, then slowly massages Lucy's breasts*) She would do anything for him. And he took her time, because she would give it, willingly handed it over to him, gift-wrapped with a pretty pink bow, let him be her main source for company, sex, he was her solitude too, because she gave that as well. She knew it was easier to give than receive, a peculiarly female thing as she saw it. She too wrote during the squeezed-out time when she was guiltily reminded why she'd held nighttime word-processing jobs for three years, since coming to the City, why she'd refused Respectability-and-Comfortable-Living, fully embracing the Suffering-Artist-in-the-City-Who-Refused-a-Bourgeois-Lifestyle-in-Pursuit-of-a-Higher-Artistic-Purpose. (*Lucy pushes Reggie's hands off her breasts, then he moves his arms around her waist and slips his fingers in her panties*) Only then, with guilt, a stinging sensation lodging in her lower reaches, would she belly-up to the unfriendly computer screen—the form of the work was rarely longer than a poem—

Finally aroused by Reggie, Lucy turns to kiss him. They start having sex. Blackout.

SCENE 4

Reggie's living room, present. Reggie is still offstage in the bathroom. Miles is nervously trying to keep busy waiting for him to return.

MILES *(To Reggie offstage)* Sam wasn't at Waldo's house or anything.

REGGIE *(From offstage)* I don't care.

MILES Sam said Waldo left his diskettes at her place last week during the workshop.

REGGIE *(Returns with a beer)* Why are you telling me this?

MILES Right, it's just that . . . when she cheated on me with Waldo, well, you heard about it on both sides. I still have this cuckold complex. *(Pauses)* Even though we're not even together or anything.

REGGIE Get over it, pal.

Reggie opens Waldo's knapsack and takes out his diskettes. He slips one into his computer. Miles notices a rifle on Reggie's shelf and takes it down.

MILES Wow. I haven't touched a rifle since the Gulf War. Won the war but left the dictator in power. *(Inspecting it)* Firing pin is broken.

REGGIE *(Looking at Waldo's text on the screen)* I found it at my ma's house and thought it would make a nice conversation piece.

MILES *(Still inspecting the rifle)* For a killer maybe. God, I wish the NYPD let us carry rifles. It looks like a model 908, discontinued in the early '60s. Not much wear on the block. You can still scare your tenants off with it. How'd the hammer break?

REGGIE It just broke.

MILES (*Stretching*) God, my arms are achy. Didn't make it to the gym today. (*Puts down the gun, takes off his shirt, and does some push-ups, then checks his watch*) I have ten after. Where are they? (*Reggie is silently reading*) Been walking much?

REGGIE If that's your roundabout way of asking whether I've been writing, the answer is yes to both. I am sick of the constant skepticism.

MILES That's Lenny, not me. I just want you to make Fred regret that he ever went to Hollywood.

REGGIE With the money they waved at him, who can blame him? I just resent the way he dumped the rest of us.

MILES If tonight's play is any good, and I'm sure it will be, you should send him a copy. (*Reggie ignores him, reading*) Where did you pick up the habit of walking and writing? You know, Thomas Wolfe used to walk a lot and then write in longhand.

REGGIE Looks like Waldo's walked a couple blocks too.

MILES How many blocks?

REGGIE Not many. He just wrote a couple pages. (*Flipping through the other diskettes*) These look like some software program. Why does the name Ricky Marvel ring a bell?

MILES (*Reading over Reggie's shoulder*) Richard Marvelli.

REGGIE Right, the AIDS casualty. Waldo could've read this to us last week.

MILES I'm glad he didn't. I like Waldo, but who wants to hear him drone on about dying?

REGGIE That's not the point. (*Flips off the computer and puts Waldo's diskettes away in his knapsack*)

MILES What's the point?

REGGIE He hasn't read anything in six months. If everyone was as encouraging to him as they were doubtful of me, maybe he'd read something.

MILES (*Opening a beer*) I think it was Hart Crane—

LENNY (*Enters, completing Miles's remark*) —who, by the by, was gay. Hey, super, any crummy, cramped, over-priced apartments available?

REGGIE Not to any bitchy, predatory queens, there aren't.

LENNY (*Combing his hair*) Puss 'N Boots here?

REGGIE Not yet, loverboy.

MILES Or was it Fitzgerald who said that he could tell from the writing if the writer was drunk?

LENNY I can tell when a writer is hungry, and this writer is famished!

REGGIE Pizza time! (*Starts dialing the phone*)

LENNY But not Dominos, they give to Operation Resuce.

MILES Pizza, I can definitely get behind that.

LENNY (*Lustfully*) Oh, let me! (*Pauses*) You're calling the place over here. (*Points east*) The only one in the city that doesn't deliver.

MILES I'll go for it. I need some air.

LENNY (*Holding his nose*) I can use a bottle of that, Reg. You don't even have a lite beer.

REGGIE (*Ignoring him, on the phone*) Two Boots? An extra large with—topping?

LENNY (*Hollers*) Everything! Absolutely everything, unexpurgated, unabashed, unedited, shameless, mylar-wrapped—

REGGIE (*On the phone*) Your special.

Lenny and Miles put their coats on.

MILES A nebula of a pizza coming up.

REGGIE (*On the phone*) A Gulf War veteran will be there to pick it up. Thank you. (*Hangs up*) Where are you going?

LENNY The corner for some lite beer and heavy air. Back in a jiff.

Miles and Lenny exit, blackout.

SCENE 5

Sam's place. There are three short blackouts as Sam is reading her story alternately to Waldo and Miles. Each one can wait in the dark background while the other is in the lit foreground. Sam should read her story without changing pace, only pausing briefly during the blackouts. Where Waldo responds supportively, Miles should demonstrate impatience, critically taking notes. The scene begins first with Waldo listening.

SAM —The next morning Lorna looked again into the wall of her apartment to see what had crawled inside. The eyes staring back at her were tiny, leading Lorna to wonder if it could be a bat. Checking again that afternoon, she was almost positive that she could see the outline of a large tree frog, the kind that lives in a hollow. Inspecting yet again, she decided it might be a lungfish in dormancy. Pressing her ear against the rotting wall, she heard what was perhaps a purring or an extended rattle. Although it continued living there for months, Lorna adjusted and ignored it. Late one winter night, she was dead asleep when the clanging from the frigid radiator revived her. Lorna was so cold her body was numb. Rolling toward the wall she felt a radiant warmth. The thing in the wall glowed steadily like a single nugget of charcoal. The next day she purchased a flashlight and again looked into the hole in her wall. From flashes and glimpses, Lorna realized that it either had a severe case of mange or it was some rare red python. She dreamed about cleaning it up, making it pretty, tying a bow around its sad little skull.

Blackout. The lights come back up and Miles is taking notes, making expressions of critical discontent. Waldo is gone.

SAM   —Lorna put out more food and some water. This time she waited all night to see it, but it didn't emerge. When she went to work the next day, though, it digested everything, and left a putrid discharge on her bed. She wasn't certain if it was defecation or regurgitation. While Lorna was out of the apartment she felt anxious about the thing's health. She wished it would trust her and climb out of the crumbling wall. Then she could bathe and fluff it and make it into a pet. Perhaps she'd teach it some trick. She decided she would name it either Frances or Terry. Finally, all out of patience, Lorna borrowed a power drill hoping to free the animal. She looked long and hard into the hole. When she saw movement she quickly drilled a hole. But as soon as the drill bit sunk into the wall, Lorna heard a bloodcurdling screech. She yanked out the drill only to find blood and sinew spaghettied around the tip. She heard the thing moaning behind the wall and felt spasmodic vibrations. Soon there was only silence and stillness. That Sunday Lorna confessed the macabre occurrence to a priest.

"You didn't even know what it was," he muttered, not even offering her the act of contrition.

She tossed a flower into a hole in the wall and muttered a prayer. Then she packed and moved out. She found a boxy studio on the the Upper West Side and got a telephone line installed. She also adopted a small sickly mutt.

Blackout, and Waldo is again listening. Miles is gone.

WALDO   (*Applauding, excited*) It's great how first Lorna has uncertainty, but then she's curious, and finally she comes to love the thing in her wall, yet just like love when you try to embrace it—you kill it.

SAM   (*Sitting happily*) It makes me feel great hearing you describe it like that. You totally get me.

WALDO (*Pauses a moment*) I think you're a wonderful writer, I really do.

Blackout, and Miles is standing there, looking discouraged. Waldo is gone.

MILES I mean, what can I say? You don't want to hear it.

SAM Just tell me what you think.

MILES It's derivative. Part of the long line of Kafka mutations that simply surrealize sexual neurosis. (*He picks up a glass, about to drink*) This glass looks spotty. (*Puts it down*)

SAM So you didn't like it?

MILES It typically deals with your frustrations as a writer, which I think is self-indulgent and lazy. In a word, and I might be saying this because I love you, I know you're capable of so much better. (*Blackout*)

⟨&⟩

SCENE 6

Reggie's living room, present. Lenny returns, taking his coat off, filled with an air of anticipation.

LENNY Reggie, do you know what's going on out front?

REGGIE Yeah, it's a mess. I'll clean it when I take out the garbage later.

LENNY I wasn't talking about that. I was talking about the spotlights searching the sky, celebs walking the red carpet, flashbulbs bursting, you take a box seat, house lights dim, stage lights rise, and it is time for the premier of *A Messenger from Valhalla*.

REGGIE That was just a working title.

LENNY Come on, now. I skipped dinner to hear this. I'm never early.

REGGIE Relax.

LENNY Let me take a peak now. I deliberately left with Miles so that no one would know we were alone together.

REGGIE Don't be so eager. I showed you my other play.

LENNY The *thee-thou* play that for some strange reason I can't tell anyone about. That's why I'm so eager to see this one.

REGGIE It's on diskette. Let's wait till everyone gets here. (*Goes to the kitchen*) Want another beer?

LENNY Yeah, but not your Coors. (*Hollering to Reggie in the kitchen*) That guy supports fascist causes! And if there's any chocolate to munch on—except Hershey's, they kill babies in India. (*Looks through Reggie's diskettes and finds the one that says "Big Play," puts it in the computer, and types*) Shit!

REGGIE (*Enters, sees that Lenny is looking at his play*) I didn't want to show it now!

LENNY (*Taking out the diskette*) Well, I'm not looking at it, am I? It's not on this diskette.

REGGIE It's not?! (*Looks at the screen, then puts another diskette into the computer*) Wait a sec. (*Looks through his box of diskettes*) Oh shit! Lucy erased it! (*Lenny smirks as Reggie screams*) HOLY SHIT! NO! THAT BITCH! (*Still checking the directory of his computer*) SHE ERASED MY PLAY!

LENNY You can stop now.

REGGIE (*Looking at Lenny*) What?

LENNY Look, Reggie, if you want everyone else to think that she erased your play, fine, I'll keep your little secret. But spare me the bullshit, okay?

REGGIE (*Angrily*) WHAT?

LENNY I figured it out last week. You didn't write a play, and Lucy didn't erase one. That's what.

REGGIE Fuck you!

LENNY Years ago you and Fred cowrote two plays that had some off-

Broadway success. He grabbed a Hollywood offer and you became a super in a basement studio.

REGGIE Oh yeah, asshole, how about the Euripides play?

LENNY That's the first thing I've seen you do in ten years.

REGGIE How about the one-act I did last year?

LENNY Now that was horrid.

REGGIE That's not what everyone said a year ago!

LENNY *Work on it*, everyone said. Remember? That's how friends tell friends their plays are dreck. (*Pauses*) It wasn't dreck. I'm just saying—

REGGIE It's pretty clear what you're saying.

LENNY I'm saying I'm your friend, and I'm telling you this all alone because I am your friend. I'm saying that for whatever the reason, since Fred left to TV land you have had a great deal of trouble trying to write. It's been visibly eating you up. And—

REGGIE (*Enraged*) You don't know shit! You're a lonely fag. You're bitter and petty and spend your time pissing on everyone's parade because you can't make your own. But I only say that out of love. How does that feel, *friend?*

LENNY I came to terms with my shortcomings long ago, princess. I've surrendered myself to it.

REGGIE Well, I haven't. And I don't need you chopping me down. I wrote a play and—

LENNY Fine, you wrote a play. I'll play along.

REGGIE Lenny, I'd like you to leave.

Lenny picks up an old magazine and reads it, ignoring him. Reggie stays at the computer, reading something. The two ignore each other until Waldo staggers in dizzily and flops facedown on the sofa, exhausted.

LENNY Hello, love boat. We've been awaiting you. (*To Reggie, quietly*) Lighten the load. (*Waldo dozes as Reggie angrily continues reading*) This is a regular bash we're having.

WALDO *(Finally stirs)* Do you smell something weird?

LENNY I smell everything weird. And this place—

WALDO No, I think I smell a gas leak.

LENNY Well, it's not me.

REGGIE *(Checks the oven in the kitchen)* No leak in here.

WALDO Strange how Con Ed keeps having those accidents. *(Pauses)* Is it Monday or Tuesday?

REGGIE Thursday. *(Rises, and Waldo lies on the couch)*

LENNY And you're on the first leg of your East Village tour.

WALDO Is what's-his-name here?

LENNY I most certainly am. Wouldn't miss it for the world.

WALDO *(Out of it)* No, the—the cop, what's his name?

REGGIE Did you sleep last night or what?

LENNY *(Goes to the kitchen and returns with a can of lite beer)* He woke up in some squatter's boudoir on Avenue C and doesn't even want to think about what he did last night. Right, Waldo?

WALDO I got fired. Did I tell you that the last time I saw you?

REGGIE You got fired? From the men's shelter at Third and 3rd? Fired?

LENNY For smelling worse than the clientele?

WALDO The boss said I exasperated him.

LENNY *(Sexually)* What in heaven's name could he mean? *(Waldo shrugs)*

REGGIE By the way, Waldo, since 1982 I stopped going for coffees at 4:00 in the morning.

WALDO I'm sorry. I'm just a little out of it. *(Starts singing softly)* Laaa, laa, laa, laaa.

REGGIE And your sublet ends next week, doesn't it?

WALDO A bathtub of sleep, a night of coffee, I'll be fine.

REGGIE I'm worried about you, Waldo. Last week you blow your savings on this impulse to go to Washington to see the Wall. This week you're fired and homeless.

WALDO It was the AIDS Quilts Memorial. And Christ, was that

last week? It seems like ages ago. Did you ever see the Quilts?

LENNY I missed it when it was here. But I did write a song of social protest which I'm prepared to read here tonight.

WALDO Oh! This is the *writer's* workshop.

REGGIE Where did you think you were?

WALDO I don't know, an AA meeting at the community center. (*Sniffs*) Maybe the Stuyvesant clinic. (*Closes his eyes sleepily*)

LENNY (*Holding Waldo's head softly*) Look at him. Did you ever see someone so much in need? He really brings out the mother in me. (*Rubbing Waldo's head*) What's wrong with my little Puss 'N Boots?

REGGIE Maybe he has feline leukemia.

WALDO I'm so tired. So what's with Lucy?

REGGIE She doesn't come anymore, remember? Why don't you sleep a little till the others get here?

LENNY Yeah, take a little nap, hon.

Waldo lays back down, Lenny rubs his back. Blackout.

꩜

SCENE 7

Reggie's bedroom, flashback. A continuation of Scene 3. Lucy is in bed with Reggie again. Reggie is sitting in his underpants, looking dejected, unable to preform.

REGGIE (*Embarassed*) Sorry about that. I thought—

LUCY (*Picks up her story and resumes reading*) The two went for a walk through Midtown one cold day, and as they walked they talked.

"The problem is," Reggie explained, "most people look at

their lives as something to get through with the least amount of effort, the path of least resistance: They're born. They get married. Reproduce. Have jobs they hate. Then they die. There's no attempt at lifting the heavy curtain, taking a peak at what lies behind. Possibilities never considered. Paths never taken—" His voice wavered into silence at the thought of life's mass incoherence.

"Surely not I, Lord!" she shouted. No, she was one of the art-making. She'd stepped out from life's routine conventions. But she wasn't ready to take a bow. Not just yet.

"Of course, the probem with being a creator is that you're also a destroyer. And I'm a monster, you know!" he said, pulling her across the street into Tompkins Square Park, squeezing her hand steadily. "I'll unintentionally use honesty and love as a means of creating havoc. The woman has to provide the controls."

"I'm all control," she said passively.

"Good, then it's time for the Control Test!"

He liked to perform the Control Test on her periodically. This consisted of taking her hand firmly in his own, then squeezing it with varying degrees of intensity. With each press he'd ask her how strong the pain was on a scale from one to ten. She never liked it too much, as her hand was the delicate instrument upon which his pain was inflicted, all in the name of—who knows? And today, with the subfreezing cold, her metacarpals, having become ungloved in the fracas, were now a frozen row of icicles. His large hand grabbed for the small collection of bones, ready to crunch them like walnuts.

"Don't hurt, this is one of only two hands I have." She tried to pull it away, but he held on, determined.

"Pain and pleasure are two sides of the same coin." Her hand was aching from his grip.

"Why don't I ever get to do the test?" she asked naïvely.

"Because," he whispered into her ear, "I'm the minister of

pain around here."

Suddenly the squeezing commenced. She closed her eyes, feeling the waves of pressure coursing through her knuckles.

"Gauge the feeling numerically!" he shouted.

"That's a four. Now a six. Ow, that's definitely an eight. That's a four. Now a six. Ow, that's a solid nine!"

As the pressure intensified, colors flew behind her eyelids. Sparks of greens, purples, reds. She squeezed her eyes tight, thinking that was the key to preventing any possible leakages. The pressure of her tightly clasped eyelids kept her from focusing on the thing at hand—*her* hand. But the agony pushed out, dribbling over her face. Teardrops cascaded down her cheeks. (*Lucy flips though several pages*) Where the hell's the next page?

REGGIE (*Disturbed*) You know, I got to say something—

LUCY It wasn't meant to be hostile.

REGGIE After all the time and help I've given you—

LUCY Here's the last page. Just hear it entirely, and then we'll talk.

(*She picks up the page and just before she continues reading, blackout*)

❦

SCENE 8

Reggie's living room, present. Waldo is dozing. Lenny is rubbing his back gently. Reggie is reading. Miles suddenly enters with a pizza.

MILES What's this, a slumber party? Hi, Len. (*To Waldo*) Hey, slacker, I've got your truffles.

LENNY Whatcha got for me?

MILES A sexually confused pizza pie.

LENNY I'm famished! *(Gets plates, Miles opens the pizza box)*

WALDO *(Discreetly)* Reg, I need to talk to you.

REGGIE Later. I'm hungry.

All gather around the pizza.

LENNY Where's the satanic Samantha?

MILES She ran home to get her story. Waldo, you left your diskettes at her apartment last week. *(Gives Waldo both his knapsack and truffles)*

WALDO *(Opens the knapsack)* Oh! My WordPerfect, I was looking for it. I'm freshening up for a word-processing job.

LENNY *(To Waldo)* So, truffles. Why didn't I get any?

WALDO Miles was in Vermont this weekend so I had him get me a box of truffles from Gershorns, the chocolate people.

LENNY You saw the chocolate people and you couldn't take a little initiative and get me some? *(Miles shrugs)*

WALDO Today's the unveiling for someone's great play.

LENNY May I try a sample from the chocolate people? I always wanted to meet them, greet them, and eat them.

WALDO I can't, they're not for me. Let's hear this politically correct bullshit you wrote.

LENNY *(Picking up a piece of paper, as if reading from it)* There once was a writer named Sam/Who had no trouble getting a man/But when they'd say, "Stay!"/She was off and away—

MILES *(Jokingly grabs Reggie's broken rifle)* Finish the sentence and bam!

WALDO Tonight's Reggie's big night. For—what's the name of it again, *Messages from Hell?*

REGGIE A *Messenger from Valhalla.* Lucy erased it.

LENNY *(Feigning surprise)* Erased? Are you kidding?!

REGGIE Cut it out, asshole.

WALDO Cut what out?

MILES Lucy wouldn't be that cruel. Would she?

LENNY Hurricane Lucy strikes again.

MILES You were almost finished with it. You know, you do nothing but complain about her.

LENNY (*Picking up her clothes from the sofa*) And she's become an utter pig

REGGIE Take it easy.

WALDO Why do you—

REGGIE Everyone just shut up about it!

WALDO I want you to answer one question first, and then not another word.

REGGIE (*Sighs*) Okay, one last question.

WALDO Why do you stay with her?

REGGIE It's a weakness. I feel sorry for her. Now, what's on tonight's menu?

WALDO I wrote an epic masterpiece, but I'm not ready to show it.

MILES Samantha is getting her short story—

LENNY I worked on my poem, but it's not really a finished draft.

REGGIE And Miles has something for us.

They all look at Miles, surprised.

MILES What?

LENNY Nothing. I never get enough of your hard-boiled-egg memoir.

WALDO You're usually the rambling rhetorician.

LENNY Innovator that I am, I'm experimenting with minimalism.

MILES Doesn't look like we're on another juice diet.

LENNY Why don't you try an innovation and hush up?

Sam suddenly enters, takes off her coat.

MILES You're not going to guess what happened.

WALDO Hi, Sam.

SAM Hi.

LENNY Gay CIA agents shot JFK and erased Reg's play.

REGGIE *(Solemnly)* Keep it up, Ollie Stone.

SAM You're kidding?

MILES Lucy did it.

SAM You didn't print out a hard copy, make a backup?

REGGIE I never owned a printer. I was just going to read it off the screen. *(Pauses)* I can't believe she'd do this.

MILES Where is she? *(Reggie shrugs, still in shock)*

LENNY The elusive Lucy. When away, she sleeps. When here, she destroys great works of art.

MILES What a ball-breaker!

LENNY She's probably at the Ukrainian National Home throwing a castration party: Everyone's chewing prairie oysters, roasting nuts, taking blind whacks at a testicle-shaped piñata.

SAM This place is such a mess.

MILES I've seen girlfriends fall out of love before, but a clean person is usually clean to the end.

SAM The last time she came to a group was—when? The '80s, I think.

LENNY I miss the '80s.

REGGIE Go back there. They're waiting for you.

Sam exits to the kitchen.

LENNY Waldo, are there any nuts in those truffles? *(Waldo shakes his head no)*

MILES Actually, they have hazelnuts with a brandy crème center. *(Lenny swoons)*

REGGIE Give the guy a break, Len.

LENNY Are you sure Lucy didn't leave you, Reggie?

REGGIE God, I wish she would.

LENNY That's what they all say when they kill the lover.

REGGIE Goddamn it, Lenny—

WALDO *(To Lenny)* I saw her driving her Honda up First Avenue.

REGGIE *(Bewildered)* She didn't—you didn't stop, or talk?

WALDO Just waved and drove.

REGGIE Well, there you go. She's not buried in the basement.

LENNY Just your play is.

WALDO Hey, what is that? Listen. (*They all listen*)

REGGIE Probably me, I've been having indigestion.

WALDO (*Solemnly*) No! I hear someone screaming or crying. (*All listen attentively*)

MILES It's New York. You're supposed to ignore it.

WALDO Probably just the pipes. Anyway, Reggie, I was really looking forward to hearing this play.

LENNY I was dying to cut it to pieces.

SAM We heard so much about it. Developments each week. Innovations at every turn.

REGGIE Wait a second! (*To Miles*) You read some of it last week?

MILES You had some of it on the computer.

REGGIE (*To Lenny*) Ah ha! (*To Miles*) Tell asshole. Tell him!

MILES Well, I just saw the format, really. I didn't get to read any of it.

LENNY Ah ha!

REGGIE I offered to let you.

MILES That's true. I had to get to the gym.

SAM (*Looking at Waldo*) So who has what to read?

WALDO I don't have anything ready.

SAM (*Muttering*) Christ, Waldo! How long has it been?

REGGIE Okay, Len, let's hear your miserable minimal poem.

LENNY (*Takes a piece of paper out of an envelope, pauses a beat, reads it slowly*) You don't leave a bed/Where the test-positive sleeps/Without wondering, is that my fate?/As the incubus spreads and reaps,/Sweat through the anxious days/Of bitterness and malaise,/Life becomes a wait/That gradually entails/Re-seeing death as great,/Since test-life always fails.

Silence, then Waldo rises and dashes into the bathroom. We hear him throw up.

REGGIE There's some constructive feeback. (*Blackout*)

◌

SCENE 9

Waldo's apartment, flashback. He is alone, speaking on the telephone, sitting before an old typewriter with paper in it.

WALDO (*Visibly rattled*) I know I was supposed to see him, but I can't this week. How is Rich? (*Pauses, listening*) Well, I'm in the middle of something and next week I'm supposed to travel, so— (*Pauses, listening*) Tell him I'll visit him as soon as I can. Love to him.

Waldo hangs up. He starts trying to work, punching the typewriter keys. Finally, he rips the page out and tears it up. Blackout.

◌

SCENE 10

Back to the present, Reggie's living room. Waldo returns to his seat.

WALDO Sorry. My stomach's doing somersaults.
SAM It's a concise poem, Len. (*Barbed toward Miles*) Least, it didn't put me to sleep.
MILES (*Murmuring*) Or deal with feminism.
WALDO (*Facetiously*) But still quite topical. You can probably get it published in *The Native* or *NYQ*.

LENNY It's a treacherous time to be gay.

REGGIE *(Yiddish accent)* No picnic being straight either, let me tell you.

MILES It was short, to the point, no loose ends—

WALDO *(Suddenly furious)* That's the fucking trouble with it! You take a vital subject and make it glib with this "since test-life always fails" shit.

REGGIE Take it easy.

WALDO No! I'm sick of watching healthy people waste life, taking the attitude, "We're all going to die anyways, so shut up and die quietly!"

LENNY Uh oh! An ACT UP rally.

WALDO When someone says to you, "Lenny, you are going to die," you are not going to say, "Oh well, life always fails." You think *(Starts panting)*, "Shit! That was it? I'm really dying? That was it and now it's over." When you die, it's like . . . the whole world dies.

LENNY Cry and you cry alone.

WALDO Go ahead make a fucking joke about it.

SAM Relax, Waldo.

LENNY Freak out, if you like. But it just hasn't been that hot for me. I've hit rerun row. I've suffered this evening before, I've had that beer and pizza before, I've heard your bullshit before. It's all just one big snooze.

WALDO Then you fucked up. It's your job to make life important. Period.

MILES Not in a compromising mood tonight, are we?

LENNY Got any suggestions for me, big boy?

WALDO For what?

LENNY Making life scrump-deli-icious?

WALDO *(Solemnly)* In a letter from Augustine to Petrarch, Augustine advocated that Petrarch should break all fetters of the world by perpetual meditation on death.

LENNY Excuse me while I hang myself. *(Waldo exits for a beer)*

REGGIE Petrarch, huh? I remember when I used to read irrelevant literary books. (*Waldo returns*)

SAM I just don't know what to look for. There's not that much to critique.

LENNY Not much to critique? Please, Waldo, don't kill her. She's not been herself lately.

WALDO Sorry if I got a little wacky. I think I had a glucose rush.

MILES So what do you look for in a poem, Waldo?

WALDO (*Starts slowly and builds up*) I don't know. Something that exalts and humbles me both at once, that I'd feel embarrassed to read aloud, but obliged to tell others about. Urgent, living, that burns to the touch, that reduces me to a mere message bearer—

REGGIE (*Sings*) Climb every mountain, ford every stream—

WALDO (*Lenny is staring at him*) What are you looking at?

LENNY You know what you just described to a tee?

WALDO No.

LENNY (*Sexually*) I think you do.

WALDO (*Joking*) Oh, a long piss after downing a six-pack?

LENNY I'll give you a six-pack. (*Pauses*) Of tall boys.

REGGIE (*Interrupting*) Actually, it wasn't a bad little limmerick, Lenny.

MILES Let me ask you something that's none of my business and has nothing to do with the poem.

LENNY I don't want to hear anything that's none of your business and has nothing to do with—

MILES Did you take the test?

LENNY Sure did, and I have a chauffeur's license to prove it. (*To Waldo*) Did you test?

WALDO I didn't get the results yet.

MILES (*To Waldo*) Why did *you* take the test?

WALDO I just did. (*Abruptly*) Is there any more beer in the fridge? (*Reggie nods yes*)

LENNY (*Staring at Waldo as he exits*) Who said a homosexual lies deep inside of every hetero?

SAM Or would like to?

LENNY I'm not the one that slept with half the male population here. *(Sees Miles gulping beer)* Miles, isn't that my beer?

MILES *(Spits the beer out)* Is this yours? *(Waldo returns with another beer)*

SAM Gays are convinced that every male from Christ to Clinton was a closet queen, and I'm bored of it.

LENNY Look who's talking. The she-wolf who thinks that every man from Christ to Clinton is a rapist—

SAM I never—

MILES *(To Waldo)* Was this your beer?

WALDO No.

LENNY I stand corrected. We're all sexually inadequate. *(To Reggie)* What was the last piece she read?

REGGIE *The Junk Male*, m-a-l-e.

MILES Lenny, is this your beer?

SAM *The Junk Male?* You loved it!

WALDO The sexual inadequacy of all your past lovers.

MILES Lenny! Is this your beer or mine?

LENNY Beats me. Drink it. I won't ask for it back.

MILES Was your bottle near empty or near full?

LENNY Let's see, am I an optimist or pessimist?

MILES I just had a cold sore and I don't want anyone getting infected.

LENNY Drink both bottles.

Miles drop both bottles, pretending it's an accident.

REGGIE Shit!

Lenny laughs and everyone helps to mop up beer.

WALDO I'm sorry for getting worked up over your poem, Len. I know your heart's in the right place.

LENNY It's okay, cupcake.

WALDO I guess I was hoping for something with more, I don't know, guilt or anxiety maybe.

SAM Guilt and anxiety have become very passé, Wald.

WALDO Well, maybe they'll come back into style. Do you know anyone who died of AIDS lately?

SAM I knew people—

MILES *(Emphatically)* I know a girl who slept with a guy who had it.

REGGIE Christ, everyone in this fucking country slept with someone who slept with someone with AIDS.

MILES God! Do you think so?

LENNY Creeks flow into brooks which flow into streams—

REGGIE *(Not pausing)* —trickling down hill and dale—into rivers.

LENNY Gays and straight, blacks and whites—

WALDO Our whole country is just glued together with sperm.

SAM —the rich and the homeless.

MILES *(Muttering to himself)* Symptom-free for years, riding on the libido. You can take away guns, but not an urge. AIDS is an amazing weapon, moving rapidly, invisibly.

WALDO What a scary thought!

MILES What is?

WALDO *(To Sam)* Pick anybody. Sexy, ugly, famous. Pick a card.

SAM The guy who plays the professor on *Nanny and the Professor.*

WALDO Okay, I'll bet you had sex with someone who had sex with someone, etcetera, who eventually made it with him.

SAM I've had sex with less than *(Quietly counting)* fift—twent—thirty different guys. And I didn't screw anyone in academia.

MILES That many!

WALDO *(Dogmatically)* But you screwed someone who screwed someone, and so on, who screwed this guy.

MILES Still, Samantha didn't make it with anyone who could've made it with *Nanny and the Professor.*

WALDO I'll bet you! Fifty bucks! Right now!

MILES You got it!

WALDO Great, I need the money. *(They shake hands)*

REGGIE (*All eyes are on Waldo*) The burden of proof is on you, Wald.

WALDO No it isn't!

MILES (*Tensely*) Yes it is! You got to show some proof. No proof, you owe me fifty, and I ain't letting you off.

WALDO (*Angrily*) Fine!

MILES So let's see this fucking proof.

WALDO They're both going to die of AIDS. How's that for proof?

SAM What?!

WALDO I got no proof. And I have— (*He empties his pockets, finds a container of pills, washes one down with beer, then counts out his change*) a dollar thirteen to my name. So you can beat me up if you want, Miles. (*Puts the pill container away*)

LENNY You okay, twinkles?

WALDO A headache.

REGGIE Bet's canceled, chemical imbalance.

LENNY I made it with the professor on *Gilligan's Island*. So if you and I— (*Makes a gesture indicating sex*) then you win the bet, 'cause you and Sam— (*Repeats the sex gesture*)

WALDO Better yet, why don't you— (*Makes a gesture indicating he should hang himself, then exits*)

MILES (*To Sam*) I've never seen him like this.

REGGIE He lost his job and next week he's out of his apartment.

SAM It's those quilts. He's been like this since he returned from Washington. (*Waldo returns*)

LENNY I've got a quick job for you if you need one, Waldo. (*Waldo shakes his head no*) Can't I have one truffle?

WALDO Look, I'm saving them for Mother's Day. My mom loves the shit.

SAM You told me you didn't like your mother.

LENNY And they call me a faggot. Read your tale of woe and humiliation, Sam. (*Exits into the kitchen and quickly returns with a beer*)

MILES Wait a second. Waldo. (*Gives him the fifty dollars*) Here, you won.

WALDO No proof.

MILES Well, hold onto it until you get a job. (*Waldo takes the money, baffled, and puts it into his pocket*) I got something to add to your poem.

LENNY Yeah, beer.

MILES I took notes. (*Opens his note pad, reads*) There's no leaving a bed, "There's," unstressed, "no," stressed, "leav," stressed, "-ing," unstressed.

LENNY I have enough stress in my life, thank you.

MILES The beats are off and you have this crazy hexameter—

LENNY I'm going to beat you crazy with a hexameter.

Waldo suddenly stomps on a shirt lying on the floor.

REGGIE Why did you just kill my shirt?

WALDO I thought I saw something else.

REGGIE Are you sick?

LENNY What's the matter, Waldo?

WALDO Sleep, I just need a lot of sleep.

SAM (*To Waldo*) When do you intend to read something?

WALDO I'm on sick leave for a while.

SAM You've been on it for months now. In fact, I don't remember the last time I heard you read. What are you here for, beer and insults?

LENNY Leave him alone, you bully. I'll protect you, bundles.

WALDO Look, Sam, I'm trying.

SAM How? (*Lenny exits to the kitchen for beer*)

WALDO I finally dumped my typewriter and got a used computer.

SAM Good, now just sit at the keyboard and wiggle your fingers. We're not even asking that it make sense.

WALDO (*Starts hyperventilating*) Sam! Please, I can't handle it right now!

MILES Okay, cool it, Sam.

SAM *You* cool it! This is a writer's group. I want a vote taken on this point. Either he brings something next week or he can't participate.

REGGIE Hold it! There is no voting in my house.

WALDO Sam, if you want, I'll quit the group. Okay?

SAM I think being a writer means writing, and if this is a support group then we're supposed to help each other. I'm trying to help!

WALDO I really am stressed out right now.

REGGIE (*Gestapo accent*) Ve have vays of making you write.

MILES (*Seriously*) During the Korean War, the Communists tortured prisoners by inserting a thin glass rod into the penis and cracking it so that—

REGGIE All right, let's try a different tactic. Waldo, have you written anything lately that you might want to share? It doesn't have to be fiction.

WALDO Sorry, but I haven't written anything in a while.

SAM What do you mean, it doesn't have to be fiction? What is he supposed to read—"Dear Abbey"? (*Miles signals for Sam to be silent*) Why are you doing that?

MILES I give up. Samantha, while you were out we looked at Waldo's diskettes and saw something.

REGGIE I put it up on the screen. I'm sorry, Waldo.

WALDO What? (*Calmly*) Oh, my memoir of Richard.

SAM Richard Marvelli?

WALDO Yeah. In fact, I just wrote about the first time you met him. (*Pauses*) Remember, you thought he was making a move on you?

SAM Yeah, it turned out he was making a move on *you*.

WALDO He probably was.

SAM (*Pauses*) So you wrote something?

WALDO It was just an account of our friendship.

MILES (*Nervously*) So who made a move on who?

WALDO Richard was omni-sexual. He moved on everything.

LENNY (*Returns, handing Miles a beer bottle*) I brought you a beer.

Drink up, Miles.

MILES *(Murmuring)* It's open. *(Doesn't drink it)*

LENNY Hold it. Richard died last fall? Now when exactly did you and Sam—

MILES *(Concerned)* We broke up in September, why?

LENNY *(To Sam)* Forget it. I just thought you and Waldo went to the funeral.

MILES Waldo and Samantha were dating by then?

REGGIE *(Pauses, then mutters)* I took an AIDS test.

LENNY Me too.

SAM So I brought a new short story—

MILES *(To Reggie)* Why'd you take it?

REGGIE Better safe than sorry.

WALDO A lot more people still die of car accidents and cancer.

SAM My point though, Waldo, is if you want to write fiction you shouldn't have an excuse. You should still submit something. I'm sorry about bringing it to a vote—

WALDO I'm just going through a lot right now, Sue.

SAM My name is Samantha. Remember?

REGGIE *(Joking)* He had something written all along. If you want a vote, it should be whether or not we read his work.

MILES *(Puts his hand in the air)* I vote we look at it.

LENNY I propose we just examine the dirty parts.

WALDO You're voting to look at my private memoir?!

SAM All we're saying is either shit or get off the pot. But stop deluding yourself and thinking that coming to this circus once a week makes you a writer. Write something!

LENNY I'm not saying that. I also propose we eat his truffles.

MILES Read your story, Sam.

REGGIE Okay, Sam, let's hear what some guy did to you this time.

SAM Fuck you. *(Takes out a short story and starts reading)* Amateur Night; An Open Mike. Why were they applauding, she wondered, as she told the series of automatic jokes. "I'm the only comic that impersonates a clitoris." With this, she stuck her tongue tip out just a bit at the right side of her wet, sealed lips, then tilted the left side of her face down so that her mouth was vertical. *(Lenny demonstrates)*

A staunch silence suddenly collapsed with a single giggle, which permitted an onslaught of male laughter and foot-stomping.

"What's so funny about that?" she finally asked into the mike. All laughed again.

"Look," she finally admitted, "I'm not a comedian, I'm just a housewife." Guys were choking on laughter.

"What's wrong with that?" *What's wrong with that?* she asked herself. It was where life had led her.

"After graduating high school, my mother threw me out of the house. I took an awful job as a cashier. I never was good in school and my roommate was a big bitch, so I'd just sit on my front steps drinking beer, smoking ciggys. One day I met him on the checkout line. He was a cabdriver, a nice guy. He wasn't too selfish during sex. Within a week I moved into his place. *(Reggie points at Waldo during this line, but then points at Miles)*

Six months later we got married, but neither of us wanted kids. That was six years ago. Now we don't talk much anymore. We don't have any intimacy. He goes to the garage early and comes back late, but he pays the bills. And lately, more frequently, I pretend I'm other people. I fantasized that I was a comedian and sometimes an actor, glamorous types, but now I'm forty-two with no family, and my figure's all but gone, and Tony doesn't even notice anymore—"

The shrieks of laughter from the audience made her realize that she had unintentionally spoken all her most intimate thoughts aloud. She froze, and her eyes melted with tears.

The comedienne whined, "They've no business! That's my life they're laughing at!" The manager climbed up to the stage and said, "Nothing personal, hon. The boys just want a good time." The laughs now were like waves nearing high tide. They receded only to hit back harder. By the manner in which she stood at the edge of the stage, she might as well have been standing on some desolate bridge. With final resolution, she let go, collapsing into the dark pool of audience before her. Hitting her head against a table's edge, she lay as flat as a squashed cockroach.

"It's only theater blood," she vaguely heard one spectator assuring another. Hands suddenly reached out of the darkness.

"Give her air," the manager said, inspecting her forehead. With a hop, she pushed the manager aside, took to her feet, and rushed out the door. Several boyish fans pursued.

They seemed to be pressing her down. Looking up Sixth Avenue, the manager could see the middle-aged woman holding her bloody scalp and running, screaming, "They're laughing at me! They're laughing at me!" Red drops trailed behind the wounded comic. The manager returned inside to introduce the next performer. *(Pauses)*

WALDO I like the setting but I wish you developed the character more. Your characters all come off a little one-dimensional.

REGGIE Unfortunately, it isn't bad.

LENNY *(Pauses)* It would be good if it didn't have this forced thesis that presents: *(Does the quote, unquote fingers sign)* "The wounded female" who we're supposed to be sympathetic to. And the: *(Does the quote sign again)* "The angry male audience" who we're directed to hate.

REGGIE *(Waldo raises his hand)* Toilet's that way, Waldo.

MILES When you said "male laughter," what did you mean? Was that supposed to be an indictment on our patriarchal society for making a woman's life laughable and empty?

SAM *(Facetiously)* Precisely.

LENNY Really, Sam, the one-note thesis is getting a bit lame. You've got a potentially cute story here that you're going to sink with all the sexual judgement.

WALDO Regarding sex in a sexually paranoid age—

REGGIE Uh oh, the AIDS interpretation.

LENNY The comic is a virus and it enters the body of this comedy club, but they purge it with laughter—

WALDO I wanted to ask how it felt being the only female in this group.

LENNY Yeah, do you feel awkward being the only sexually inconsistent member here?

SAM No, do you? *(Lenny shakes his head no)*

MILES I miss Lucy.

WALDO Yeah.

REGGIE Well, let's not talk about it.

MILES I wonder why she quit.

REGGIE Don't blame me.

SAM *(Muttering)* She'd dress like a slut.

LENNY Ah ha!

SAM Ah ha *what?*

LENNY It's the strongest form of bigotry. Gays who hate gays, blacks who hate blacks, and *(Points to Sam accusingly)* a woman who hates women.

SAM What are you talking about?

WALDO She's a flaming feminist.

LENNY She hates other females. She *loves* being the only female here.

WALDO Lucy wasn't bad either. You used to come down hard on her. *(Muttering)* Which was probably why she quit.

SAM What?!

REGGIE Give it a break, Len.

LENNY It's true. You critiqued her work like an Iraqi terrorist with a Silkworm missile.

MILES You *were* hard on her.

SAM I was, I'll admit it. I thought she was an excellent writer. But just like the tight miniskirts and low-cut blouses she wore, she sold herself short. She lacked confidence. Every time there was a choice between a challenge or some stupid little pleaser, she'd do the cute thing. Well, it was our job to be ambitious for her.

WALDO Is humiliation a practical form of criticism?

SAM You're not one to talk. All you wanted to do was fuck her.

REGGIE (*To Sam*) Yeah, once Lucy quit, you went off and la-dee-dah behind Miles's back with Whimsical Waldo over here. (*Miles moans*)

WALDO (*Angrily*) Hey, what does that mean?

REGGIE Nothing, sorry.

WALDO No! What exactly are you saying?

REGGIE You're jobless and homeless. Life's a whimsy.

WALDO You take that back! That's just not true!

REGGIE Okay, I'm sorry.

Lenny begins to rub Waldo's back.

WALDO Don't touch me! Please.

SAM (*Quietly to Waldo*) You okay, hon?

WALDO (*Muttering angrily*) Calling me fucking whimsical.

MILES You are in a bad way tonight, pal.

LENNY See, that's why I asked when you and Sam broke up. 'Cause I remember hearing that Waldo's friend died when (*To Sam*) you were cheating on Miles with bubble-ass over here. Amazing how the mind links distasteful events.

SAM For Christ sake.

MILES Wait a second! Are you saying that you two had sex that long ago?

SAM Let's not go into this, please. I told you *all* about it.

LENNY Who's reading next?

WALDO Miles, he's the last. Then I got to get some sleep.

SAM What, are you sick? (*Feels Waldo's forehead*)

LENNY You've got a weird rash there. (*Points to Waldo's forehead*)

WALDO I'm just running a sleep debt, with all my other debts.

MILES You should see a doctor. Run some tests.

WALDO I'm okay.

REGGIE Do some exercise. It'll build up your muscles.

LENNY Join the Marines. It'll build your character.

WALDO I slipped a disk or something a couple months ago. It gets real painful. (*Stretches with a grimace*)

LENNY What a pansy! Want a back rub, dove? (*Waldo consents with a nod, and drinks his beer*) I defend him from menacing women, verbose writers, rub his aching back, and I can't even get his little brown truffle.

REGGIE Miles, time's passing. Better start your engines.

MILES (*Reads proudly and slowly, all listen with interest*) This is a part of my ongoing cop memoir that you've all been hearing since I've known you, by New York Police Officer Miles Gallo, entitled, *Gallo Humor*, dedicated to twelve honorable years of Republican presidency—

LENNY No political acceptance speeches!

MILES *Gallo Humor*, copyright 1993.

LENNY No one will steal it. Just read.

MILES Then shut up and let me read it. *Gallo Humor.*

LENNY (*Softly*) We've memorized the title. *Gay Low Humor.*

SAM We're never going to leave here unless you let him read it.

LENNY I'm just saying we remember the title.

MILES (*Pauses*) *Gallo Humor*, Chapter 14. Being a cop didn't always mean being a prick. Frequently it meant staring into mysteries that would never be explained. One steamy night last summer, I was heading home after a long day in Neighborhood Stabilization. Off-duty, I was walking up Houston when I heard the shrieks of a man who said that his neighbor had just been condo-jacked. Two people had just taken over his apartment. Best as I could tell, a crazy-looking older guy and his cutie-pie chick had literally broken in and dug a hole in the middle of a yuppie's living room floor. Problem was, the apparent vic, Mr. McYup, who was naked except for his boxers, kept insisting the probable perps were his friends and that no crime had occurred.

Without a plaintiff, or any real evidence, a charge simply couldn't be filed. My own instincts told me that the cutie-pie was a hooker. The perverted property owner probably did it with her in the hole. Who the hell knows why? Later, when the yupster refused to pay, the geriatric pimp showed up. (*Lights begin to fade*) These situations had become a dime a dozen, half-baked no-plaintiff cases that would never float in court, but the type of bilge water that swamps a beat cop's day—

Blackout. Moments later the lights rise as he is reading another section. The group is bored or restless, looking at their watches, reading magazines, whispering amongst themselves.

MILES —So I was stuck in Quality of Life, a pretty phrase for a scummy, thankless assignment. Basically, I became a babysitter for the local homeless. This was their routine: They spend the nights canvassing through the garbage cans in the area. The more desperate of them burgle or steal from the local merchants, or just smash and grab from parked cars. By rush hour, they collect along Astor Place, where they put their crap on display to convert their spoils into street drugs. I don't like playing the heavy, but when you warn these people over and over, what choices are you left with? Morality fades. After a while brutality becomes the common language, and abuse hides in the gray area of intent. How hard do you have to hit to get the job done? How much force is just enough? The law covers only the black and white, so cops are stuck doing the black and blue work—bruising and scaring the scarred and beaten. (*Lights slowly fade*) If the homeless are society's unsympathetic victims, we are made into society's unwilling bullies. Loathed and looked at as eroders of constitutional rights, but let's see them operate without us—

Blackout.

SCENE 11

Reggie's bedroom, flashback, a continuation of Scene 7. Lucy has just finished reading her story. Throughout the scene she is slowly dressing.

REGGIE Did I ever treat you like that?

LUCY It was just a story.

REGGIE It was cute and all, but did I ever squeeze your hand?

LUCY You squeeze other things. Don't worry about it. *(Pauses)* I know this is a stupid question, but do you think I'm better than Sam?

REGGIE Sure, I never even copped a feel off of her.

LUCY I mean as a writer!

REGGIE *(Amused)* I know. Sure, sure.

LUCY Why?

REGGIE I don't know, she's into surreal feminist crap.

LUCY Oh God! You're just placating me.

REGGIE Actually, I'll tell you what I do like. Remember that batch of juvenile writing you did in college?

LUCY *(Sarcastically)* Sure, my batch of juvenile writing. I have it here somewhere. *(Points to a box)*

REGGIE You had a curtain-riser with some kind of dumb title like, *Some Rot, Others Die.*

LUCY *(Sighs)* I wrote that in a summer writing workshop. You would like that. It's the most maudlin, pretentious—

REGGIE *(Angrily)* Well, I'm fucking sorry, but I liked it. And I really thought it could be developed into something.

LUCY About a great writer who can't write. You probably see yourself as the great writer, don't you? Here. *(She locates it and drops it in front of him, he doesn't pick it up)* It's yours.

REGGIE *(Pissed)* All right, you want my opinion? I really think you come incredibly close, but ultimately I don't believe you have the commitment. You're not willing to make the sacrifices to be a serious writer.

LUCY *(Checks her wristwatch)* I got to get going.

REGGIE Hold on a sec. I'm sorry.

LUCY Save it for your next protégé.

REGGIE *(Facetiously)* All right, you're the exciting voice of your dull generation. Is that what you need to hear?

LUCY I don't need anything from you.

REGGIE What an ingrate! Here in the middle of the night, trying to suck reassurance from me when you need it. But when you hear something that's uncomfortably honest, albeit a little impolite, you bail out.

LUCY You're half right—I am a hypocrite. But what I really get from you isn't reassurance. In fact, it's the opposite, it's the strength to quit this writing bullshit altogether.

REGGIE What does that mean?

LUCY It means I hate writing. And for the record, all you can do is tear people down because the simple fact is—*you can't write.*

REGGIE Hey, hon, I would've been writing right now if you didn't bribe me with sex to hear your whiny prose.

LUCY You know, that's the only thing you ever really need a woman for—blame for your goddamned inabilities. From now on, you'll have all the time you need to write, and you can go fuck yourself. *(She exits, blackout)*

SCENE 12

Reggie's living room, present. Before the lights go up, we can hear Miles still reading his short story. As the lights rise, we see Reggie staring off sadly. Lenny, who has headphones on, is giving shirtless Waldo a back rub. Sam is sleeping.

MILES —Had I gone nuts? Did I really permit some crazy Dr. Mengele–type scientist to perpetrate his insane mind-control experiment, designed to microwave a criminal into a model citizen? Yes, he claimed the man had murdered his wife, and for some reason I believed it. Weeks later, I inspected his behavioral results. I walked into Frankenstein's castle on Avenue C and heard screams coming from the basement. The scientist's body had grown in strange proportions. His arms had blown up to the size of oak trees. His massive granite hand had the poor criminal by the neck. He was choking the life out of his human guinea pig. As I struggled to loosen the monster's steely fingers, the lunatic grabbed me with his free hand and, clamping it like a bear trap around my neck, he proceeded to strangle me as well. I could feel the blood constricted in my arteries and oxygen blocked in my throat. Slowly, feeling my consciousness literally dissipating from my body, I struggled to reach for my service revolver. It was the first time I had ever drawn the gun in the line of duty. Not even sure if I was actually doing it, or only dreaming I was, I pointed my .38. It seemed to take forever and required all my strength to pull that little metal trigger, finally—BANG!

WALDO *(Suddenly bolts up from his sleep, covered with sweat, fighting with Lenny above him)* HELP! Don't! STOP!

LENNY Stop?

WALDO Sorry, I dreamed something awful happened.

REGGIE Were you shot by a verbose cop?

WALDO No, I—I got to take a leak.

LENNY *(Sensitively)* Waldo, may I just have one truffle?

WALDO No! For the last time—no! What the hell's wrong with you? *(Exits to the bathroom)*

LENNY Asshole! He's not peeing. He's abusing himself wickedly in there.

SAM I wish someone would abuse *you* wickedly.

LENNY I rubbed his pimply back. He used me! Now he owes me a truffle. (*Opens Waldo's knapsack*)

MILES That's his mom's, Len. I don't think—

LENNY What have we here? (*Takes out some diskettes*)

REGGIE That's the memoir he wrote. It's only a couple pages.

SAM Leave the poor boy's stuff alone.

MILES (*Awkwardly to Reggie*) There was nothing in that memoir that might've suggested— Well, they didn't share the same razors or lovers—

LENNY Or drink from the same bottle?

MILES Yeah, that sort of thing.

LENNY That rash on his forehead troubles me.

MILES Why?

LENNY What are these diskettes? (*Reads the label on one*) WordPerfect?

REGGIE (*Half asleep*) It's just a software package.

SAM It's his private diary. Put them away.

LENNY (*Puts a diskette into the computer*) Don't worry, Sam, I'm sure it doesn't say anything about your little indiscretion.

REGGIE He's going to be out in a minute. (*Lenny is reading the screen intently*)

SAM (*Yawns*) What's that sound?

MILES Sounds hydraulic. Like a garbage truck.

SAM No, I hear someone crying.

REGGIE (*Alarmed*) Oh shit! The cans!

MILES What cans?

REGGIE (*Pulling on his shoes*) The building's garbage cans. I'm supposed to pull them out front. Help me, quick!

LENNY No way. This is my good shirt.

MILES I'm in the middle of my story!

REGGIE We'll be back before Pee Wee's out of the john.

MILES *(Irate)* Goddamn it! *(Miles and Reggie dash out)*

LENNY *(Holding up a diskette)* This is the only WordPerfect diskette. *(Keeps reading)* Hey! He really did write a lot of pages here. *(Takes the diskette out of the computer)* This file says *Novel Number One.*

SAM What?!

LENNY It's a fucking novel!

SAM *(Rises)* You're kidding. *(She chuckles)*

LENNY *(Counts the diskettes in the box)* He's got eight, nine, ten diskettes filled up.

SAM What does that mean?

LENNY *(Slips another diskette into the computer)* There's writing on each of them. There are over a thousand pages here!

SAM Over a thousand pages? But why hasn't—

LENNY He's done a sequel to *Valley of the* fucking *Dolls.*

SAM And I yelled at him for not writing.

LENNY This is too much. Wait till Reggie sees this.

SAM Lenny, do me a favor and keep a lid on this.

LENNY Why?

SAM I know how Waldo works, he'll freeze up if he finds out we know. He shouldn't be forced. He'll read when he's good and ready.

LENNY Gosh, imagine if he's really written something.

SAM Just imagine.

LENNY *(Reading the screen)* I don't want to pry, but did you and Waldo— *(With difficulty)* What I'm trying to say is, were you cautious?

SAM Please, I get my share with Miles the hysteric.

LENNY Why is Miles such a germ phobe?

SAM Remember when he said, "I knew a girl who slept with a guy who had AIDS"? *(Lenny nods yes)* That was his sister. So far she's tested negative. Also, his mother died of a virus. She was a nurse, always fastidious about sterilizing and sanitizing. So Miles has become obsessive.

LENNY *(While reading the computer)* I really didn't mean anything. The reason I asked is that this memoir goes into a certain intimacy between him and Ricky Marvel.

SAM *(Takes the diskette out of the drive, puts it back in Waldo's bag, and turns the computer off)* You can play that crap with the others, Len, but please don't try it with me.

LENNY What the hell are you talking about?

Miles and Reggie return, Miles is pressing a napkin to a bloody gash on his hand.

SAM *(Sternly)* About Waldo, not a word.

REGGIE About Waldo, not a word about what?

SAM I was just telling Lenny that I haven't heard Waldo read a word in the past year.

MILES I don't think pressuring him is helpful, Sam.

REGGIE I'll get a bandage for you, Miles.

MILES It's just a scratch and it wasn't rusty.

SAM What happened?

REGGIE Miles cut himself on an old garbage can.

MILES I'm all right. Does Waldo seem okay to you?

LENNY I think he's taking drugs. I really do.

SAM That's not his style.

MILES Has he been in the bathroom this entire time?

SAM *(Goes to the bathroom door)* Waldo, you still alive? *(Knocks)* Waldo! You okay?

LENNY He's not answering!

MILES *(Banging on the door)* WALDO, OPEN UP OR I'M GOING TO BREAK DOWN THIS DOOR!

WALDO *(Emerges from the bathroom, his eyes wet)* I'm sorry, I just fell alseep.

LENNY You look misty-eyed.

REGGIE You fell asleep on the toilet? *(Waldo shrugs)*

MILES That's where Elvis died.

REGGIE And Lenny Bruce.

WALDO That's great—me, Elvis, and Lenny Bruce finally have
something in common. Finish your story, Miles.

SAM I'm sorry for yelling at you about not writing, Waldo. All right,
Miles, finish your story.

Reggie goes back to sleep. Sam stares at Waldo. Lenny resumes massaging Waldo's back. Miles stands before them with his manuscript.

MILES Let's see, going directly to Chapter 28. *(Flips through some
pages and resumes reading, lights slowly dim)* What they don't
tell you at the Academy is that most copwork is paperwork.
Paperwork is tedium, and tedium is the interconnective tissue of life . . .

Blackout.

ACT TWO

Reggie's living room, Miles is still reading his story. Sam, Waldo, and Reggie have dozed off to sleep, snoring softly. Lenny, who has headphones on, has managed to get Waldo's shirt off and is softly stroking his back.

MILES —So, after twenty years on the force, with a half-salary pension and full benefits, not to mention Social Security and Disability— *(Looks up for a moment and no one is even pretending to listen, so he goes over to Sam, who is sleeping, and gently whispers)* Sam, can you hear me? I'm sorry for—

WALDO HEY! *(Leaps to his feet)*

REGGIE *(Awakens)* Excellent. That was wonderful, mellifluous—

LENNY *(To Waldo)* Just relax.

SAM *(To Waldo)* What happened?

WALDO He knows damned well what happened!

LENNY Miles, did you shoot another innocent bystander?

WALDO He didn't do anything. *You* did!

LENNY Methinks he doth protest too fucking much.

SAM I'll protect you, Waldo. Sit next to me. *(He does)*

REGGIE *(Returns to his supine position)* Continue reading, Miles.

LENNY I didn't do anything. Little homophobe.

MILES Where was I? *(Searches for his spot in the memoir)*

WALDO Am not. Someone sure as hell touched me. And I wouldn't let a woman stick her fingers up there either.

SAM Good for you. *(To Lenny)* He's tired. Read, Miles, read miles and miles.

*Reggie and Sam lie down again. Waldo rises and returns to the bathroom.
Miles waits, Reggie opens his eyes and sees him waiting.*

REGGIE Finish the damned story, Miles.

Lenny moves over to Waldo's knapsack.

MILES Waldo is back in the bathroom. And what the hell are you
    doing?
LENNY Mind your own boring business. *(Gobbles down another one
    of Waldo's truffles)*
SAM Len! Waldo is clearly having serious problems.
LENNY Yeah, they were caused by my eating his truffles. *(Muttering)*
    I didn't even touch him.
MILES They're for his mom. I don't think—
LENNY *(Searching through Waldo's knapsack)* I just took one.
MILES Bullshit, you've already had three truffles—
SAM Lenny! Cut it out! *(Grabs the box of truffles from him)*
LENNY Hey!
SAM Why don't you grow up?
MILES Calm down, Sam.
SAM He's past forty and still acting like a baby.
LENNY Fuck you.
SAM If any other person here acted the way you're acting—
LENNY Wait a second. What exactly are you implying?
SAM I'm saying what I'm saying.
LENNY No you are not. You're referring to my sexuality.
SAM Oh, give me a break.
REGGIE Hey guys, just chill.
LENNY You can only imply and keep secrets because you're a hos-
    tile little bitch.
SAM I think you got me beat there.
MILES Guys, I'd like to finish my story—

LENNY She asked me to keep a secret from you guys.

SAM Oh God!

REGGIE Lenny, let this blow over, please.

LENNY Fine, but I just want to get off my chest that Waldo has written a blockbuster that looks like *Remembrance of Dirty Things Past. (Sam sighs)*

MILES What are you talking about?

REGGIE I already checked. It's only a couple pages long.

SAM Len, I apologize. And for the record, I'm sure that you did not squeeze Waldo's butt. Now, can we please move on?

LENNY Sam, I accept your apology and I bare no grudge, but I simply cannot deceive my friends.

REGGIE What are you talking about?

SAM Lenny's just teasing. *(Impatiently)* Miles, to hell with Waldo, finish your fucking story.

LENNY Waldo has written a hot tell-all memoir. Look for yourselves. *(Slips one of Waldo's diskettes into the computer)*

SAM *(Gets up and tries to turn the computer off)* It's his private memoir. Put it back!

Lenny blocks her for a moment as Miles reads the screen. Reggie remains seated and amused.

REGGIE Relax, Sam, we're writers. We have great insight and compassion. What does it say?

MILES *(Reading)* This sure ain't a WordPerfect program.

LENNY See! See! *(Eats another truffle)*

SAM Reggie, will you help me here?

REGGIE Okay, boys, put the toys away. He's probably wiping as we speak.

MILES *(Holding up a diskette)* This is the one WordPerfect diskette. Lenny's not kidding. *(Takes the diskette out of the computer and looks at it)* This file says *Novel Number One*.

REGGIE What?!

MILES (*Still reading*) Memoir, shit! This has chapters. That's a scene.

REGGIE (*Shoving in*) A scene?

MILES And characters. It looks like a novel.

SAM Lenny, how can you live with yourself?

LENNY By not lying to friends. You should try it.

REGGIE (*Reading*) What I saw was just a couple of pages.

MILES Will you guys be quiet? I'm trying to read. Sam, when did you first do it with Waldo?

SAM None of your goddamned business.

LENNY Sleeping with Waldo makes it Miles's business.

MILES Sam, listen, he refers to a "burden that is engulfing him." Read this.

REGGIE I got a critical disk error once when I had a hundred and twenty pages on a diskette.

MILES (*To Sam*) If he did it, and caught something, I want to know if he was able to transmit by the time— (*Toilet flushes*)

SAM He's coming!

Miles puts the diskette back in Waldo's knapsack, Reggie turns off the computer. Everyone returns to their former positions. Waldo enters and lies back down.

WALDO Go ahead, finish your story.

LENNY When drinking beer, piss is clear. Clear as the nose on your face.

REGGIE (*Solemnly*) I've got to pee.

LENNY I'm getting some ice cream. (*To Miles*) I got to cool myself down. (*Heads to the kitchen*)

MILES Waldo, I have to ask you a difficult question.

WALDO Cross my heart, hope to die, I didn't drink your beer.

MILES Did you ever do anything sexual with this Ricky guy? (*Waldo is surprised*)

SAM Miles!

MILES (*Anxiously whispering*) I'm entitled! (*To Sam*) The last time we did it was last August. You're at risk just as much as I am, Sam. More so. More so!

SAM *(To Waldo)* Did you do anything?

WALDO *(Torturously)* I didn't do enough. Not nearly enough.

LENNY *(Returns with a glass of ice cream)* Cherry Garcia, with brandy.

REGGIE *(Returns with a bottle of tequila, from which he takes a deep gulp)* I feel crappy.

WALDO You shouldn't drink like that, Reggie.

REGGIE You shouldn't give me a reason to.

SAM He's pissed about Lucy erasing his play.

WALDO You have to call Lucy. She'll talk to you. Trust me.

REGGIE *You* wrote the Yellow Pages!

MILES Waldo, please—

WALDO What the fuck is going on here?!

SAM They had a preview of your memoir.

WALDO *(Angrily)* What? I already told you! That's a personal account of my friendship with Richard.

REGGIE *(Accusingly)* Then why is it structured in chapters? *(Waldo is dumbfounded)*

MILES He's asking a reasonable question, Waldo.

WALDO I find it distances me. Okay? Like it didn't happen to me. It's not for public scrutiny.

SAM I'm sorry.

REGGIE I suppose I am too. I just feel like—

WALDO You're just pissed about what Lucy did, but she—

LENNY Oh, right, she erased the poor boy's play.

REGGIE Yeah, yeah. Getting back to Miles's story. Does anyone want to comment?

LENNY You're going to lose the sympathy of some readers for shooting an unarmed civilian.

MILES *(Frantic)* What I wrote about was fear of death. *(Bewildered, Lenny silently pronounces the word "death")* Once you're introduced to it, you never forget it. Waldo, please!

SAM You're not finished, Miles. Keep reading.

MILES It's over. I need to know. *(Waldo shakes his head no)*

LENNY Our little love boat's walking on water.

SAM I think Miles's cop memoir is a little tedious.

MILES *(To Sam)* You goddamned hypocrite!

REGGIE That's a rather violent response to criticism.

MILES Miss Hillary Clinton. But when she was alone with this whacko *(Points to Waldo)*, she was on her back with her legs in the air. *(Lenny giggles)*

WALDO Leave her alone.

MILES Fuck you, it's your fault!

REGGIE Slug it out!

WALDO You have nothing to worry about. Nothing.

LENNY Are they talking about literature?

WALDO No, Miles's autobiography. He's not finished, but it does seem a little long.

LENNY *(To Waldo)* Coming from you—

REGGIE *(Rapidly questioning Waldo)* Yeah! How'd you like Miles's characterizations? Or his prose style? How about his plot structure? What'd you think of his plot structure?

LENNY There was a plot?

WALDO *(To Reggie)* I'll criticize your plot structure.

REGGIE *(Angrily)* Take some notes, Miles, 'cause this man is a fucking expert. He's *written* and he *knows*.

WALDO Hey, Reggie, I know your little problem, your little secret—

REGGIE Lenny, have you and Waldo been talking?

LENNY *(Slightly nervous)* Waldo wouldn't talk with me if I begged him.

WALDO I just don't need the prostate test—

LENNY I didn't touch you! Christ, I feel like Clarence Thomas.

SAM Lighten up, both of you.

LENNY *(To Reggie)* Do you have more lite beer? Or do I have to board another boat.

REGGIE I have some tequila. *(Offers the bottle)*

LENNY Tequila? I'm not twenty anymore. I can only drink polite aperitifs and lite beer.

SAM We're out of beer.

LENNY Oh, right. Miles finished all the beer, and he didn't even drink any. Some trick, Mr. Safe Sex.

MILES So go out and buy some. You never invite people over to your hovel for a group.

WALDO This place is getting a little stuffy. I'm going out for a beer run. *(Moves over and collects his diskettes)*

REGGIE What the—? Oh, looky here, he's taking his toys with him.

MILES *(Disbelief)* You're packing up your diskettes? That is a little insulting.

WALDO You looked at them before.

SAM Everyone's just blowing off steam. I'll take care of them, Waldo. It won't happen again.

REGGIE *(Sets the tequila bottle on his groin)* Yeah, she'll take good care of me. I'm next.

MILES Fuck you, asshole!

LENNY Reggie, do you have any more lite beer or not?

WALDO Be patient with him. Reggie's going through a hard time.

REGGIE I am? All right, I am. Waldo, will you help someone going through a hard time?

WALDO Just ask, Reggie.

SAM *(Takes cash out)* Let me give you some money, Waldo.

MILES I just gave him fifty. He's getting it from both of us.

LENNY *(Muttering)* That's what I've been saying all along.

REGGIE *(Suddenly flares)* I mean—I've organized this group for years. I've given honest advice, tried to be encouraging, tried to be sensitive. I gave what I had!

WALDO What the fuck are you talking about?

REGGIE Beer.

SAM Maybe we've all had a little too much already.

MILES I don't want any more.

REGGIE YES YOU DO! And so does Lenny and so do I. You owe us!

WALDO All right, I'll get some beer. *(Exits quickly)*

LENNY I never thought he'd leave—

Miles grabs Waldo's knapsack and tosses it to Lenny, who is at the computer, then Miles blocks Sam.

SAM What the hell are you two doing?

LENNY Just getting another truffle. *(Eats another truffle, then shoves Waldo's diskette into the computer)*

SAM Stop it! *(Miles holds her as she tries to stop Lenny)* Reggie, help!

REGGIE I'm just minding my own beeswax here.

SAM *(To Lenny, who is reading the screen)* Christ sake, his friend died. Can't you leave him alone?

MILES *(Struggling with Sam)* During that little skirmish in the Gulf, I learned that you can't be both afraid and sympathetic of the same thing.

SAM He's your friend, Miles.

LENNY A friend doesn't cheat on you behind your back.

SAM I can't believe you're saying that, Lenny.

REGGIE A little more friendly with some than others.

MILES *(Calmly, at the keyboard)* Look, you should be more worried than I, because if he had intercourse with that man and caught a virus, there is a far greater chance that you have it.

LENNY Tell it like it is.

SAM Stop it!

MILES Damn it! You heard him earlier, saying that you and the professor were going to die of AIDS.

SAM He was just being weird.

MILES That fucking pill he popped wasn't an aspirin, sweetheart. Did you see how quickly he tucked the container in his pocket?

SAM For Christ sake.

MILES And do you want me to tell you about that lesion on his forehead? What more do you want?

SAM Reggie, Waldo's your friend. He wouldn't let this happen to you.

REGGIE (*Drinking tequila*) A better man than I, Waldo Din.

SAM You're not that drunk, so don't bullshit me.

REGGIE He could have mentioned he was writing. As it is, he didn't write anything. He'll tell you that himself. So I don't know what they're looking at.

SAM You guys are all cowards. Cowards and bastards.

LENNY I'm just putting the word "sodomy" on search. Is that so scummy?

SAM Yes! Goddamn it, I gave him my reassurance.

REGGIE You shouldn't have written a check that you couldn't cover, honey.

SAM You guys are all scum.

LENNY (*Reading at the computer*) There's kind of an oblique reference here—

MILES What? What do you think?

REGGIE Share it with us. You've written book reviews before. Does the boy got any style?

LENNY (*While reading*) Only style. (*Pauses*) It's actually sad. A poor speller, choppy episodes, very touching, sickly sweet. Oh, here's a potential doppelgänger emerging. Crappy syntax, unrequited love, verbs as nouns. *Hello*, split infinitive. An inorganic symbol, twelve o'clock high. Dangling modifiers, for shame. He doesn't really give anything away. I can't read anymore. (*Tries to move, but Miles shoves him back into the chair*)

MILES You just keep sitting there. Where's this oblique reference?

SAM You really don't think Waldo has any talent?

LENNY He babbles in a way that tries to hide something but completely crumbles—

MILES Hide what?

LENNY I don't know. A self-pity or something. It lives in just a couple of words—it's really just a bunch of cathartic shit. He tries to be commanding, but it's too flimsy. It's like a bad rewrite of *The Runaway Soul*.

MILES Screw that, get to the hard facts.

LENNY God, he wrote a lot though.

REGGIE SHIT! I studied for years how to be a writer, undergraduate, graduate, post-graduate. I mean, what've you go to know?

LENNY Admit it, Reggie.

REGGIE What?

LENNY You know what. What I said earlier, about your alleged full-length play. *(Reggie ignores him)*

MILES *(Reading)* He said he didn't do anything. Shit, he doesn't give away a thing here.

REGGIE Right! What a liar. How can he be called anyone's friend?

MILES I don't mean that. I mean—

REGGIE *He* was the one with the writer's block. Week after week he'd come with nothing. He wouldn't even be holding a book, just helpless arms.

SAM Which is why I was pushing at him, while you guys were so supportive of his *not* writing.

MILES I can't deal with him anymore. This is it for me.

REGGIE I don't want to see that prick again either.

SAM This isn't an election.

REGGIE Is this a vote, Miles?

MILES It sure is. And I vote him the hell out!

SAM What?

REGGIE Me too. He's out of here.

SAM Wait a second!

REGGIE We need a majority. Lenny, how do you vote?

SAM You guys are all insane. Lenny, Waldo's your friend. He's everyone's friend.

LENNY Just leave me out of it.

REGGIE That means you abstain.

SAM This guy is out getting us beer. What did he do?

REGGIE *(To Sam)* How do you vote? Expulsion or remain?

SAM Reggie! Don't do this. Not even as a joke.

MILES That's two for, one against, one abstention. Resolution passed: Waldo is the fuck out of here. (*Takes a swig of tequila*)

REGGIE This is bullshit. If he wrote a memoir, that's one thing. But you write a novel to be read. TO BE SOLD! He was just being greedy. He used us. Punishment should fucking fit the crime. (*Bolts up and exits*)

LENNY (*Sarcastically*) The punishment? How delightful!

MILES (*Frantically to Sam*) That man has exposed us to a virus. He's got details in this thing that are— We could be dead as we speak!

LENNY (*With disbelief*) He's dead. I love it!

REGGIE (*Reenters concealing a pair of scissors, grabs Waldo's floppy diskette*) Punishment's going to fit the crime.

SAM What are you doing!?

REGGIE A little editing. (*Starts cutting Waldo's diskettes in half*)

LENNY Scissors! (*He easily grabs the scissors away from Reggie*) Shit!

Miles is still reading as Waldo enters.

WALDO What's going on?

SAM I'm sorry—

REGGIE (*Jumps at him drunkenly, but Lenny intervenes*) Where does a little twerp like you come off writing a novel behind our back?

WALDO What?!

LENNY (*Holding Reggie*) You were voted out of the group.

REGGIE Where does a pimple like you come off writing all those pages? Whenever it was your turn to read (*Mocks Waldo's voice*), "Sorry, pals, I didn't write nothing today."

WALDO It's therapy, asshole.

REGGIE Making money is great therapy.

WALDO That is a private journal. My psychiatrist recommended I keep it to control my depression.

MILES (*Turns from the computer as Waldo begins to collect his diskettes*) Did he fuck you too?

WALDO Fuck you!

Miles punches Waldo in the face, knocking him to a sofa.

MILES Admit it! That's why you've been acting so weird all night, isn't it? *(Waldo struggles, Miles pins him down)* Say it! Say it! You got AIDS! *(Sam tries to intervene, but Miles shoves her away)*

SAM Lenny, help!

MILES So help me, Len, I'll break your fucking arm.

REGGIE You've got his blood on your cut.

MILES Oh shit! *(Frantically exits to the bathroom to wash out his wound)*

LENNY *(Finds Waldo's pill container, which fell out of his pocket during the scuffle and reads)* Prozac. *(Pauses)* For AIDS?

WALDO *(Getting up quietly)* Richie and I grew up like brothers. When he told me he was HIV-positive, I felt uncomfortable around him. *(Angrily)* I didn't reject him! I just felt— strange. During most of his sickness, I couldn't deal with him. And then, like that *(Snaps his fingers)*, he's dead. And it's the oldest cliché in the world, but there's no making peace with the dead. I mean, who do you talk to? Loose ends just stay that way, and you kick yourself until you're just tired of kicking. So then I saw a shrink and he gave me that *(Points to the capsules)* and then Halcyon, and then I was taking too much. Last week, I had some electrotherapy. He said to try to find a substitute. Writing is no substitute. Writing is bullshit. *(Throws the diskettes across the room)* I didn't do shit with him. Or for him.

MILES *(Regretfully)* Shit, Waldo—

WALDO Fine, apologies accepted. That's the big pathetic secret, Reggie. Don't worry, Reggie, I won't tell about yours. *(Exits)*

MILES *(To Sam)* Go with him, please. Please. He shouldn't be alone like that.

SAM Shit. *(Exits)*

REGGIE *(Pauses)* Lucy left me a week ago.

LENNY Good. You said it yourself, she was keeping you from working. Now you can finish your *Messenger from Valhalla*.

REGGIE *(Quietly)* She wrote that play we read. In fact, I tore it apart. I tore everything of hers apart.

MILES *(Thinking about Waldo)* My God. Why'd I hit him?

REGGIE We'd fuck, and then Lucy would sit there, read her stuff, and then listen to every word I uttered, like I was some kind of literary god, declaring, *This is great. This is crap. (Pauses)* Smart girl. Much better writer than me. Great lay too. *(Pauses)* Shit, I should've went to law school.

LENNY So that was what Waldo was talking about when he said "your big secret."

REGGIE How he found out about it—

MILES *(Disconnected from them)* I remember that day my mom came home and said, *Amyotrophic Lateral Sclerosis, Lou Gehrig's Disease. Outlook, grave. Prognosis, a couple years.* I was thirteen years old. Once you really feel—this is fucking it! No illusions. No "pray to God my soul to keep," or harmony with nature. Just death. If you've ever watched someone die, you die yourself, without even the benefit of an end.

LENNY Have a beer. *(Gives his beer to Miles, who chugs it down)* So I was right.

REGGIE *(Angrily grabs Lenny)* You have a fucking gift. There was no play. There's no writer. If you feel some sense of victory over that.

LENNY I just didn't want you to lie about it.

MILES *(Muttering sadly)* How could I have hit him?

REGGIE All I ever wanted was to be a writer.

MILES Didn't Hemingway call it a soldier loyal to the impatient imagination and the blank page?

LENNY Or the blank imagination and impatient page.

REGGIE You know what it was that got me so fucking mad? *(Lenny shakes his head no)* Well, Waldo seemed so—

LENNY Out of it?

REGGIE Yeah, but in that youthful, energized, enlightened way. All the illusions still in place. I was once like that. Obscure references. I used to get outraged over profound ideas. Now I'm just grumpy. And then suddenly I'm hearing he's written volumes.

LENNY But the writing turns out to be psycho-babble and the enlightenment is battery-charged.

REGGIE Don't say that. He's young. Maybe, hopefully, he'll get his shit together and write something. Lucy was right. I've become an asshole, an official Olympic asshole.

MILES Why didn't I believe him when he first told me?

LENNY Got your car? *(Miles nods)* See you next week.

REGGIE No you won't. This is the end of it for me.

MILES Hey, what was that thing you had on the screen last week if it wasn't A *Messenger from Valhalla*?

REGGIE It was the one-act I cowrote with Fred ten years ago. Let it be remembered that that play got mixed reviews, which for me is all the immortality I'll ever see. But it's more than most people.

LENNY Now we need two new members.

MILES You know, some writers are late bloomers.

LENNY That's right.

MILES Ibsen never even began writing until—

REGGIE Spare me the anecdotes. *(Miles leaves)* What do you think Waldo meant by "writing is bullshit"?

LENNY I have no idea, but I'll tell you this: The only reason I write is because, well, people, parties, places, for the most part, they've become a screaming bore. I mean, why else would anyone spend hours upon hours of their precious life all alone? No pay, no recognition. The reason I come here is to read my stuff. Writing is a concession to the fact that life is basically *blah*. So if it's of any comfort, Reg, I think being a failed writer might mean there's still hope for you.

REGGIE Yeah.

LENNY There's no reason to be both lonely and unproductive. Waldo said Lucy will speak to you. Give her a call.

Lenny exits. Reggie takes out the portable TV and turns it on. Fade to black.

PLEA BARGAINS

To my brother Patrick

Plea Bargains was produced at La Tea Theater on November 23, 1994.

Professor Euclid Von Bootum	Billy Lux
Woodrow	Caliph Haines
Isadora Von Bootum	Stephanie Tashman
Officer Miles Gallo	Joe Wyka
Director	Thomas Morrisey
Sound and Music Designer	Brad Kaus
Stage Manager	David Oreklin
Carpenter	Michael Granville
Light Designer	Jen Primosch

The playwright would like to gratefully acknowledge that lines of poems by Ginsberg, O'Hara, Di Prima, Ferlinghetti, Kerouac, Oppenheimer, Levendosky, Creeley, Waldman, Levertov, and Sirowitz are used.

Production note: The style of this play—with the disintegrating character of Von Bootum who suffers a split personality, the Frankenstein experiment performed on Woodrow, and the avenging ghost of Isadora—should be a bit campy, perhaps in the tradition of a low-budget horror film. Isadora is a ghost through most of the play and should look the part; in the recurrent subway sequence she is forced to relive her death over and over. Although she sometimes alters the words, she is stuck in performing the same doomed actions. A low-level crackling sound might be employed when she uses her electrostatic powers. Her passage into heaven at the end can be done with a piece of bloody fabric from her dress attached to a simple pulley that is lifted over the audience's heads.

ACT ONE

ACT TWO

ACT ONE

SCENE 1

Darkness, then a strobe of light. The sound of a subway passing is accompanied by a gunshot. Isadora screams and footsteps are heard running away. Lights rise on a ghost lifting out of Isadora's dead form. Then fade to black. Lights rise again to a simple unlit living room, with chairs, a table, and a wheelchair. The only unusual object is the Polk tank. This is a small structure with a door. The interior looks like a space-age microwave. It should be able to hold two people and is controlled by a computer. Professor Von Bootum enters, wearing a false mustache and glasses. He is carrying an unconscious man over his shoulder—Woodrow. He walks over to an awaiting wheelchair and lowers the man onto it. A beanie drops from Woodrow's pocket onto the floor. Von Bootum locates a pair of handcuffs and locks Woodrow's hands to the wheelchair's armrest. On a counter is a prep kit containing some chemical vials, a container of grain alcohol, a syringe, a bottle of formaldehyde, and cotton gauze. Von Bootum proceeds to inject the man in a variety of places. When he finally jabs a hypodermic into the man's jugular, Woodrow starts awakening.

WOODROW Don't shove, I'z getting off the train.

VON BOOTUM *(With a slight German accent)* No, Woodrow, you just relax. We haven't quite arrived yet. *(Takes the syringe out of Woodrow's neck)*

WOODROW *(Struggles with the cuffs until he realizes his hands are secured)* What the fuck's this? HELP! HELP!

VON BOOTUM *(Places cotton gauze over Woodrow's face, talks at a slow two-beat)* Inhale, exhale—nice, and—slow—we hope—you like—our show. *(Removes gauze when Woodrow's semisedated)*

WOODROW *(Groggily)* What are you, one them sick psycho sadists?

VON BOOTUM I just wanted to have a pleasant talk.

WOODROW So did Dahmer. You want to chop me up and fuck me.

VON BOOTUM I beg your pardon!

WOODROW Chop and fuck. Chop and fuck. Let me go!

VON BOOTUM Admittedly I have no social life, but I have no libidinous desires either.

WOODROW No what?

VON BOOTUM May I chat with you?

WOODROW Say what?

VON BOOTUM May I talk to you?

WOODROW *(Trying to calm down and gain control of the situation)* Talk? Sure, okay, bud.

VON BOOTUM Bud, yes, buddy. Yes. We're buddies, that's good.

WOODROW Sure, it's good. We're good buddies, man. So let's get down, rap.

VON BOOTUM This is good because I am not from here. My accent betrays me, I'm sure.

WOODROW I wouldn't betray you, man.

VON BOOTUM No, I know you wouldn't. I'm just saying I am from elsewhere. I have not had a buddy since before the war. I miss having a buddy.

WOODROW But there are two kinds of buddies, you know. Your butt-dy and you wine-drinking buddy, you see what I'm saying?

VON BOOTUM Exactly, a wine buddy. I believe you are my Rhinewine buddy. *(He laughs aloud, Woodrow joins in laughing)* We are having a good time, no?

WOODROW Oh yeah, this is where it's happening. But buddy, what's this here? *(Rattles his chains)*

VON BOOTUM Oh my, you're right! Buddies don't treat buddies like this. Let me unlatch your cuffs, buddy.

Von Bootum uncuffs Woodrow, who lunges at Von Bootum but falls to the ground in a heap. Von Bootum helps him back into his wheelchair and recuffs his hands.

VON BOOTUM I injected high-potency relaxants in all your limb muscles. But as much as they might awaken, I think I'll take the precaution of the restraints.

WOODROW So fucking kill me, you fat fag. That's what you're going to do, so fucking do it!

VON BOOTUM Hush now, my buddy.

WOODROW Kill me, you fat-ass fuck in tight-ass slacks.

VON BOOTUM Silence! *Dunkopf!* I've observed the Geneva conventions, I am not hurting you. I'm not wearing slacks and my gluteus maximus isn't—

WOODROW KILL ME, YOU COCKSUCKER! JUST KILL ME!

VON BOOTUM Okay! I'll kill you. *(Fills the hypodermic needle, holds it up, pushes the syringe until the bubbles are out, then takes out a Sony Walkman and puts headphones on Woodrow)*

WOODROW *(Groggily)* What are you doing? Will you just do it and quit fucking with me?

VON BOOTUM Fine. *(Injects him)* Your awful little life is *kaput.*

WOODROW I'm really—dying?

VON BOOTUM Not only are you dying, but for all intents and purposes, you are dead. Now will you please relax? *(Locates a medical bag behind the counter)*

WOODROW Dead?

VON BOOTUM Just an hour ago you were peddling rubbish on Second Avenue, trying to sell me a broken VCR.

WOODROW *(Groggily)* It weren't broke! If that was what all this is about, you should'a tested it before killing me, man. All you had to do was just plug it in.

VON BOOTUM Yes, well, that wasn't the garbage I bargained on. I bargained on you, my Rhine-wine buddy.

Von Bootum opens a medical bag and spreads out surgical equipment. He pulls on surgical gloves and mask, turns on a bright lamp and a small drill. He operates on Woodrow's brain while talking. Occasionally he holds up blood-covered props, like bone shards, liver, and bloody gauze. From time to time he throws down scalpels and picks up other surgical tools.

WOODROW *(Barely conscious)* Wait a sec! If I'm dead, what are you doing to me?

VON BOOTUM A procedure called the Von Bootum–Polk. There are no sensory nerves on the surface of the brain, and you have local anesthesia along the temple where I'm making my present incision.

WOODROW I don't want my round bottom poked.

VON BOOTUM Von Bootum–Polk. It will make your mind more limber. Calm your anxieties. Permit greater focus.

WOODROW What is this guy howling about in my ear? *(Tries shaking off the headphones, but a piece of his brain falls out)*

VON BOOTUM Be still!

WOODROW Sounds like Ed Koch on an acid trip.

VON BOOTUM Much like yourself, the brain is a great garbage collector. Every little thing you hear piles up. *(Holding a vial)* This miracle drug refunds all those little beer cans from the shopping cart of your subconscious.

WOODROW *(Panting desperately, trying to stay awake)* What are you saying? I won't remember my friends or nothing?

VON BOOTUM *(Disapprovingly)* They must share in the fault of your existence. As they are learning in L.A., one shouldn't build on a fault line. *(Grabs a large needle and thread)* I'm closing the incision now.

WOODROW *(Drifting in and out of a dream state)* Joey, help! This guy's fucking with my cauliflower—

VON BOOTUM *(Takes the syringe out, ready to inject)* We'll blot that Joe right out of your head with the serum that makes it all possible, the Recallol, which I discovered and refined.

A ghost, Isadora, materializes wearing the bloody garment she was killed in. A bullet hole is visible on the front of her blood-dried dress. No one can see or hear her except Woodrow, who is terrified.

ISADORA'S GHOST *(Replying to Von Bootum's remark)* Bullshit! You lying bastard.

WOODROW *(Horrified)* Oh shit!

Isadora's ghost points her hand at Von Bootum and we hear static electricity. He suddenly grabs his crotch.

VON BOOTUM Ow! I never felt static electricity in this room before. *(Suspicious about the rug)*

WOODROW *(Utterly terrified)* Yo, Jack, you got a roommate? A dead roommate?

VON BOOTUM Uh oh! Woodrow, I gave you a drug with hallucinogenic properties. Now just the other day you saw a violent film.

WOODROW I saw a film?

VON BOOTUM You saw a rather intense double feature. *No Good 2 No 1* and *Dun'a Completely Foolish Thing.* So if you are seeing anything disagreeable—

ISADORA'S GHOST Remember me? Isadora, that wicked witch of the F?

WOODROW *(To Von Bootum)* She says her name is Isadora.

VON BOOTUM *(To himself)* How did he know her name? He must have seen it on a wall diploma.

ISADORA'S GHOST What the hell?

VON BOOTUM *(Taking Woodrow's headphones off)* Okay, tape is over. Before I blot you out in the Polk tank, I want you to focus on this tape you heard. Now be kind, rewind, and replay what you heard.

WOODROW (*Recites it at high-speed, the way he heard it*) I saw the best minds of my generation destroyed by madness, starving hysterical naked, dragging themselves through the negro streets—

VON BOOTUM (*Insanely dancing around*) Yes! It works! The monster recites poetry!

DETECTIVE GALLO (*Offstage, knocking and pounding*) Open up!

ISADORA'S GHOST (*Yelling*) It's the cops! Nail his ass!

VON BOOTUM Oh shit! One second. (*Jumps up and wheels Woodrow back into the closest while whispering*) Shut up!

ISADORA'S GHOST Keep reciting or I'll cook your balls like hard-boiled eggs! (*In terror, Woodrow keeps reciting the poem*)

VON BOOTUM (*Whispering*) Shut up! Damn you.

WOODROW (*Offstage*) —at dawn looking for an angry fix, angel-headed hipsters burning for the ancient heavenly connection to the starry dynamo—

VON BOOTUM (*Knocking intensifies*) Who is it? I have inalienable rights!

GALLO Dominos Pizza.

VON BOOTUM (*Opens the door*) I didn't order Vomitos Pizza.

GALLO Dominos. (*He enters*) We no longer give the pizza free if we get it to your door past twenty minutes, but I still tried to get here quickly. (*Faintly hears Woodrow reciting the poem*) Do you hear that? (*Von Bootum shakes his head no*)

ISADORA'S GHOST Of course he hears it, you dumb fuck. (*Screams to Woodrow*) Louder in there! (*We hear Woodrow mumbling louder*)

VON BOOTUM (*Tranquilly*) Oh! That's my tape machine. I put poetry on before I take my afternoon nap, and like ether it rises into the sinuses of my subconscious.

ISADORA'S GHOST I'll rattle your fucking sinuses! (*Exits*)

GALLO (*Shows a receipt*) The pizza is $12.75.

VON BOOTUM I didn't order any such pizza. (*Woodrow's recital intensifies until he starts howling*)

GALLO You want to turn it off?

VON BOOTUM It's the only thing that you're going to get from me. I didn't order your incredibly fast food which has ruined the fighting spirit of your country.

GALLO Is your number (*Checks the receipt*) 555-7463?

VON BOOTUM No, that's the number for information, you idiot. Aren't you a little old to be a pizza delivery boy?

GALLO Here in the East Village people aren't afraid to grow old in their menial jobs—

VON BOOTUM I see they also have no fear of growing tedious and wasting other people's time.

GALLO Shit, your tape machine sounds like it's in misery, man.

VON BOOTUM All right, I'll purchase that inedible disc of dough if you just leave. (*Takes out his wallet and finds he doesn't have any money with him*) Damn!

Von Bootum exits. Gallo scouts around, picking Woodrow's beanie off the floor, and he notices the cotton swabs. Von Bootum returns just as Gallo finds the hypodermic.

VON BOOTUM I shouldn't leave that out. (*Takes it from Gallo*) My wife and I are—we're both very important scientists. She had a laboratory in the basement.

GALLO Maybe your wife ordered the pizza?

VON BOOTUM She's away. Here's your extortion money, with no tip to insure that you'll never return.

GALLO Maybe she ordered it from somewhere else.

VON BOOTUM She vanished in the snow last February.

GALLO What are you saying?

VON BOOTUM She didn't survive the past winter. Now outz!

GALLO That's cold-blooded, man, making jokes about your dead wife. (*Turns to go*)

VON BOOTUM (*Dramatically grabs his forehead*) You'll have to forgive me, I'm still in the denial stage. I'm one of those people who down bitter pills and fart the woes away.

GALLO Well, then that pizza should help you. (*Turns to go*) Remember, if you don't want to put on your clothes, call us at Dominos.

VON BOOTUM I hope you people drop like dominos. (*Closes the door on Gallo, glances at a photo of his wife as her ghost reenters*) Poor Hynie Mama.

ISADORA'S GHOST Quit calling me that!

VON BOOTUM (*Holds up the photograph*) I did love you— in a pendular, irrational, eleemosynary, torpid sort of way.

ISADORA'S GHOST Same to you, shithead. (*Von Bootum exits and returns, wheeling out Woodrow, who is still reciting "Howl"*)

WOODROW (*At the top of his lungs*) —Carl Solomon! I'm with you in Rockland (*Howls like a dog*) where you're madder than I am (*Howls*), I'm with you in Rockland (*Howls*) where you must feel very strange— (*Howls*)

VON BOOTUM Stop that infernal howling before I have to put you to sleep!

ISADORA'S GHOST Shut up! (*Woodrow stops*)

VON BOOTUM Now, before I blot that little piece of bubble gum in your skull, do you still see a certain blood-soaked fishwife?

ISADORA'S GHOST Tell him you see that Leona's healthy, swine.

WOODROW (*Terrified, confused*) I see Leona Helmsley fine.

VON BOOTUM What is this you're saying?

ISADORA'S GHOST No, *Leona*, my snake!

WOODROW Leona Helmsley's a snake.

ISADORA'S GHOST Howl for that pizza boy again. HOWL! (*Woodrow howls in fear*)

VON BOOTUM What is this, an outbreak of lycanthropy? We'll have to start you from scratch, tabula rasa. Do you like poetry? It's the styrofoam peanuts of memory stuffers. (*Types into the computer, then fastens suction cups onto Woodrow's forehead*)

Seventy-two hours of babbling Beats right up to the Nuyorican pottery-wheel poetry. That should do the trick. In you go! *(Slides Woodrow back into the Polk tank)* Still, in order to successfully complete the experiment, we must find another guinea pig to help you develop a conscience. But who?

Fade to black.

∞

SCENE 2

It is dark and silent. We hear a train, as if in the distance. It grows louder until it sounds as if it is rushing into a station. Lights come up on a littered subway station, with graffiti-profaned billboards and a Second Avenue station sign. Although Isadora's voice is heard first, Von Bootum dashes onto the platform hoping to catch the train.

ISADORA *(Offstage)* Come back here when I'm screaming at you, you Kraut clown!

VON BOOTUM *(Hyperventilating)* There's always a train on the opposite track.

ISADORA *(Ignores him and pulls her coat tighter)* We're in a filthy fucking subway station in a fucking ghetto! You miserable cheapskate bastard.

VON BOOTUM You saw me, Hynie Mama, trying to *Sieg Heil* that infernal taxi cab. *(Having trouble breathing)*

ISADORA *(Swatting him with each word)* You fat, fag, fuck, failure! Your life is a big pile of stinking shit. And the only reason you married me is to turn my life into stinking shit too.

VON BOOTUM Please, all I need is a human subject to show that my experiment is both successful and—

ISADORA (*Looking down the subway tunnel*) Somebody ought to do an experiment on you, you horn-hatted fart-machine.

VON BOOTUM (*Holding his forehead painfully and looking into the tunnel*) Is that a train's headlights?

ISADORA It's two thirty-watt lightbulbs wondering the same thing I am: How did I get screwed here? You shit.

VON BOOTUM (*Puts his hand over his heart and breathes steadily, then slowly squats until he is sitting on the ground*) Please, Hynie Mama, I'm having intensifying palpitations in my xiphoid process!

ISADORA Good. Maybe you'll die before Simon Wiesenthal catches you! Vile Visigothic vomit!

VON BOOTUM (*Sitting on the ground, struggling to breathe*) At least I tried—what's your excuse? You were supposed to invent the great crime serum, the pharmaceutical approach. The only breakthroughs you've had were through your waistlines, whereas I just have one final push to go.

ISADORA I'd like to give you a final push.

VON BOOTUM (*Notices something offstage; nervously, laboriously, he rises, still holding his chest.*) Hynie Mama, Hynie Mama—

ISADORA Will you quit calling me that, you anal Oedipal asshole?

VON BOOTUM But I have something important to tell you—

ISADORA Fuck off, I'm fantasizing about a real man. Someone with a ticklish chest whose spout isn't tucked away under a beer-keg of a belly.

VON BOOTUM I think there's someone behind the pillar.

ISADORA Pissing probably. (*Curious*) Where?

VON BOOTUM (*Points offstage*) There, by the— (*Suddenly his voice booms loudly*) By the way, did you pack all those Deutsche Marks neatly in your purse?

ISADORA What?

VON BOOTUM (*Covers his mouth in surprise and questions*) Did I say that? (*Strangely loud again*) All that money in your purse is going to fall out. (*Loud*) Hundreds of Deutsche Marks!

ISADORA With you as the breadwinner, this purse is costume jew-
elry.

VON BOOTUM Come on, this way. (*He grabs her and they exit, but we
can still hear them talking while offstage*)

ISADORA Hey, Octoberfest's over! Where are you taking me?

VON BOOTUM Just move it! Shit, the exit's locked.

*Woodrow enters, stage right. He follows behind them and exits stage left,
where he grabs Isadora's purse offstage.*

ISADORA My purse!

*Woodrow tries to run with it, but Isadora holds on and Woodrow drags
her back onto the stage.*

ISADORA EUCLID, HELP!

VON BOOTUM (*Offstage*) My Angina!

ISADORA (*Fighting for the purse*) HELP! Euclid! Help!

VON BOOTUM (*Enters, moving around to the side of Woodrow where
Isadora can't see him, speaking in a loud demonic tone*) Give him
the purse! He's got a gun! (*Von Bootum pulls out a gun*)

WOODROW No I don't! (*Woodrow holds up his hands when he sees
Von Bootum's pistol*)

VON BOOTUM (*Shoves his gun into Woodrow's pocket so Isadora doesn't
see it, speaking in a diabolic whisper*) Take mine!

WOODROW (*Pulls out the handgun*) Give me that fucking bag.

ISADORA You human garbage. Euclid! (*She hits Woodrow*)

VON BOOTUM (*Holding his chest, terrified*) That's my gun! Oh God!
Don't shoot, please. I'll give you all the money in the world.
(*Back in demonic voice*) If you kill her!

WOODROW What?!

ISADORA HELP! Token booth clerk! Fellow New Yorkers! Wait a
second, all this already happened. (*She slaps the gun out of
Woodrow's hand*) Oh my God! I can't believe I did that.

(*Realizes she can't release her purse*) Just take the fucking bag. Pull it out of my fucking hand!

VON BOOTUM (*Grabs a stick on the ground*) I'll hit you, so help me! (*Woodrow recovers the pistol*)

ISADORA Just take the purse and go!

VON BOOTUM (*In a diabolic tone to himself*) I'm doing this for you, bud. (*Hits himself over the head and falls unconscious*)

ISADORA (*Still fighting with Woodrow, but speaking calmly*) Did what for who? Did you see what just happened? (*Digs her nails into Woodrow's face*)

A *gunshot blast sounds, Isadora falls. Fade to black.*

CX&

SCENE 3

It is a few days later. Von Bootum pulls Woodrow out of the Polk tank. He is still bound in his wheelchair. He uncuffs Woodrow's restraints and helps him up. Looking blankly, Woodrow sits up and coughs.

VON BOOTUM So how are we today, my wine buddy?

WOODROW (*Slowly and deeply introspective*) The hollow eyes of shock remain. (*Pauses*) Electric sockets burnt out in the skull.

VON BOOTUM You're not angry with me, are you, Woody?

WOODROW (*Suspicious, accusatory*) We are tired of your dreary tourist ideas of our negro selves.

VON BOOTUM Do you remember anything before the poetry submersion? (*Pauses*) Anything about a certain female?

WOODROW (*Tactfully*) —The young man asked plaintively whether Lenin had ever wondered about the cup sizes of fellow revolutionaries.

ISADORA'S GHOST *(Suddenly appears)* Oh, kiss my ass!

WOODROW *(Scared)* Kiss the ass of the devil and eat shit! Fuck his horny barbed cock.

ISADORA'S GHOST *(Infuriated)* I'm going to fucking fling you out the window!

WOODROW *(More frantically)* Flung me across the room, and room after room, hitting the walls rebounding—

VON BOOTUM Relax, Woody. You don't remember about any woman, do you?

WOODROW *(Regains control)* The female is ductile and, stroke after stroke, built for masochistic calm.

ISADORA'S GHOST Keep it up and you'll learn masochistic calm, prick.

WOODROW *(Frantically)* She in whose lipservice I passed my time, whose name I knew, but not her face.

ISADORA'S GHOST You can't talk outside of that poetry shit, can you? *(Woodrow shakes his head no)*

VON BOOTUM *(Takes out a small pocket light and looks into Woodrow's pupils)* Poor boy, I'm afraid that some of those drugs I gave you are hallucinogenic.

ISADORA'S GHOST I'm reduced to an acid trip. *(She sits)*

WOODROW Lady, do not banish me for digressions. My nature is a quagmire of unresolved confessions.

ISADORA'S GHOST If only you knew. *(Sighs)* I'm never going to get justice.

VON BOOTUM *(Reading from the computer)* Let's see, now that we have completely blotted out your former identity, the real work begins. What character-matrix shall we fill you with?

GALLO *(Kicking open the door with his gun drawn)* Freeze! Goddamn it!

ISADORA'S GHOST Got you, you bastard.

VON BOOTUM All right! *(Slowly open his wallet)* I'll tip you, pizza boy.

GALLO *(Shows his badge)* Detective Gallo, Ninth Precinct, Homicide. I know all about your wife.

VON BOOTUM She was killed two weeks ago.

GALLO That doesn't excuse this. (*To Woodrow*) You okay, partner?

WOODROW May I go now? Am I allowed to bow myself down in the ridiculous posture of renewal—

GALLO Knock yourself out.

VON BOOTUM Forget him.

GALLO You shut up! In the corner. (*To Woodrow*) You tell me what happened here.

WOODROW I—I—saw— (*Frustrated, unable to speak*)

GALLO Tell me?

WOODROW I saw the—

GALLO What'd you see?

WOODROW The best minds of my generation—

VON BOOTUM Officer, you don't understand—

GALLO SHUT UP! (*To Woodrow*) What happened to these minds? What'd he do?

WOODROW (*Sadly*) Destroyed—

GALLO Did you murder your wife?!

WOODROW (*Slowly and distinctly*) By madness—starving—hysterical—naked—

GALLO You're worse than that nut on 9th and C who cooked his roommate.

VON BOOTUM It's a poem. He speaks the language of post-modernist poets. It's the first part of an experiment. And it's a success.

GALLO Success?! He sounds like a freakin tax form.

VON BOOTUM He'll die unless I prepare him for the second stage, his character-matrix experiment.

GALLO Don't touch him. (*Stares into Woodrow's eyes*) What the hell did you do to him?

VON BOOTUM He would score astronomically on any IQ test.

WOODROW It takes a fast car lady to lead a double life.

GALLO Sounds like good advice. The DA would have a field day cross-examining your IQ genius.

VON BOOTUM Officer, he was a vagrant without skills, without any hope of ever becoming a contributing member to our great society. Now you be the decider of truths here. I haven't hurt a hair on his head and have only helped him.

GALLO (*Looks closely*) There's a hole in his head!

VON BOOTUM That is not a hole, it's an aperture.

GALLO It's a fucking hole!

VON BOOTUM All right. But it's a very small hole. It's where I put the Recallol.

GALLO You can't just grab the homeless and change them.

VON BOOTUM The great judicial theorist Strippelgram once said, "To genuinely improve the abject human condition must involve cruel, irreversible change."

GALLO You have no authority, we have a legal system.

VON BOOTUM Let me tell you about your system. We pay $20 billion a year, that's $125 a day per prisoner, 62% of which return to prison in three years.

GALLO You have a right to remain silent. In fact, I'd prefer if you'd remain silent. Where's the phone?

VON BOOTUM Officer, you arrest me and all the work I've done will be undone. He'll be free to kill again.

GALLO Not likely, if he didn't kill before. (*On the phone*) Put me through to Wojahowitz.

VON BOOTUM Oh, but he did.

GALLO (*On hold*) He did what?

VON BOOTUM This is the man who killed my wife and knocked me unconscious two weeks ago.

ISADORA'S GHOST Justice served! I'm out of here.

GALLO (*Hangs up the phone*) The crime report said you couldn't make an ID. You got proof this is the guy?

VON BOOTUM He told me exactly where in the East River he disposed of the murder weapon.

GALLO That'd do it.

VON BOOTUM He said he stole the gun from a dealer in his building on 7th Street where he purchases the notorious crack-cocaine.

GALLO How did you find him?

VON BOOTUM I recognized him immediately as one of the regulars who sell refuse on the sidewalk near Astor Place.

GALLO Why didn't you have him arrested?!

VON BOOTUM Crime is a disease. As a doctor of criminal behavior, I refuse to join with the medieval approach of incarcerating these mentally ill. I really think I can cure this man if you just let me. And I believe the fact that he killed my wife—the vaccine to all my wants, the antidote to all my desire— (Sniffles) entitles me to some say in this matter.

ISADORA'S GHOST This sauerkraut's turned me into a guinea pig acquisition form!

GALLO I don't see evidence of rehabilitation. In fact, I've heard livelier car horns in Bensonhurst than this man.

VON BOOTUM I'm not just drilling holes in skulls. I have spent the past twenty years developing a three-part program that destroys recalcitrant behavior, imposes an iconographic character-matrix, and then educates that matrix. With time, the former identity breaks through. The result is the same person with an advanced education—a human being with a purpose.

WOODROW (Watching Von Bootum) Lonely men stand in lines at the candy counter of the porno flick. Their pale crumpled popcorn bags heavy with sperm.

GALLO Yuk! That's some contribution to society.

VON BOOTUM This is the blotting stage. After it's done, a character-composite is constructed. Then he gets educated. In a week he'll have a high school education. In four weeks he'll have a college education.

WOODROW (Slowly, sensitively) Am I the person I did not want to be? That talks-to-himself person? Am I the loony man? In the great serenade of things—

GALLO (To Woodrow) 'Fraid so. (To Von Bootum) All right, this guy's obviously a throwaway.

ISADORA'S GHOST A throwaway? What the hell kind of cop are you?
(*Exits*)

VON BOOTUM I salute you, sir. In this vile age of politically correct
cowardism, of multicultural snivelling, all diluting or deni-
grating the intellectual genetic purity, you stand tall.

GALLO You got one week to show me that you have created a
human being who can "contribute to society," and in return
I'll see that you don't get booked. But you hurt another hair
on his pin-sized scalp and I'll put an aperture in *your* head.

WOODROW How much longer will I be able to inhabit the divine
sepulchre of life, my great love? Do dolphins plunge bot-
tomward to find the light?

GALLO I don't know, but I do know that I have to deal with drug
dealers, murderers, scum of the earth. And none of them
make my skin crawl worse than poets. I mean, I'm a writer
myself, you know, but these guys don't know when to quit.

VON BOOTUM I see your point, detective, I can mix any character-
matrix.

GALLO Don't Dan Quayle him, but look to the good old days when
folks were gentler, things were kinder.

VON BOOTUM Yeah, yeah, I see what you're saying. (*As Gallo turns
to go, Von Bootum injects him in the neck*) I can't have him
ready in a week. But I can have you ready before anyone
notices you missing.

GALLO Why did you do that? (*Instantly becomes weak, Von Bootum
helps him into the same wheelchair that Woodrow was in*) Boy
am I tired.

VON BOOTUM There is one vital part of the experiment I failed to
mention. For this I will need your civil services for just a few
days.

GALLO (*Giggling*) Shoot or I'll halt. I mean—

VON BOOTUM I will halt all this out of your mind. And you will
shoot your sense of humanity unto him. So we're off to see
the wizard—

GALLO The wonderful wizard of ours . . . (*Sings to sleep*)

VON BOOTUM (*Typing at the computer*) Let's look into America's past for an affable character-type for you, Woody. From tabula rasa to—Rastus! That will be your trigger-name, before I pull the trigger on you.

ISADORA'S GHOST (*Rematerializes*) Pull the trigger?

WOODROW Pull my daisy, tip my cup. Cut my thoughts for coconuts—

VON BOOTUM Although young Woodrow's operation will be successful, the patient, as the old adage goes, shall die. We can't let poor Hynie Mama's death go unavenged.

ISADORA'S GHOST (*Looking at Woodrow*) This is too pathetic. I don't know which of you I feel worse for. (*Exits*)

VON BOOTUM (*Adding diabolically*) Even if she did deserve it. (*Sinister laughter as lights fade to black*)

❦

SCENE 4

It is dark and silent. In the distance we hear a train again. It grows louder until it sounds as if it is rushing across the front of the theater. A blast of wind and a strobe of light might suggest its crossing. We are back on the same subway platform as in Scene One. Isadora should behave comically. All the others should ignore her, as they are still stuck in their original roles and attitudes. The scene begins in mid-action.

VON BOOTUM (*His voice is still diabolic*) By the way, did you pack all those Deutsche Marks neatly in your purse?

ISADORA With you as the breadwinner— (*Realizes she is reliving her death*) Uh oh. Here we are again. (*Sees Woodrow*) Knock knock, who's there? Come. Come where?

VON BOOTUM Come on, this way. (*Points in the distance, they exit stage left*)

ISADORA It's like sex, the guy ignores you and you're left to deal with your own climax. (*To Von Bootum*) Ten to one, the exit's locked.

VON BOOTUM Shit, the exit's locked!

Woodrow enters stage right. He walks nervously behind them and also exits stage left, where he grabs Isadora's purse.

ISADORA (*Offstage*) I was expecting you, stranger. (*Woodrow tries to run with Isadora's handbag, but she holds on and is pulled back onto the stage*) Hey, Euclid, what do you have that rhymes with a woman's genitalia?

VON BOOTUM My Angina!

ISADORA (*Fighting for the purse*) No, I insist, you take it. You take it!

VON BOOTUM (*Still offstage*) He bit the bait. Give him the purse, he's got a gun! (*Pulls out his gun*)

WOODROW No I don't. (*Holds up his hands seeing the pistol; Von Bootum shoves his gun into Woodrow's pocket*)

ISADORA Wow! I knew I recognized that gun.

WOODROW (*Pulls the pistol out of his pocket and points it in Isadora's face*) Give me the fucking bag!

ISADORA Take it! (*She involuntarily slaps Woodrow across the face*) This is a splendid opportunity to show you're more forgiving than I.

VON BOOTUM That's my gun! Oh God. Don't shoot, please. I'll give you all the money in the world. (*In a different voice*) If you kill her!

WOODROW What?!

ISADORA No! What's on first. (*Slaps the gun out of Woodrow's hand*) Who's on second, and this is the third time I've been killed. Take it way, Euclid!

VON BOOTUM (*Grabs a stick off the ground*) I'll hit you, so help me!

ISADORA *(Before Woodrow has retrieved the pistol)* Nice knowing you. Don't forget to feed the snake.

VON BOOTUM *(In a diabolic tone)* I'm doing this for you, bud. *(Hits himself over the head and falls unconscious)*

ISADORA That bud's for you. Hey, you've got a pimple on your face, mind if I pick it?

Isadora unwillingly digs her fingernails into Woodrow's face, and just before she rips them down, Woodrow shoots her. She screams and falls, still holding the purse.

ISADORA Another bad fucking joke!

Isadora dies, blackout.

♋

SCENE 5

Back in the living room. Woodrow's wearing an apron, yet between household chores he is supposed to be studying books. His character and accent should be composites of various black stereotypes from Rochester to Aunt Jemima. He is taking care of Detective Gallo, who is sitting in the wheelchair curled up. Occasionally, Gallo blurts out street phrases. Since Woodrow and Gallo have undergone an empathy experiment, Woodrow regards the officer as a part of himself. Isadora's ghost appears increasingly haggard and tattered.

ISADORA'S GHOST No sooner is he moving around than Professor Henry Higgins has made Eliza the killer into a domestic.

WOODROW Thank you, missy! *(Belatedly, his eyes widen in a minstrel fashion and he shrieks, jumping into the air)* I dink I juz saws me a hobgoblin! (*He rubs his eyes and checks again*) Shoo, spook! I don't want me seein dat. (*Covers Gallo's eyes*)

GALLO Smoke, coke, TNT—

ISADORA'S GHOST Believe me, kid, Miss Scarlet doesn't want to see that either.

WOODROW Da bossman sez I got da mojo on my tinkin 'cause of de tonic dat I'm a drinkin.

ISADORA'S GHOST Ted Danson at the Whoopie Goldberg roast?

GALLO (*Slightly garbled like the subway PA system*) Please stand clear of the moving platform as trains enter and leave the station. Thank you.

WOODROW (*Gently holding Gallo's head in his hands*) Leastways I ain't Lucy-nation, which's what you is.

ISADORA'S GHOST Why are you holding him like a baby? And what is that crap he's blurting out?

WOODROW (*Still holding Gallo*) Who's him? I ain't holding no him.

ISADORA'S GHOST Okay. Von Bootum must have educated you himself.

WOODROW Sure done did. I'z got me a high school edjy-cation.

ISADORA'S GHOST A New York City high school education—figures. You're supposed to get a college education.

WOODROW Yes'm, but I'z got to ease up awhile, on account the doctor don't want me gettin brain overload. I'z suppose to do some of that page-turnin book-learnin.

ISADORA'S GHOST You're reading books and you don't know pronouns?

WOODROW Pronouns? Indicative? Possessive? Personal?

ISADORA'S GHOST What about history? Do you know anything about Alexander the Great? No, wait, let's give Von Bootum's experiment more of a test. Do you know anything about Great Alex's dad?

WOODROW (*Using the same mock black accent*) Philip of Macedon who lived from 359 to 336 BC conquered villages southward from his native town. These included Amphipolic and Pydna and finally Delphia in 356. He was stopped in Thermopylae in—

ISADORA'S GHOST Please drop the accent. I'm in no mood.

WOODROW Not meaning to be uppity, and I know I'z using the wrong auxiliary verb, but I is what I is.

ISADORA'S GHOST (*Pauses*) Oh! That's very shrewd of him. Any other character-type would have turned rebellious when educated with a history of racial oppression.

WOODROW You sound whiskey-crazy, ma'am. Who you be?

ISADORA'S GHOST I am the increasingly late Mrs. Von Bootum. Who are you?

WOODROW (*Does a little tap dance*) Who's da boy dat runs da fastest, why it's lil'o me—Rastus.

GALLO Animals don't wear your skin. Don't wear their fur!

ISADORA'S GHOST Where is Dr. Franken-Bootum anyway?

WOODROW (*Holding Gallo in his arms*) If'n you really be his dead wife, you'd know de honorable professor educates during the day.

ISADORA'S GHOST Oh, go wet nurse.

WOODROW (*Cleaning up*) Pshaw! I isn't wettin on any nurse. I'z workin on my feces.

GALLO Pray to end abortion! Human life is sacred.

ISADORA'S GHOST (*Referring to Gallo*) You're not getting any of this?

WOODROW Any of what?

ISADORA'S GHOST Forget it. Why are you working on a thesis?

WOODROW He wants me to prove dat I'z reformed. So I've drawn up some feces proposals. (*Reads from a list*) "How to create either an automated train porter or watermelon deseeder or tapdancing robots."

ISADORA'S GHOST (*Disgusted*) Okay, turn that on. (*Points to the computer*) Let's see what Mr. PC did to you.

WOODROW Oh, I ain't supposed to handle the master's gizmos.

ISADORA'S GHOST Look, you're a human guinea pig in an experiment that uses pop caricatures from a time when this country didn't attempt to hide its racism. Now you want to regress your way back to the plantation? Or shall we try to emancipate you?

WOODROW You sayin it's all shinola?

ISADORA'S GHOST 'Fraid so.

WOODROW (*Grateful*) Hallelujah! I had this awful recollection of us colored folk being slaves.

ISADORA'S GHOST I'm afraid that part is true.

WOODROW Missy, either you lyin about everythin, in which case I is plum-wine crazy, or—

ISADORA'S GHOST Why can't I be telling the truth?

WOODROW How come I'z talking to a dead lady?

ISADORA'S GHOST If I told you, you'd freak out.

WOODROW Why's that, ladybug? Why you helpin me?

ISADORA'S GHOST Because I can't do anything with you—or *to* you—in the condition you're in.

GALLO How do you get to McSorley's? Where's the Statue of Liberty? What train takes you to the World Trade Center?

WOODROW You talkin monkey-shine.

ISADORA'S GHOST Do you want to take responsibility for your life or not?

WOODROW That's what I'm tryin to axe you!

ISADORA'S GHOST You already shot me, please don't axe me.

GALLO Accommodation! Not prohibition! Sing a petition for smokers' rights.

WOODROW So let me get this straight, I'z gonna be responsible.

ISADORA'S GHOST That's right. You wouldn't just be some servile appendage. You'll feel pride when you've accomplished something good, and even more important, you'll be plagued with guilt when you've done something wrong. Put your finger on the keyboard, and when you feel a slight electrostatic sensation, let your fingers do the walking. (*He does so, and she puts her hands over his and reads while typing*) Look at this. He's got everything from Aunt Jemima to Butterfly McQueen in here.

And you're somehow connected with this clone. (*Referring to Gallo*)

WOODROW I'z the only clown here.

ISADORA'S GHOST (*Reading the computer*) Yeah, yeah, you've empathized with each other so much, you think you're part of each other.

GALLO (*Speaking with a "ghetto" accent*) Yo! Hon, don't walk by, I love you, so let's give it another try— Then fuck you, bitch! I don't want yo' ass anyways.

ISADORA'S GHOST (*Reading*) No wonder he's like that. He's supposed to be blotted on the poetry stuff, but the tape malfunctioned. For the past two days he was submerged in a program on the sounds of the street.

GALLO Big savings, little time! GOING OUT OF BUSINESS!

ISADORA'S GHOST Let's put you both out of business. What influences can we fill you with? Okay, here's some from the '70s: *Blacula, Blackenstein, Shaft, Superfly, Get Christy Love!* Let's fast-forward through Blaxploitation. Here's some good responsibility-accepting types. Okay, get back in there. (*Woodrow sits in the wheelchair with Gallo*) Let's see about the new trigger-name—you will be Marvin.

GALLO (*Musically*) Hammer time! Can't touch this! Can't touch this!

ISADORA'S GHOST (*Replies to him*) Want to bet? I'll unblot you both at the same time.

WOODROW Wait a second, it's all comin back to me.

ISADORA'S GHOST What is?

WOODROW (*Slides himself and Gallo into the Polk tank while muttering*) I saw da best minds of my generation destroyed by madness—

ISADORA'S GHOST Oh God, here I go again, back into my late-night rerun in the subway that doesn't run—

Fade to black.

ACT TWO

SCENE 1

Back in the living room. The scene begins with smoke, coughing, screams, alarms. Woodrow is banging from inside the locked Polk tank. Gallo is quietly sitting behind him.

WOODROW Help! Set me free! HELP!

ISADORA'S GHOST *(Lights rise on her)* I can't! Didn't you ever see the movie *Ghost*? I can't touch anything.

VON BOOTUM *(Dashing in)* Oh my. Rastus! What happened?! How'd you— *(Helping him out, coughing)* How'd you get in there? Who remixed your matrix tape? *(Checks the computer screen)*

WOODROW *(Speaking in a grandiloquence reminiscent of Malcolm X)* I have seen the great divide and yonder!

VON BOOTUM Oh my God! *(Gallo is still coughing)* How'd you two peas get in that pod, huh? You were supposed to be preparing a thesis proposal—

WOODROW Mine eyes have seen the glories as well as your evils! I cast my sights upon the prize! Yes sir! *(To Gallo, who remains in the back of the Polk tank)* Who's unfairly consigned to the rear of this bus?

VON BOOTUM Rastus!

WOODROW *(Instantly reverting)* Yes'm.

VON BOOTUM *(Inspecting Gallo's pupils)* Oh my. The detective is coming to. Somebody sabotaged my invention. Let's check out the damage in here. (*Crawls inside the Polk tank*)

ISADORA'S GHOST Marvin! He's going to reprogram you. Lock him in!

Woodrow locks Von Bootum in the tank. He angrily starts typing at the computer.

WOODROW I'll tie the oppressors to the whipping post!

ISADORA'S GHOST Type in the adult-film category, look up Long Dong Silver.

VON BOOTUM (*From inside the tank*) I hear you clicking out there, but to no avail. The tank's ruined. Open up, Rastus.

WOODROW (*Opens it*) Yes'm, boss.

ISADORA'S GHOST Marvin! Wait!

WOODROW (*Angrily*) Your chickens have finally come home to roost. And I'm leaving before they do!

ISADORA'S GHOST Good for you. Get the hell out of here.

VON BOOTUM You're the subject of my test. You can't go! Rastus, come to me.

WOODROW (*Reverts to Rastus*) Howdy, boss, can I get your dogs out from under you?

ISADORA'S GHOST Marvin!

WOODROW (*Reverts to Marvin*) I'm unshackled from both you blue-eyed devils.

VON BOOTUM Your trigger-name is supposed to revert you permanently. I don't understand why it isn't working.

WOODROW I'm free, thank God almighty, I'm free at last! (*Turns to go, takes a couple of steps, and mutters vacantly, fitfully*) Spare any change? Spare any change? Spare any change?

ISADORA'S GHOST Marvin! (*He comes to*) Get the hell out of here.

WOODROW (*Takes another few steps and reverts*) Spare change?

ISADORA'S GHOST Marvin! (*He comes to*) What did he do to you?

VON BOOTUM You've got a brain-cuff on, which prevents you from attacking me or leaving here. It works regardless of character profiles. Now listen, Rastus or Marvin or whoever you are. During the Renaissance, an apprentice would study under a master until he fully learned his trade, then he would submit his masterpiece.

WOODROW (*Indignant*) Don't I know what a master's piece is? Don't I know what submission is? Don't I know the slave trade? Don't you dare presume to teach me anything, white motherfucker.

VON BOOTUM I'll uncuff you when I have my masterpiece.

WOODROW (*Lunges at Von Bootum, but reverts before touching him*) Spare change?

ISADORA'S GHOST Marvin!

VON BOOTUM I'm sorry that you can't slaughter me the way you murdered my Hynie Mama, but I will remove your brain muzzle when you've completed a scholastic thesis of some kind. (*Takes off his jacket, exchanges it for a lab coat, and removes his shoes, which he exchanges for slippers*)

WOODROW You held us as slaves years ago—

VON BOOTUM I beg your pardon. Russian Wolfhounds, perhaps. But the Von Bootums never owned slaves.

WOODROW Then what the hell is all this?

VON BOOTUM This is a one-room empowerment zone. A tiny gesture of affirmative action. A one-man war on poverty.

WOODROW Another forty-acres-and-a-mule failure is all.

VON BOOTUM Failure? Listen to yourself, Woodrow. Look at the clarity of your thought. Your righteous indignation! Life! I've given you a reversely discriminated life.

WOODROW YOU TOOK MY LIFE AND GAVE ME A ROLE! WHERE AM I FROM? HOW THE HELL DID I GET HERE?! WHO AM I?!

VON BOOTUM An ingrate. Suffice it to say, you were broken when I found you. I gave you food, board, an education—

WOODROW But you haven't given me my freedom!

VON BOOTUM There is a library in that computer. Use it and present me with a suitable thesis proposal, and you're free.

WOODROW Okay, how about a stinging indictment of White America.

VON BOOTUM Cliché. Unacceptable.

WOODROW All right then, I'd like to prepare a declaration for an independent African-American state.

VON BOOTUM I don't know who downloaded that mumbo jumbo into your character profile, but let me advise that you watch some daytime soaps and flush all those revolutionary clichés out of your head. They're only going to make you bitter.

ISADORA'S GHOST Tell him you've theorized a preventative to injustice.

WOODROW (To her) That's not mine.

VON BOOTUM Nothing is yours until you sit down, crack open some books, and study, whatever your name is.

WOODROW My name is Marvin.

VON BOOTUM Look, I don't want to fight. I'm going to revive the cop since I'm done with his part of the experiment. Can I persuade you to change into proper attire and join us for dinner?

WOODROW I will neither turn away an olive branch nor uncock a gun. (Exits)

VON BOOTUM (Sits Gallo up) Officer, listen to me. Stand up and keep your eye on the watch.

GALLO Andy Warhol wore khakis!

VON BOOTUM You've got an ad campaign stuck in your brain. (Takes out a pocket watch on a chain and swings it pendulously, back and forth) You can hear me, can't you?

GALLO Big Mac attacked khakis.

VON BOOTUM You broke in, found me experimenting on my wife's murderer, and agreed to give me three weeks, yah?

GALLO Leonard Bernstein wore khakis!

VON BOOTUM When I awaken you it's three days later. You'll forget your entire time here. In fact, you are just joining us for hasenpfeffer burger and for the hundred-hour head-cleaning of our little blockhead, yah?

GALLO Jackie wore khakis.

VON BOOTUM Good. Put on your jacket and wait outside. When I open the door, you will awaken. Then you can begin your inquiry, yah?

GALLO Pataki wore khakis.

VON BOOTUM (*Puts away the pocket watch angrily*) Don't tell me who wore khakis no more! I don't care who wore these khakis. Now out!

Gallo exits. Von Bootum takes a mint from a bowl, sits in a chair, removes his slippers and socks, and scratches his feet while reading The Bell Curve.

ISADORA'S GHOST You got everything you wanted. The law outside waiting at your beck and call, picking your stinking feet. Only you replaced me with Woody as your domestic. Maybe that's an improvement, I wasn't a great cook. We didn't have sex in years, always fighting. But I loved you. How could you do this to me?!!

Woodrow returns, dressed as Malcom X.

VON BOOTUM What's this? You look like a disgruntled bellhop.

WOODROW You promised food, white man!

ISADORA'S GHOST Pew, I can smell his socks from the great beyond. Do him a favor, Rastus, and toss them into the can.

WOODROW Yes'm. (*Throws Von Bootum's socks into the garbage*)

ISADORA'S GHOST I'm sorry, I meant *Marvin*. I accidentally used your old trigger-name.

VON BOOTUM My God, why did you discard my socks?

WOODROW The smell was oppressive.

VON BOOTUM (*Starts blinking and acting feverish*) My wife used to do that.

ISADORA'S GHOST *(Smiles smugly)* Do me a favor and smack him, just once for me.

WOODROW Woman, please!

VON BOOTUM Well, under the right circumstances or for the right amount of money, they do indeed please. Would you like a bitter, Woody?

ISADORA'S GHOST Would you mind if I offered a thesis proposal?

WOODROW Yes! *(Von Bootum extends the bowl of mints)*

ISADORA'S GHOST I thought of a great proposal and I can dictate it to you.

WOODROW No!

VON BOOTUM Do you want one or not?

ISADORA'S GHOST Marvin, I just want to help you and—

WOODROW It's just that I have to find my own way.

VON BOOTUM As you wish, I'll put them here. *(Sets the bowl down)*

ISADORA'S GHOST Once he's finished with you, he'll dispose of you like a lab rat, unless you impress upon him that you have a great discovery that he can use—the man's a blatant thief.

WOODROW Actually, I was thinking about the sciences.

VON BOOTUM What about the sciences?

ISADORA'S GHOST Tell him you need to use the lab.

WOODROW Well, downstairs you have a lab, don't you?

VON BOOTUM That was my wife's work place, a permanent shrine to endless nagging. It's off-limits.

WOODROW I'm sorry, I didn't mean to trouble you about her.

ISADORA'S GHOST Hell no, don't trouble anyone on my account.

VON BOOTUM She was a brilliant pharmaceutical biochemist. For years we researched along the same lines.

ISADORA'S GHOST My lines!

VON BOOTUM When she died, I tried to decipher some of her notes, but they were entirely illegible—

ISADORA'S GHOST Deliberately, you plagiarist.

VON BOOTUM Brilliant yet unfeeling woman.

ISADORA'S GHOST *(Spits on his face)* Feel that, monster.

VON BOOTUM *(Lovingly)* Yet sometimes I can almost feel her moist lips on my cheek. *(Woodrow coughs nervously)* You okay, Woodrow?

ISADORA'S GHOST Come on, push him! Needle him! Don't let up! You have a terrific science project.

WOODROW *(Holding his head)* I have a terrific headache.

VON BOOTUM Isadora used to give me migraines. But you mustn't be in any pain when I awaken our friend. *(Referring to Gallo, Von Bootum exits)*

WOODROW Pardon me if I seem a bit unsure of myself, but who the hell are you again, and how'd I get here?

ISADORA'S GHOST I'm sorry, that's right. You just went through another character-matrix designed to give you a maximum sense of responsibility. You shot me to death on a subway platform. And because that fat fuck doesn't believe he committed a crime, he doesn't see or hear me. Only you can.

VON BOOTUM *(Returns)* Here we are, some Acetylsalicylic Acid, also known as aspirin. *(Gives Woodrow some pills)* I think I hear a knock. I'll get our guest and we're off to dinner, yah?

WOODROW *(Stares at Isadora in disbelief as Von Bootum exits)* WHAT?

ISADORA'S GHOST You shot me to death during a botched robbery attempt.

WOODROW I don't believe it.

ISADORA'S GHOST The memory cells are still in your head. You can remember if you think hard enough.

WOODROW There must be a misunderstanding.

ISADORA'S GHOST There isn't, and the good news is, I'm going to spend every waking second with you. Every minute, every moment, I'll be *(Shouts in his ear)* right here with you!

VON BOOTUM *(Enters with Gallo)* Look who's here. *(Low tone)* He doesn't remember you. *(Normal tone)* Allow me to introduce. Detective Gallo, this is Rastus.

GALLO How do you do, Rastus?

WOODROW *(Wide grin)* How's do I do what, boss?

ISADORA'S GHOST Marvin!

GALLO Excuse me?

WOODROW The name's Marvin. *(Gallo looks familiar to him)* How do I know you? *(They are about to shake hands when Gallo soulfully hugs him)*

GALLO Sorry, I guess I just needed a hug.

VON BOOTUM I made some reservations for Anal Bark, the exquisite new Indian restaurant on 6th Street.

GALLO Sounds delish! God, I'm famished. *(To Woodrow)* So, how we doing?

WOODROW *(Militantly)* How are *we* doing? One third of *us* live in poverty and a quarter of *us* are in jail by the time *we're* thirty. That's how we're doing! *We* make up 12% of the nation's population, yet 50% of the nation's prisoners. That's how *we're* doing!

GALLO *(Defensively)* Hey, I voted for Clinton. *(To Von Bootum)* Why's he acting like that?

VON BOOTUM If I can have a word alone? *(Gallo and Von Bootum step off to one side, away from Woodrow)* You remember our deal about Woodrow, yah? *(Gallo nods yes, and leading him off-stage, Von Bootum keeps talking)*

WOODROW *(To Isadora)* Look, I truly regret any harm I might have caused you, but I don't remember a thing.

ISADORA'S GHOST Shut up, I'll make you a deal. There's one thing I didn't complete before my bothersome bloodbath.

WOODROW What?

ISADORA'S GHOST My experimental serum Rehabilitol. Von Bootum didn't know it, but I almost finished the theoretical side of it.

WOODROW The hieroglyphics in the basement?

ISADORA'S GHOST Right, I did most of the preliminary experiments, I just never pulled them all together.

WOODROW This Rehabilitol is the cure for crime you were mentioning?

ISADORA'S GHOST It's more of a corrective.

WOODROW And once it's done, you're gone?

ISADORA'S GHOST Once it's done *and* tested, I'm gone.

VON BOOTUM (*Reenters with Gallo*) Sorry for taking so long. I just wanted to familiarize the good detective with some of the latest developments.

GALLO So, locked in the microwave with Spike Lee, I hear.

WOODROW Better than being locked in there with *you*.

GALLO (*Blank-eyed*) O.J. wore khakis. (*Grabs his mouth*) Why did I say that?

VON BOOTUM We're operating without the Polk tank now, so we're going to need more time than anticipated.

GALLO Now wait a sec, we had a deal. (*Unsure*) Didn't we?

VON BOOTUM I didn't know that the Polk tank would break.

ISADORA'S GHOST Have him agree to your thesis now. He won't refuse you in front of the cop. Then I'll leave you alone.

WOODROW Actually, professor, I've given this a lot of thought and I came up with an exciting thesis proposal.

VON BOOTUM (*Bored*) I'm all ears.

WOODROW Inspired by you, I'd like to try to undertake a pharmaceutical remedy to crime.

ISADORA'S GHOST Good—make him the inspiration.

VON BOOTUM But your concentration is in the humanities. Your mind isn't designed for the sciences.

GALLO Just say no to drugs, Woody. (*Blank-eyed, chants*) Smoke, coke.

WOODROW Who the hell do you think you are? How dare you presume to know what my mind is designed for?

VON BOOTUM (*Nervous in front of Gallo*) I just mean you have no training in pharmacology.

WOODROW Percy Julian, a fellow African-American, did pharmaceutical research that resulted in successful treatments for glaucoma and arthritis. When he died, he held over a hundred patents.

GALLO You'd be great at *Trivial Pursuit.*

VON BOOTUM Why this sudden interest?

WOODROW It was sparked while reading the late Mrs. Von Bootum's textbooks—

ISADORA'S GHOST Name's Isadora.

WOODROW —*The Chemicals of Criminals, The DNA of a Repeat Offender,* and, of course, her breakthrough work, *The Calcium of the Recalcitrant.* I'm quite prepared on the subject.

GALLO *(Skeptically)* Prepared on the subject?

ISADORA'S GHOST Suggest a test of any kind.

WOODROW You can test me on the subject if you wish.

VON BOOTUM I don't think so, Woody.

GALLO Wait a second, doctor, I'd like to see some kind of test. I want proof of you—of his—change. I believe I'm here for *(Goes into a sudden trance)* hasenpfeffer hamburger and for a hundred-hour head-cleaning of our blockhead, yah?

WOODROW Screw you too.

VON BOOTUM All right, Marvin, I'll quiz you, but you get just one question wrong and you're back in the humanities, yah?

WOODROW Fine.

VON BOOTUM Methocarbanol, what does this drug do?

ISADORA'S GHOST It's basically a muscle relaxant for spasms.

WOODROW It's a muscle relaxant.

VON BOOTUM What is the precise location of this drug's action?

ISADORA'S GHOST It's a trick question. The location's not fully clear. It's thought to act on the nerve pathway in the brain and spinal cord that are involved in the reflex activity of voluntary muscles.

WOODROW It roughly acts on the nerve pathways in the brain and spinal cord that are involved in the reflex activity of voluntary muscles.

VON BOOTUM Wrong! So sorry.

ISADORA'S GHOST Bullshit! Open that book. (*Points to one on the shelf*) Check out chapter three. (*Woodrow goes to the shelf and opens the book, Isadora looking over his shoulder*) Keep turning, keep turning. (*Finally coming to the right page, she yells*) THERE! (*Woodrow shows it to Von Bootum and Gallo, who skim the section*)

GALLO Whoops, there it is! Can't touch that! I mean, very good.

VON BOOTUM Okay. (*Takes the book from Woodrow, flips through it, and stops at another page*) Ephedrine, what year was it introduced? Where was it used in crude form for centuries?

ISADORA'S GHOST China for five thousand years and introduced in (*Looks over Von Bootum's shoulder*) 1924.

WOODROW China is where it was used and it was introduced onto the open market, I think, in May 1924.

GALLO Is he right?

VON BOOTUM (*Slams the book closed*) I vastly underestimated the strength of his memory retention.

GALLO Why don't you give him a shot at the lab?

VON BOOTUM A regurgitative mind is not the same as an inventive mind. I am very hesitant to set someone loose in a room where he could hurt himself.

WOODROW Doctor, I have no intention of making this into a long endeavor. I'll surprise you with my speed.

GALLO I took a chance on you. Take a chance on him.

VON BOOTUM (*Resumes flipping through the book*) All right.

ISADORA'S GHOST I'm gone. (*She vanishes*)

VON BOOTUM You really worked out a complete program then?

WOODROW I have. I know exactly what I'll be doing and—

VON BOOTUM (*Stops on a page in the book*) Oh, here's a question that'll assure me that you soundly know your phamaceuticals. Answer this—

WOODROW But I thought the test was over.

GALLO The trial doesn't end till the judge leaves the room.

VON BOOTUM Final jeopardy question: List the drug families.

WOODROW Drug families?

VON BOOTUM All the major drug families, yes, Rastus.

WOODROW (*Reverts to Rastus*) Let's see, you means like Whalens, Duane Reade—

GALLO No, the *drug* families.

WOODROW Oh! Da drug families. You mean like da Genovese, Columbo, Gotti—

GALLO WHAT?

ISADORA'S GHOST (*Appears*) Marvin! (*Gallo bolts to attention*)

ISADORA'S GHOST & WOODROW (*Isadora's ghost speaks breathlessly along with Woodrow*) Amphetamines, Analgesics, Antiarthritics, Antiasthmatics, Anticoagulants, Antidepressants, Tricyclics, Antidiabetics, Antigout, Antihistamines, Antihypertensives, AntiParkinson's, Antispasmodics, Atropines, Barbiturates, Benzodiazepines, Cortisone, Decongestants, Diuretics, Monamine, Oxidase-Inhibitors, Nitrates, Penicillin, Phenothiazine, Sedatives, Sulfonamide, Tetracyclines, Thiazides, and Tranquilizers, mild and strong.

GALLO Now that was thrilling. (*Von Bootum applauds*)

WOODROW I can also list the dynastic families of Xhosas, Zulus, and other African tribes.

VON BOOTUM Not necessary. And though I'm genuinely impressed, I'm afraid that in all good conscience, I still can't permit you to go into a lab.

WOODROW Is the master afraid of being usurped by the servant?

GALLO You know, doc, if he really did create some brilliant kind of serum, that'd mean you could take (*Quietly*) criminals and turn them into geniuses. Now that's Nobel Prize–winning stuff.

VON BOOTUM (*Muttering*) Nobel Laureate Von Bootum. All these people who laughed at me and said, "Von Bootum, you *dunkopf!*"

GALLO They'd be fools!

VON BOOTUM Yah! *(To Woodrow)* Tell you what. I'll give you two weeks, that's up until the tenth of this month, to show early results.

ISADORA'S GHOST I need much more time.

WOODROW *(To Isadora's ghost)* More time? Another week?

VON BOOTUM Fine, another week, but that's the limit. *(Gallo takes out his appointment book)* How does that fit with your tax-paid schedule, detective?

ISADORA'S GHOST NO! I need at least a month! *(Woodrow shakes his head no)*

GALLO Fine. In fact, I'll stop by once before then.

ISADORA'S GHOST Look, I'm dead, I don't need sleep, but be warned: The next three weeks are going to be the roughest, most exhausting weeks in your life.

VON BOOTUM Fine. All right, at 3 o'clock on the seventeenth of the month, I will be ready for your experiment.

WOODROW *(Grabs his coat and heads toward the door, speaking to Isadora's ghost)* I just want to get the whole thing over with quickly.

GALLO What motivation. I have to tell you, Woody, I thought you lost it when you started listing those drugstores.

WOODROW Just having a laugh. Actually, all modesty aside, I also wrote a little poem.

ISADORA'S GHOST & GALLO Yikes!

VON BOOTUM *(Admiring Woodrow)* Arts and sciences! If only Isadora was like that.

ISADORA'S GHOST *(Suddenly pointing to Von Bootum's shoulder)* Look, Woody, there's a waterbug crawling on his arm. *(Woodrow slaps his shoulder)*

VON BOOTUM Ow!

WOODROW Sorry, I thought I saw something.

VON BOOTUM Well, come on, Marvin, recite us your marvelous poem while we're going to dinner.

ISADORA'S GHOST I'll see you in the lab later. *(She vanishes)*

WOODROW *(Takes out a piece of paper)* I saw the best minds of my
generation—

GALLO Eating, I bet. In an Indian restaurant. *(Grabs his coat and
rushes for the door)*

WOODROW No, destroyed by madness— There's more.

VON BOOTUM Maybe after dinner, Marvin. *(All exit, fade to black)*

SCENE 2

*It is dark and silent. In the distance we hear a train again. It grows
louder, until it sounds as if it is rushing into the front of the theater; a
gust of wind and a strobe of light might suggest its crossing. We are back
on the same subway platform as in Scene One, only this time Isadora
refuses to speak in her dance of death. Everyone else is in mid-action.*

VON BOOTUM Just move it! Shit, the exit's locked. *(Woodrow enters
stage right, walking nervously behind them, until he also exits
stage left, where he grabs Isadora's purse)* My Angina! *(Still offstage, we hear him demonically)* He bit the bait. *(Voice reverts
to normal as he enters the stage)* Give him the purse! He's got
a gun! *(Pulls out a gun)*

WOODROW No I don't! *(Holds up his hand upon seeing Von Bootum's
pistol)*

VON BOOTUM *(Shoves his gun into Woodrow's pocket so Isadora doesn't
see it, then in a diabolic whisper)* Take mine.

WOODROW *(Pulls out the gun)* Give me the fucking bag!

VON BOOTUM *(Holding his chest)* That's my gun! Oh God! Don't
shoot, please. I'll give you all the money in the world!
(Alternate demonic voice) If you kill her!

WOODROW What?! *(Isadora slaps the gun out of his hand)*

VON BOOTUM (*Grabs a stick off the ground*) I'll hit you, so help me! (*Woodrow recovers the pistol*) I'm doing this for you, buddy.

Von Bootum hits himself over the head and falls unconscious. Isadora involuntarily digs her fingernails into Woodrow's face, and just before she rips them down, Woodrow shoots her. She screams in agony, still holding the purse.

ISADORA No! No! No!

WOODROW Shit! (*Helps her to the ground, then pulls the purse away*) All I wanted was the fucking purse! (*Fade to black*)

☙❧

SCENE 3

In the lab downstairs, there is a mouse in a cage and an unseen snake in a terrarium. A variety of chemicals line a spice rack against the back wall.

ISADORA'S GHOST (*Looking into the terrarium, seeing the snake*) At least the monster didn't kill you, Leona. This is my little baby python.

WOODROW Yes, I remember you mentioning her. Well, I'll be upstairs working on my *Call to Revolution* pamphlet. Let me know when you're done.

ISADORA'S GHOST Wait a second. I can't hold things, I'm a ghost.

WOODROW Surely you don't expect me to be your step-and-fetch-it.

ISADORA'S GHOST You have to.

WOODROW Have to? I beg your pardon, but I—

ISADORA'S GHOST Rastus! Will you help me, please?

WOODROW (*Reverts*) Yes ma'am.

ISADORA'S GHOST Open that drawer. (*He does as she says*) Put that notebook on the counter. (*Points*) Flip to the last page and stand aside. (*Muttering*) God, I created a monster.

WOODROW Who's dat, missy?

ISADORA'S GHOST Let's just say he was driving Miss Daisy crazy. Please open that drawer. Grab those test tubes.

WOODROW What else can I do for you, ma'am? Just name it.

ISADORA'S GHOST You really are a kind person, Rastus.

WOODROW Thank you, ma'am, but it's easy dis way.

ISADORA'S GHOST What do you mean *this way*?

WOODROW I means being told what to do. Not having to make any difficult decisions like some man, or given any re-spon-so-bil-i-ty. Just being made into a—a—good boy.

ISADORA'S GHOST Only Marvin could make me feel this ashamed.

WOODROW Caught hiding in the woodshed. (*Pauses*) Rastus has faded. So has Militant Marvin. I'll miss his causes and slogans.

ISADORA'S GHOST What do you mean they *faded*?

WOODROW (*Sadly*) I can't remember anything I learned from Polk Tank University.

ISADORA'S GHOST (*Delighted*) His experiment is a flop? That's terrific! (*Suddenly contrite*) I'm so sorry.

WOODROW (*Visibly depressed, facetious*) Actually, not all is lost. I do remember everything I read on my own. And considering I went through most of Von Bootum's library, that's substantial. On the bright side, maybe I'll win a basketball scholarship. On the dark side, other things are coming back to me—and they're terrifying.

ISADORA'S GHOST What other things, Marv?

WOODROW Woodrow. My name is Woodrow Bishop. I'm twenty-eight years old, from 148th Street. My older brother Lyle was killed during a gang fight when I was eight. I don't recall ever meeting my father. I had some sisters, but everyone seems to vanish with time. By twelve, I was on my own, petty crimes and jail time. To employ the vernacular, hanging out in the hood. After a long stretch in jail, I'm suddenly released into a world without friends, skills, direction. Into an isolated day-to-day street existence. There are no vacations, no birthdays, no real family. My only glories came from finds in garbage cans, charity I was given, or things I conned away or stole from people. Have you any idea what it's like living without family, security, or any future? (*Long pause*)

ISADORA'S GHOST Why did you do that just now—pretend you were Rastus?

WOODROW You were *my* guinea pig. I wondered, between compromise and tyranny what a decent person would choose.

ISADORA'S GHOST I'm embarrassed. You're free to do what you want.

WOODROW Unfortunately I'm not, so let's get to work.

ISADORA'S GHOST We can divide the world into those we injure and those who injure us.

WOODROW Yet if we don't forgive we'll never really be free, will we?

ISADORA'S GHOST I guess not. (*Flipping through data and graphs*) Look, if Von Bootum learns that his experiment is a failure, he'll try to dispose of you. So let's get this done and you out of here. (*Points to a list in the notebook*) You read the inventory of chemicals, I'll check if we have them or not.

WOODROW (*Reading*) Sodium Chloride? (*She looks*) Just for the record, I don't believe that Von Bootum's life has been cruel enough to convert him into a murderer. He's not some Nazi fugitive, is he?

ISADORA'S GHOST (*Searching*) We're out of Sodium Chloride, or salt, and we're going to need it immediately, so put it on top of the list. Von Bootum's father was executed by the Nazis for publicly denouncing them when they first came to power. His mother brought him to the U.S. after the war.

WOODROW He's not Jewish, is he?

ISADORA'S GHOST No, but I am. Any problem with that?

WOODROW Just asking.

ISADORA'S GHOST I was one of the founding members of Cut

Crime, a project in the Justice Department cut by Reagan in '81. Von Bootum only came on the scene after our early findings. I was chief of pharmaceuticals research. He was head of surgery, big phoney.

WOODROW If he did rehabilitate me from a criminal, he must have done some research. *(Reads)* Lithium?

ISADORA'S GHOST Check. He followed the instructions on the can.

WOODROW Please, I'm not microwaveable. He did more than that. Why do you hate him so much? What wrong did he really do? *(Reads)* Cotton swabbing?

ISADORA'S GHOST *(Locates it)* Check. You only really know someone when he kills you, trust me.

WOODROW But I thought I killed you. *(Reads)* Guanidine?

ISADORA'S GHOST Out. *(Pauses)* You seized an opportunity. Hell, he even provided the weapon. But since he thinks he got away with it, he's grown even worse.

WOODROW I don't think he's worse.

ISADORA'S GHOST Then you won't believe that he's plotting to kill you, or that his existence stands in the way of my going to heaven, or wherever the hell.

WOODROW Calcium? So what's the undiscovered country like?

ISADORA'S GHOST *(Finds it)* Check. It's like living near an airport, I just keep dying over and over, but never really taking off. And I keep regretting everything I never did. *(Angrily)* Shit! *(Grabs her head painfully)*

WOODROW What's the matter?

ISADORA'S GHOST I've got this tremendous headstone somewhere in Queens and that's my only monument. Death removes all the bullshit. You become your achievements. If I could have finished this fucking experiment, it would have given my life some real value.

VON BOOTUM *(Offstage)* Detective! I thought you were coming later.

GALLO I just got out of my writer's group and was in the area. *(They enter)* You've been on my mind a lot, kid. *(Gallo hugs Woodrow)*

WOODROW What's this, the Vulcan mind probe? Get off!

GALLO Sorry, I just feel a part of you.

WOODROW Think about that the next time you arrest a black man on little or no evidence.

ISADORA'S GHOST (*Facetiously*) Yeah! Justice for Woody!

VON BOOTUM Woodrow, we didn't mean to disturb you, we were just hoping for a little preview.

GALLO What exactly is this experiment supposed to do?

ISADORA'S GHOST & WOODROW I'm working on an accelerant that contains Smartypanzine, a growth hormone which injected into the blood system will accelerate the rate of muscle growth or atrophy based on the amount of Hezzamoron in the brain.

ISADORA'S GHOST Now out!

GALLO What is this Hezzamoron?

WOODROW & ISADORA'S GHOST It's a protein that a team of pathologists in France have theorized is linked to one's ethical clarity. They found no traces of this in outlaws, cops, or criminal researchers. Now go!

VON BOOTUM So it essentially makes the virtuous stronger?

ISADORA'S GHOST And the wicked weaker, you bastard.

WOODROW Right.

ISADORA'S GHOST Now get the hell out!

GALLO But since this stuff would probably be used on convicts, isn't it going to be unfair to the poor? Not that that really bothers me, but won't this make the poor weaker?

WOODROW (*To Isadora*) Hey, that's a good point.

ISADORA'S GHOST That's why we're going to dump the whole brew into the New York reservoir—so it'll work on the whole goddamned city, rich and poor alike.

WOODROW (*To both Isadora's ghost and Gallo*) Well, the poor will have to worry about that one, right?

GALLO I've got to admit it, doctor, you really have done something impressive.

ISADORA'S GHOST Tell them what I said!

VON BOOTUM Thank you, detective.

GALLO (*To Woodrow*) You are incredible, pal. And handsome. (*Embarrassed*) Sorry.

WOODROW By the way, doctor, I'm going to need a few things. (*Gives Von Bootum the list*)

VON BOOTUM (*Reads*) Iodine-free salt. Isadora probably depleted it making dinner. She was an awful cook.

ISADORA'S GHOST (*Electroshocks Von Bootum and Gallo's crotches*) GET OUT!

VON BOOTUM & GALLO Owww!

VON BOOTUM Did you— Forget it. (*Von Bootum and Gallo exit, muttering*)

WOODROW If I was a shitty person before, is Von Bootum's approach—making me completely different—a remedy?

ISADORA'S GHOST I don't know. My Smartypanzine serum keeps character intact. That's the superiority of it.

WOODROW But Gallo had a point too. Your notion of a "cure" for injustice doesn't cure injustice at all. In fact, cheap NRA-protected handguns basically allow the physically weak to prevail over the strong, so even if we find your cure it'll only have marginal value.

ISADORA'S GHOST Many offenses, such as rape and domestic abuse, are physical-domination crimes.

WOODROW A Freudian would say that this alleged cure is nothing more than a result of some kind of female hysteria.

ISADORA'S GHOST Freud wasn't killed by two males in a train station. Now, grab that test tube rack and put those tubes in them—

Slowly fade to black.

☙❧

SCENE 4

It is dark and silent. In the distance we hear a train again. It grows louder until it sounds as if it is rushing into the front of the stage. A gust of wind and a strobe of light might suggest its crossing. We are back on the subway platform. Isadora is more closely bonded with Woodrow in this scene than with Von Bootum. Everyone is in mid-action.

VON BOOTUM Just move it! Shit, the exit's locked! *(Woodrow rushes nervously behind and also exits, offstage he grabs Isadora's purse)*

ISADORA Woody! *(Woodrow tries to run with it, but Isadora holds on and he pulls her back onto the stage)* It's me, Woody! And I'm stuck, I can't let go.

VON BOOTUM My Angina!

ISADORA *(Yelling behind her while fighting for the purse)* Woody, fucking listen to me! There's only ten dollars in this bag, it's not worth it.

VON BOOTUM *(Still offstage, we hear him demonically)* He bit the bait! *(Voice reverts to normal)* Give him the purse! He's got a gun! *(Pulls out a gun)*

WOODROW No I don't! *(Holds up his hands upon seeing Von Bootum's pistol)*

VON BOOTUM *(Shoves the gun into Woodrow's pocket. In a diabolic whisper)* Take mine.

ISADORA *(To Von Bootum)* What did I ever do to you?

WOODROW *(Pulling the purse and Isadora onstage, he draws the gun)* Give me that fucking bag!

ISADORA Please, I can't!! *(Crying as she hits Woodrow)* Christ sake, listen to me.

VON BOOTUM *(Holding his chest, terrified)* That's my gun! Oh God! Don't shoot, please! I'll give you all the money in the world. *(Alternate demonic voice)* If you kill her!

WOODROW What?!

ISADORA Try to remember. We're a team, working in a basement for the past three weeks. *(Slaps the gun out of his hand)* I'm sorry! I beg you, Woody.

VON BOOTUM *(Grabs a stick on the ground)* I'll hit you, so help me! *(Woodrow recovers the pistol)*

ISADORA God! Please, Woodrow, I know you're not a killer. Don't hurt me, please. Just this once, please. Try!

VON BOOTUM *(In a diabolic tone)* I'm doing this for you, bud. *(Hits himself over the head and falls unconscious)*

ISADORA Your name is Woody Bishop, twenty-eight years old, from 148th Street. Your brother Lyle died when you were eight. You never met your father. You had sisters, but by twelve you were on your own—

Isadora involuntarily digs her fingernails into Woodrow's face, and just before she rips them down, Woodrow shoots her. She screams in agony, still holding the purse.

ISADORA No! No! No!

WOODROW Shit! *(Grabs Isadora and helps her to the ground, then takes the purse)* All I wanted was the fucking purse!

Sudden blackout.

ᴏ℀ᴏ

SCENE 5

It is pitch black. Isadora's scream carries over from the last scene. Lights come up on her laboratory. Woodrow jumps out of his chair when he hears her. It is apparent that he is overworked, in need of a shave, shower, and sleep.

WOODROW *(Tiredly)* What?

ISADORA'S GHOST It's killing me!

WOODROW You had that dream again?

ISADORA'S GHOST It's not a dream, it's death. *(She catches her breath, recomposes herself, and looking into the mouse cage, she sighs)* SHIT! The specimen is dying. The experiment is a failure.

WOODROW No, it can't be!

ISADORA'S GHOST *(Still preoccupied with the memory of her own death)* It's just a fucking specimen.

WOODROW I know, but—I—I'm a specimen too.

ISADORA'S GHOST I can't take it anymore. You keep killing me over and over and over and over.

WOODROW I honestly don't remember anything.

ISADORA'S GHOST Well, let me refresh your memory.

WOODROW It's not necessary.

ISADORA'S GHOST You fire that fucker's gun into my chest. I feel the bullet cracking through my sternum, the blood boiling up out of me—

WOODROW I didn't mean to—

ISADORA'S GHOST —lying faceup in that filthy train station, all alone, feeling life rush out. You're running off with my handbag. Von Bootum is on the ground grabbing his stingy heart—

WOODROW I—I—oh God. Oh shit! I remember rummaging through the purse as I'm walking up First Avenue—lipstick, mascara, an appointment book, eyeglasses. Oh God, I remember putting the cash in my back pocket!

ISADORA'S GHOST Every time I make the same fucking mistake. I can't take it anymore. It's killing me. I can't die anymore.

WOODROW *(Remembering)* Can that be me going to a liquor store and buying a big bottle of Ripple? Then going into a bombed-out tenement on Avenue B, guzzling it down, trying to forget that awful moment—that *is* me! *(Emptily)* The next morning waking up, hungover on the rooftop, in the rain, realizing I'm broke again. Realizing that I had . . . killed you.

ISADORA'S GHOST The only one that really knew what was happening was him. That prick. You just reacted, I even hit you repeatedly.

WOODROW I've done some pretty awful things, but I never killed anyone before, I swear.

ISADORA'S GHOST I know you didn't. (Looks away coldly)

WOODROW Your average household pet was cared for better than me. I was treated far less than human—

ISADORA'S GHOST (Furious) And I'm still dead! (Pauses, regains composure) Please, do me a favor and let's move on. We have another problem to deal with. (Examines the dead mouse) I have to rethink all this.

WOODROW I'm so tired. What could have killed the mouse?

ISADORA'S GHOST I don't know, I'm not a pathologist. I wouldn't know where to begin.

WOODROW (Picks up the mouse and examines it) Meal time, Leona. (Drops the mouse in the snake's terrarium)

ISADORA'S GHOST Get that out of there. Whatever killed the mouse might kill Leona!

WOODROW (Looking in the terrarium) Oops, too late. She just gulped Mickey down.

ISADORA'S GHOST SHIT! All right, pick up that rack, load the tubes, turn on the Bunsen burner—

WOODROW Hold it. Isadora, I need a nap.

ISADORA'S GHOST We don't have time.

WOODROW I've been awake for days!

ISADORA'S GHOST You were the one who said three weeks, not me.

WOODROW How long am I expected to be a pair of gloves from the netherworld? And it's too late. (Checks his wristwatch) They're supposed to be home in a couple minutes.

ISADORA'S GHOST Just pick up that test tube and pour that damned Guanidine into it and—

WOODROW Sorry, I need a break. *(Sits down)*

ISADORA'S GHOST Pick up that damned test tube!

WOODROW *(Explosive)* I'm exhausted!

ISADORA'S GHOST Then you shouldn't've shot me.

WOODROW And you should've just given me your purse.

ISADORA'S GHOST *(Zaps his testicles)* You bastard!

WOODROW Owww! *(Clutching himself)* You bitch! You drove Von Bootum mad. Instead of him killing you, I got stuck with the dirty job. Well, I'm the goddamned victim here.

ISADORA'S GHOST How dare you.

WOODROW When you first met him, was he a whacko?

ISADORA'S GHOST What?

WOODROW Did he always have all that repressed hostility? All those freaky habits?

ISADORA'S GHOST No, but—

WOODROW Well, who do you suppose did that to him?

ISADORA'S GHOST If you're implying—

WOODROW I'm just saying, he didn't start out this way. I mean, he's pathetic and lonely, but he really tried to do something.

ISADORA'S GHOST Yeah, turn you into a voicemail announcement for *The Amos 'N Andy Show*.

WOODROW Look, instead of killing me or sending me to prison, he tried to repair what he thought was broken. Now, I'm not saying what he did was right—

ISADORA'S GHOST Taking a human being and experimenting on him against his will is cruel and insane.

WOODROW Lord knows, he had his own vainglorious reasons.

ISADORA'S GHOST Vainglorious reasons? Listen to you, you sound like the *Christian Science Monitor*.

WOODROW That's right, words I never dreamed I'd know. Ideas that he opened me up to. By accident a madman helped me, so my question is, what drove him mad? Who pushed him off the deep end?

ISADORA'S GHOST Wait a fucking second. If you're suggesting that his insanity is due to my occasional nagging—

WOODROW Occasional nagging? You're a fault-finding pain in the ass who was bitter and jealous of his talent.

ISADORA'S GHOST You have no right to judge our marriage.

WOODROW Not once in the last three grueling weeks have I heard you say "relax" or "good work." It's been, "You killed me, now pay up." Or trying to turn me back into Rastus. Well, I got news for you, lady. If I were married to you for ten years, I'd, I'd—!!

ISADORA'S GHOST What? You'd do what? SAY IT!

WOODROW Divorce! I'd divorce the hell out of you!

ISADORA'S GHOST Well, I can live with that. *(Notices her snake)* Leona!

WOODROW *(Reaches into the tank and pulls out an earthworm)* She shrunk to a fraction of her original size.

ISADORA'S GHOST The mouse ate the corrective, it killed him. The snake ate the mouse and it affected her too.

WOODROW It made her small and puny.

ISADORA'S GHOST But she's still alive! We might presume that it made her body strength relative to her moral state.

WOODROW Was your snake immoral?

ISADORA'S GHOST No, but reptiles do have an acute absence of Hezzamoron. Put some serum into a syringe.

WOODROW *(Does as he's told)* Now we just need another subject.

Von Bootum sneaks into the room, looking feverish and disheveled. Hiding, he listens to Woodrow.

ISADORA'S GHOST How about Von Bootum? If he's a murderer, he'll be made weaker and punier. But if he's what you think he is, he'll be stronger and bigger.

WOODROW He's a sour kraut not a guinea pig.

ISADORA'S GHOST Either way, he's still a pig. Have you seen his room up there? It's a mess. You'd think it'd hurt him just to pick up. *(Woodrow smiles)* What are you grinning at?

WOODROW Maybe I should kill Von Bootum while forcing him to mop his floor. Then he'd have to keep reliving the hell of housekeeping.

ISADORA'S GHOST You were right about me being a bitch. I wasted my life getting angry and frustrated. He'd spend hours doing his research and I'd furiously clean up after him. But finally dead, I'm doing the work I should have been doing all along. This should have been my life. That's why I don't want to stop now. Not till it's finally done.

WOODROW All right, let's beat him at his own game. That'll really boil his beets and burn his bratwurst.

ISADORA'S GHOST He's in enough pain. Over the past few days, I'd sneak upstairs and see him sitting all alone at that dining table, holding his forehead, tormented in that roach motel that I can't and he won't clean up. You know what? For the first time, I really, truly feel sorry for that man.

VON BOOTUM *(Leaps out from his hiding place with a gun)* Boil my beets and burn my bratwurst? Who can this be you're speaking to?! Why are you saying such nasty things about me?

WOODROW I was thinking aloud.

VON BOOTUM *(Insanely)* I too think aloud. Sometimes, as at the moment when my poor Hynie Mama was killed, my loud thinking takes control, and I feel crazy all over. A tingly, itchy, achy, kooky, nutty craziness.

WOODROW Maybe a nice shower—

VON BOOTUM Oh no, this is what happens when the most ruthless aspect of your personality is pulled out of you like a limb torn from its socket. It compels you to have your Hynie Mama blown away.

ISADORA'S GHOST I wish he'd stop calling me that.

WOODROW Sounds like the basis for a temporary-insanity defense.

ISADORA'S GHOST Sounds like the basis for a lobotomy.

WOODROW You can surrender to Gallo. He'll vouch for your character, a deal with the DA—

VON BOOTUM I have no intention of dealing with any DAs. You see, my schizophrenic side was correct in forcing me to do this. Just as yours is right in wanting to kill me while mopping my floor. I should clean my room. It's a real pigsty up there.

WOODROW Look, you accidentally helped me. Let me help you.

VON BOOTUM Better yet *(Cocks his pistol)*, let me help put a hot piece of lead into the soft folds of your brain.

ISADORA'S GHOST Better still, hire a maid.

WOODROW Doctor, I know a little about killing. The person you kill doesn't just die, they're always with you. And no matter what you do, you can't ever be forgiven. Because we can kill but we don't have the power to unkill.

VON BOOTUM Tell that to the filthy ashes of Isadora Von Bootum.

ISADORA'S GHOST Filthy? When I static him, you jump for the gun. Ready? *(Woodrow nods his head yes)*

VON BOOTUM Why is your head bobbing? *(Isadora electrifies his crotch)* Oww!

Von Bootum drops his gun, Woodrow rushes him, and they struggle. The gun is kicked to the far side of the laboratory counter. Von Bootum reaches over, stretching to grab it. The syringe is sitting on the counter top.

ISADORA'S GHOST He's going for the gun. Quick, the syringe!

WOODROW No!

ISADORA'S GHOST Don't spend the rest of your life regretting a stupid decision!

Woodrow grabs the syringe and injects Von Bootum on the gluteus maximus.

VON BOOTUM Ow! Ohhhhhhh!

Von Bootum starts rolling on the ground behind the lab counter as his body sprouts into a hideous mix of large and small limbs. These can be sculpted from foam rubber.

VON BOOTUM What have you done? What's happening to me?

WOODROW What have we done? What's happening to him?

ISADORA'S GHOST *(Sadly)* Shit! Parts of him are becoming strong. Other parts are shrinking. What could've gone wrong?

WOODROW No one's all good or bad. We're a mix of both—that's what's happening to him.

ISADORA'S GHOST Poor Euclid. I'm sorry, forgive me, Hynie Papa.

WOODROW I'm going to put him out of his misery. *(Tries to grab the gun from Von Bootum)*

VON BOOTUM No! *(Grabs Woodrow's neck and strangles him)* Now I have the strength to snap your neck like a twig. You miserable fly!

WOODROW *(Gasping for breath, struggling)* HELP!

ISADORA'S GHOST *(Trying to zap Von Bootum)* It's not working.

GALLO *(Offstage)* Hello, you there, my Woodman?

WOODROW HELP!

GALLO *(Enters)* Christ, he's on you like a pair of khakis!

WOODROW *(Turning blue)* HEY!

Von Bootum grabs Gallo's neck with one hand while still strangling Woodrow with his other. Gallo pulls out his service revolver and shoots Von Bootum in the chest. Woodrow gasps for air.

GALLO Are you okay, buddy? *(Woodrow nods his head yes; Gallo tries speaking to the dying Von Bootum)* Doctor, can you hear me? He stopped breathing!

Gallo starts performing CPR on Von Bootum's body. Over the amplifiers we hear a train rush into the station and almost inaudibly we hear an exchange that gradually grows louder. It should be played only loud enough to be recognized, never interfering with the dialogue between Gallo and Woodrow, who don't hear it.

VON BOOTUM Just move it! Shit, the exit's locked!

ISADORA My purse! EUCLID, HELP!

VON BOOTUM My Angina!

ISADORA HELP! Euclid, help!

VON BOOTUM He bit the bait! Give him the purse. He's got a gun.

WOODROW No I don't.

VON BOOTUM Take mine.

WOODROW Give me that fucking bag!

ISADORA You human garbage! Euclid!

VON BOOTUM That's my gun! Oh God. Don't shoot, please. I'll give you all the money in the world. *(Alternate voice)* If you kill her!

WOODROW What?!

ISADORA HELP! Token booth clerk! Fellow New Yorkers!

VON BOOTUM *(In a diabolic voice)* I'm doing this for you, bud— *(We hear a gunshot)*

ISADORA'S GHOST Do you hear that?

WOODROW No, hold on. *(Trying to find Von Bootum's pulse)* It's me, professor, your old Rhine-wine buddy.

GALLO *(Regarding Von Bootum)* It's no good.

ISADORA'S GHOST Something's happening to me.

WOODROW What?

GALLO *(Assuming Woodrow was addressing him)* I didn't say nothing. *(Pauses)* He's dead.

WOODROW *(Sadly)* It's like losing a sadistic father. He tortured and abused me but I have a solid grasp of the humanities and *(To Isadora)* because of you, the sciences—

ISADORA'S GHOST That's right, listen to me, damn it, you've got a rare opportunity. You're intelligent, educated, and young. Do something with your life, because it all ends too quickly.

(*Starts focusing on a distant spot offstage, then moves behind Gallo*)

WOODROW I'm scared.

GALLO I'm right here, man. Listen, I know this sounds weird, but that's what it is, isn't it?

WOODROW What are you jabbering about?

GALLO I'm coming out of the spiritual closet, Woodrow. I love your spirit, man.

WOODROW What?

GALLO I can't explain it. It's not sexual, it's spiritual. I just can't stop thinking about you. It's like you're part of me and I'm not ashamed.

WOODROW Oh! That's just the aftereffects of Von Bootum's empathy experiment. We were psychically connected.

GALLO That might be, but that doesn't excuse me from presuming you guilty of murdering his wife.

WOODROW It wasn't so far-fetched.

GALLO Why? Just because you're a poor-looking black guy, I'm supposed to believe you're a murderer?

WOODROW (*Moving beside Isadora*) No, because I *was* the murderer.

GALLO You're still innocent until proven guilty. I don't know what Von Bootum did to me. I mean, I keep hearing strange street sounds, and I like wearing khakis. Most of all, though, I really want to help you. (*Turns to leave, as does Isadora's ghost*)

WOODROW Where are you going?

GALLO (*Thinking Woodrow's talking to him*) I need to call the police and get a drink. (*Heading toward the exit*)

ISADORA'S GHOST My murder's been avenged! Hey, Pat Swayze, wait up! I'm finally out of that damned subway station. Bye, Woody!

She vanishes and a small piece of fabric from her dress with a tuft of her hair is pulleyed across the top of the stage over the audience's heads.

WOODROW *(To Isadora's ghost)* Hold on—you're all I got!

GALLO *(Rushes back and hugs him)* If you want to stay with me, just till you get on your feet, no problem. You're not alone, Woody. We're in this big scary world together, okay, buddy?

WOODROW I'll need a place, I guess.

GALLO Want a beer? *(Exits)*

WOODROW No thanks— *(Speaking in the direction of where Isadora's dress is pulleyed)* I'm sorry for killing one of the best minds of my generation. I'm so sorry. *(Whispers)* And Isadora, if from where you are, you think you can forgive me, try and give me one final sign.

GALLO *(Offstage)* Owww! *(Drops a beer bottle)* My balls!

WOODROW *(Smiles, lights dim, he whispers)* Thank you.

Blackout.

SPARE CHANGE

To Thomas P. Burke, Esq.,
an uncle's uncle

Spare Change was first produced by Sometimes Thespians at the University of St. Francis in Joliet, Indiana, on February 3, 2006.

George Regan	Kevin Leonard
Cleopatra	Jamin Gahm
Mozambique	Jessica Jannusch
Jesus	Arturo Insurriaga
Anthony	Keith Hernandez
Officer Gallo	
Cop #2	
Dealer	
Jogger	
Psycho	
Walking peddler	
Junkie	

Walk-ons: four businessmen, six men, three women, two teenage boys

Voices: thirteen male voices, eleven female voices, four teenage boy voices, three teenage girl voices

Director	Chris Bersano
Lighting/Sound Director	Trevor Lynn
Stage Design	Chris Bersano
Set Construction	USF Sometimes Thespians
Stage Manager	Carrie Monaco

Acting notes: Although the voices and walk-ons are from a passing crowd, the voices can be pretaped or actors offstage can alter their tone and volume to allow for multiple roles. Walk-ons with slight cosmetic variations can double and even triple up on roles. The "voices" lines are meant to be short excerpts from lengthier conversations and should be spoken as such. Also, the volume of the voices should rise slowly as they pass the stage.

Production notes: Life-size puppets can be used in a revolving carousel. Substitutions for puppets, however, can be done with any number of improvizations, including clothes on hangers or large black garbage bags. They can be fastened to ropes above the view of the audience so they are wheeled through a pair of pulleys at both ends, offstage. This carousel of puppets represents two lanes of pedestrian traffic. They should move at a standard walking pace.

ACT ONE
Time: early 1990s, mid-spring, late morning
Place: a stretch of sidewalk near Astor Place

ACT TWO
Time: about an hour later
Place: same

ACT ONE

A street scene, late morning. From downstage toward upstage is the gut-ter, the curb, and then the sidewalk, covered with the usual degree of lit-ter. Off to stage left, against the building is a garbage dumpster on wheels. Inside the dumpster should be some cardboard boxes for Mozambique's three-card monte game in Act Two. The "stores," where the vendors sell their merchandise, should be on the sidewalk, upstage from the path of passersby. The vendors move around, alternately lean-ing up against the wall of the building or out in front of the passersby. The set might include such street paraphernalia as a public garbage can, a street sign, or a fire hydrant. Extremely bright lights should convey that it is a sunny day. A loop of street noise should be played throughout.

Lights come up slowly. Anthony is alone, curled up like a cat and sleeping upstage next to the dumpster. As the play opens, Zach has just been arrested, his store/merchandise is cast about haphazardly on the sidewalk. Mozambique, a black woman in her fifties, enters cautiously. Cleopatra, a tall black transexual in her thirties, follows. They are both carrying bundles of clothes, books, and other objects for resale.

CLEOPATRA Maybe we should wait awhile longer. (*Looking nervously both ways*)

MOZAMBIQUE (*Starts collecting the clothes and magazines that are scat-tered on the ground*) Poor Zach had some nice things.

DEALER (*Walking through the set quickly*) Sess, sess, nickel bag, sess . . .

CLEO He should've hauled ass. When they come, you got to move it or lose it.

MOZAMBIQUE The pigman's got it in for him.

CLEO You talking about that officer, Gallo?

MOZAMBIQUE Yeah, fucking Gallo.

CLEO Least he left most of Zach's stuff.

MOZAMBIQUE (*Giving Cleo some of the merchandise*) Here's his car radio.

CLEO He toted this around all week trying to peddle it. I'll sell it in his honor.

MOZAMBIQUE If that fucking three-card monte dude didn't rip off that old guy, Gallo never woulda come.

CLEO Yeah, but three-card Monte got away with, like, a hundred bucks.

MOZAMBIQUE That's true. We oughta try that shit. (*Squinting up at a building clock*) What time does that clock say?

CLEO That old bastard just kept putting down twenties. Probably his whole SSI check. (*Looking up at the clock*) Five after 11. You missed the breakfast special.

MOZAMBIQUE And it's too early to take the cans back. Screw it, I'm setting up my store now. Catch the lunch-hour crowd.

CLEO But they just left here with Zach.

MOZAMBIQUE He's got bench warrants.

CLEO A two-day lockup in Central Booking.

MOZAMBIQUE I'll take my chances. (*Puts her bag down*) They ain't coming back for a while.

George, a black man in his twenties, enters, pursuing Businessman #1.

GEORGE I don't steal. I never hurt anyone. I served in Vietnam—

Mozambique and Cleo listen to George while unloading their bundles and placing the items on a blanket or newspaper on the ground, up against the building so the crowd will see it as they pass.

MOZAMBIQUE Will you look at this kid go? I saw him talk his way into the shelter after it closed last night.

BUSINESSMAN #1 I'm grateful. Now will you stop following me?
  (*Races ahead, trying to evade George*)

CLEO What were you doing there?

Cleo sets up her store and fusses with the merchandise display when she's not doing anything else.

MOZAMBIQUE I was with Zach. They wouldn't let him in, but then that boy talked his way through. (*Watching George*) I have a boy about his age—somewhere.

GEORGE (*To Businessman #1*) I don't use drugs. I have a wife. And a child—children. (*He picks up a cigarette butt, slips it behind his ear, then blocks Businessman #1*) All I'm asking for is a penny. A lonely penny.

CLEO He's cute in kind of a gritty way.

BUSINESSMAN #1 (*Angrily*) You followed me for two blocks. Now leave me alone!

GEORGE Please, sir, all I'm asking for's a penny. (*Businessman #1 tries to move out of the way, George stays with him*) Once you get to know me you'll—

MOZAMBIQUE (*Amused*) Got a yuppie by the neck.

BUSINESSMAN #1 I don't want to know anything about you.

GEORGE Well, I know you—

BUSINESSMAN #1 No, you don't.

GEORGE I know you got a wallet stuffed with bills.

BUSINESSMAN #1 And how would you know that?

GEORGE I saw you take it out at that ice cream place. But I ain't robbing you. Am I?

CLEO Puts the G in gauche.

BUSINESSMAN #1 (*Finally dropping a quarter before George*) Now leave me the hell alone. (*Exits*)

GEORGE (*Picking up the quarter*) Cheap mothafucka!

CLEO Grateful. (*Attends to the display of her store*)

MOZAMBIQUE All piss and vinegar, just like my Willy boy. (*Setting up her own store*)

FEMALE VOICE #1 So, did you get the summer share?

GEORGE (*Moving toward the two female designates*) Summer share any change? I need it now, but you might need it later, and I'll—

FEMALE VOICE #2 (*Ignoring him*) Yes, it's just a little more than we intended to spend, but—

GEORGE I'll take a little less.

FEMALE VOICE #1 Sorry, we have no money for you.

George sees Cleopatra from the rear as she is fussing with her store. Not knowing she's a transexual, George removes the cigarette butt from behind his ear and offers it to Cleo.

GEORGE You look like a smoker. What's your name, love?

CLEO (*Taking the cigarette into her mouth*) Cleopatra, darling. Spare a light?

George realizes she is a tranny and plucks the cigarette out of her mouth. He shoves his hands in his pockets looking for a light, then unknowingly drops nail clippers shaped like a crucifix.

GEORGE Shit, I thought you were someone else—like a girl. (*Begging toward the puppets*) Spare any change—

CLEO I can spare a change, honey puddle.

GEORGE (*Takes a liquor bottle from his back pocket and swigs from it, then spits it out into the gutter*) You mind if I park here a minute? I feel sick.

MOZAMBIQUE Just don't vomit.

GEORGE (*Sits for a little while begging toward the puppets*) Spare any change? Can you spare some change? Change? (*A jogger runs by with headphones on*) CHANGE?

CLEO I think you might find a more sympathetic crowd down on Broadway.

GEORGE I was down there. And down the block beyond that. And the one beyond that.

WALKING PEDDLER (*Enters, holding a pair of women's high-heeled shoes*) Brand-new women's shoes, a pair of ladies' shoes, size 8, real cheap, cheap. (*Shows the shoes to Cleo and Mozambique, who both shake their heads no, then he tries selling to the puppets as he exits*) Women's shoes—cheap . . .

GEORGE (*Still sitting on the curb*) You got the easy life. Just sit back, let them come and buy.

MOZAMBIQUE (*Noticing him taking out the liquor bottle*) Looks like you're not exactly breaking rocks either.

GEORGE Want it? There's still a swallow in there. It's good. I got it this morning from an all-night party I went to.

MOZAMBIQUE (*Takes the bottle*) Then you must be lying. 'Cause I saw you go into the shelter last night.

GEORGE They don't let women in there.

MOZAMBIQUE (*Opening the bottle*) I was seeing a friend off and I saw you talking up that guy on duty.

GEORGE (*Snatches the bottle away and pours the remainder into the gutter*) That's the last time I ever be nice to anyone.

MOZAMBIQUE You are an asshole.

Street sounds, puppets passing.

TEENAGE GIRL VOICE #1 —So I coughed up these chunks in class and I wasn't sure whether to swallow them or spit them out.

TEENAGE GIRL VOICE #2 Ewww!

GEORGE (*Walking alongside Teenage Girl #1 designate*) I'll take any chunks you can cough up. Spare anything?

CLEO (*Bends down to the sidewalk*) Look what I found. Born-again nail clipper.

GEORGE (*Grabbing it out of her hand*) With the dead guy on it. They're mine, Mr. Ed.

CLEO The name's Cleopatra. And the dead guy's Jesus. It's called a crucifix.

GEORGE *(Begging from passing puppets)* Spare any change? Spare any change? Spare any change . . .

CLEO *(Playfully competing with George's begging, she steps up, holding bras, and starts hawking)* Brassieres at bargain-basement prices! One day only! Brand new!

GEORGE *(Trying to outdo Cleo)* I've got AIDS! I fought in 'Nam! I'm an ex-junkie!

CLEO *(Louder)* Lace panties that'll drive him mad! Cheap! Fire sale! It's sizzling hot! Elastic bands! Fits all shapes and sizes!

MOZAMBIQUE SHUT UP!! The both of you! *(After a pause, to George)* How come they let you in? They wouldn't let Zach in. Poor guy's sitting in a cell now.

GEORGE *(Angrily)* Hey! You didn't see me at any fucking shelter last night!

MOZAMBIQUE I did see you. And so did Zach.

GEORGE *(To Cleo)* Who the fuck is Zach?

CLEO He got arrested about ten minutes ago.

GEORGE Arrested! Don't talk to me, neither of you. *(Sitting tiredly on the ground)* Change? Change? Change . . .

CLEO *(Carefully adding a prefix to George's chant, so they're saying "sex-change")* Sex—sex—sex—

GEORGE Cut it the fuck out! *(Cleo makes an innocent expression and George resumes)* Change? Change? Change . . .

MOZAMBIQUE I never could beg, I swear.

CLEO Men just have no shame.

GEORGE *(To a puppet)* Spare any change? Spare any change? *(Yells across the street)* Is them flowers for me, darling?

TEENAGE GIRL VOICE #3 *(Offstage)* They're for your grave, asshole. *(Mozambique and Cleo laugh)*

CLEO *(Yells to Teenage Girl Voice #3)* You tell him, honey child!

GEORGE *(To Teenage Girl Voice #3)* Fuckin' ho! I'd fuck y'ass out of pity—

CLEO (*Coyly*) Who, me?

GEORGE (*To Teenage Girl Voice #3*) —but you too ugly for even me, and I live on the street. (*Proudly to all*) I'll say it, I ain't ashamed—

MALE VOICE #1 —No, I don't want to hear another word about it.

MALE VOICE #2 I'm sorry, but I do love you and I can't change that.

MALE VOICE #1 Cut it out this instant, I have a wife and child. Do you understand?

GEORGE (*To specific puppets*) Can you help a poor black get back on the fast track?

MALE VOICE #2 Can't you see we're talking?

MALE VOICE #1 You're an insult to your people.

GEORGE Fuck you.

CLEO (*Laughs*) An insult to your people! You poor boy.

GEORGE Fucking faggots.

MOZAMBIQUE (*To Cleo*) See that, I'd rather just collect bottles or something. The day I got to ask some white motherfucker for even a penny—

GEORGE I can beg from 'em or kill 'em. Don't matter. Never saw 'em before. I'll never see 'em again. Like they're not real.

MOZAMBIQUE Maybe *you* ain't real. (*Pauses*) Shit. This whole day hasn't been real. I haven't made a cent and I'm hungry. I need another dollar before I can get a fuckin' sandwich.

CLEO If I get any hungrier, I'll eat my implants.

MOZAMBIQUE (*Pauses*) I'm ready to just chuck the whole fuckin' mess in the garbage—aw, fuck it! (*Angrily begins to pack up her store*)

TEENAGE BOY VOICE #1 (*While Cleo is speaking*) Who's the name of the lead singer of Twisted Sister?

CLEO You just got here, where you gonna go?

TEENAGE BOY VOICE #2 Fuck Twisted Sister. Whitesnake, man—

MOZAMBIQUE Away. Find some food.

CLEO Here. (*Flips through her things and locates the remainder of a large pack of M&M's*)

MOZAMBIQUE I ain't taking what little you got.

CLEO Take 'em, my dentures are rotting right to hell. *(Mozambique takes the M&M's)*

GEORGE *(To teenage boy designates)* I got— *(Counting his change)* twenty-five, thirty, thirty-five . . . All I need is sixty-five cents to get on the PATH and get back to Jersey City. Can you guys—

TEENAGE BOY VOICE #1 *(Ignoring him)* Whitesnake—shit! It's Twisted Sister—

GEORGE Your twisted sister's fucking a white snake, asshole.

TEENAGE BOY VOICE #1 Fuck you, man.

MOZAMBIQUE *(To George)* How much you got?

GEORGE Why?

MOZAMBIQUE Truth is, I pity you, I really do. And I'm tired of lugging this shit around. So I thought I'd offer you my entire store for a buck. The easy life for a dollar.

GEORGE *(Counting change)* I'll give you what I got—thirty-five cent—and owe you the rest.

MOZAMBIQUE I'm giving you a hundred dollars worth of goods for thirty-five cents? No way.

Businessman #2 enters and surveys Mozambique's store. George keeps checking his pockets and looking on the ground for change. He briefly exits stage right.

BUSINESSMAN #2 How much is the—ah—marital aid?

MOZAMBIQUE That's a five-dollar apparatus. Never opened. Secret Santa gift to an infection-free nun.

CLEO *(Muttering)* The Little Sister of the Good Vibrations.

MOZAMBIQUE And it's got clip-on pieces here. *(Points to the box)*

BUSINESSMAN #2 *(Picks out a small plastic item and holds it up)* What's this?

MOZAMBIQUE Three bucks.

BUSINESSMAN #2 What is it?

MOZAMBIQUE Like I says, it's three dollars.

BUSINESSMAN #2 (*Smugly*) You don't even know what it is.

CLEO It's a butt plug. (*Businessman #2 drops it and picks up a vibrator*) The prior owner had a small leak.

GEORGE Look, man! (*Holding his coins up*) I got forty-two cents now, and—

MOZAMBIQUE Not while I'm doing a sale, man.

CLEO (*To Businessman #2*) You put a little coke on the tip of that, stick it up your ass, and you is in for one tingly treat.

BUSINESSMAN #2 (*Regarding the dildo*) I'll give you a buck for it and the attachments.

MOZAMBIQUE That cost twenty-five dollars in a store. All I'm askin' is one-fifty, and— (*Businessman #2 puts it down and storms off*) Okay! Sold, man. Take it! Shit. There goes my fuckin' sandwich.

GEORGE Look, what am I holding here?!

CLEO (*Grabbing her crotch*) Look what I'm holding, homeboy.

GEORGE (*Opening his palm*) Fifty cents.

MOZAMBIQUE More than a white fuckin' asshole, I hate a lyin' black bastard, 'cause I just saw someone give you change.

GEORGE Listen, I had a dime, the suit gave me a quarter, I founds a dime. (*Points offstage*) The lady gave me five pennies— (*Mozambique ignores him and he returns to the puppets*) Can you spare a penny, 'cause I was in Vietnam and all this Asian Orange got sprayed in my face—

CLEO It's Agent Orange, Rambo.

GEORGE (*Ignoring Cleo, counting coins*) I got enough so if you put it to your dollar you can get an egg salad sandwich from the A-rab deli. (*Stops counting and declares*) Fifty-five cent!

MOZAMBIQUE Hey! (*Points to a stack of porn magazines, picks one up*) There are folks fucking in there. (*Holding up the dildo*) A double-A battery, and this will give a woman a lifetime of satisfaction. Not to mention all these fine ladies' garments. Now, you think I'm gonna part with that for fifty-five cents?

CLEO Oh, sell it to the boy. Zach's been toting it for the past six months. You don't have to carry that torch for him.

DEALER *(Enters)* Nickel bag, sess, nickel bag . . . *(Lingers, chanting to the crowd)*

GEORGE *(Looking at the vibrator)* Thing looks like a Yuletide log. You know why he couldn't sell it? 'Cause you can't fit it in any human-size hole.

CLEO I can argue that, but—

DEALER Sess, nickel bag . . .

GEORGE *(Frisking himself and finding the crucifix clippers)* I'll throw these holy cutters into the deal.

MOZAMBIQUE I'm going to say it one last time: My store's a dollar. Not owed or in little pieces or anything. It's one dollar, and if you keep bitching it's going up to two.

GEORGE Spare any change? *(The Jogger comes back carrying a paper bag, George jumps up and deliberately blocks his passage so that he's jogging in place)* What'd you get me?

JOGGER *(Yells and points to his headphones)* Sorry, but I can't hear you. *(Tries to get around George, who blocks him, also running in place)*

GEORGE I need new soles on my Nikes.

JOGGER Can't hear you.

GEORGE *(Screams)* CAN YOU SPARE SOME CHANGE?

MOZAMBIQUE *(Jogging alongside)* Want to buy a back massager? Good after a long day of exertion.

JOGGER *(Pointing to his shorts)* No pockets, no cash. *(Exits)*

CLEO *(Singing)* You're so vain, you probably think this song is about you. Don't you, don't you . . .

GEORGE Just want to check out the merchandise a sec. *(Picking up a porn magazine)* Shit, they're fucking wet.

MOZAMBIQUE They're moist. One of them fucking street-cleaning trucks sprayed my shit this morning.

GEORGE *(Flipping through it)* Hey, what the hell is this? *(Reading covers)* Chicks with Dicks? Knocked Up and Milky? Lactating Lassies? *(Quickly flips through the remaining ones)* These are all fag shit.

CLEO For shame! Selling fag rags!

MOZAMBIQUE *(Snatches them from George and puts them back on the ground)* It's for straight guys too. I think.

FEMALE VOICE **#3** —So I'm watching Donahue discussing the g-spot orgasm, you know? I turn to channel 7 and there's Oprah discussing the same thing—

FEMALE VOICE **#4** No!

FEMALE VOICE **#3** I'm telling you. The exact same panelists were on both shows.

FEMALE VOICE **#4** No!

GEORGE *(Sings rhythmically)* She ain't kidding/And neither am I/ When I say help/Or I'm going to die/Spare just a penny/Spare any change—

CLEO *(Adding to the rhyme)* Give it quick/'Cause he's deranged.

GEORGE *(Begging Woman #1 as she walks by looking at Cleopatra's store)* All I need is a penny, ma'am, please. How can you sleep in your warm bed tonight knowing you couldn't spare a single penny to a homeless man? *(Woman #1 opens her purse in front of George, who points in it)* Look at all that change.

WOMAN **#1** You asked for a penny. Here's one penny. *(Exits)*

GEORGE *(Throws it back at her)* Fucking penny! They make 'em just to annoy people.

BUSINESSMAN **#3** *(Picks up a porn magazine and looks through it)* How much?

MOZAMBIQUE *(Points to the price)* It says nineteen dollars and ninety-five cents on it. I'm asking a buck. *(Businessman #3 gives her a dollar)*

GEORGE Spare any change? *(Businessman #3 gives George a coin and exits)* Shit! He bought the only one that wasn't wet. Shit! Now you'll see, you ain't going to sell another one.

MOZAMBIQUE Don't worry. It was one of the fag mags which you were too proud to sell.

A well-dressed couple enter. She's crying and he's absorbed in his own thoughts. She talks as the Walking Peddler enters.

WOMAN #2 *(Weeping)* —Then after years, you realize it's all bull-shit. You've wasted your entire youth!

WALKING PEDDLER *(Holding up items)* Children's clothes, child's shirt and pants and shit . . . *(All shake their heads no, he keeps chanting and exits)*

WOMAN #2 You detest your coworkers. Your job is utterly meaningless! You're always angry. And you can't seem to take hold.

MAN #1 Say, what was that dish Martha served at her little soiree last Thursday?

WOMAN #2 I'm talking about—

GEORGE I know what you're saying, lady. I'm blowing my youth too. But I'm starving, please— *(Man #1 gives him some change and they exit, George counts eagerly)* Shit, I think—I might— ninety-two fucking cents. SHIT! I got ninety-two cent and— *(Stoops over and picks up the penny and holds it up, then sees Anthony sleeping and gingerly starts picking through his pockets)*

ANTHONY *(Waking up)* What! What!

GEORGE Sorry, thought you were Charley. Someone I knew back in Baltimore. Spare any change? *(Resumes begging the crowd)*

MOZAMBIQUE This boy's got a case of the sticky fingers.

ANTHONY *(Sleepily)* Mi nombre es Antonio . . . *(Falls into nonsense)* Antonio mi casa. Mi madre, mi Antonio . . .

CLEO You're Anthony, I'm Cleopatra. You know, Queen of the Nile, like Elizabeth Taylor.

ANTHONY *Tu no eres* Elizabeth Taylor—*eres feo. (Falls back asleep, Mozambique starts picking up her store)*

GEORGE *(To Mozambique)* I got ninety-two cent, and you can frisk me.

CLEO I'll give the boy a full cavity search for you, Mozy.

MOZAMBIQUE All right. If you were praying you can stop, 'cause they were just answered. I got enough for a egg salad with lettuce, tomato, and a side of— *(Takes the money out of George's hand and throws away the two pennies)*

CLEO Just talking about it is cruel, girl.

MOZAMBIQUE Sorry. Good luck, boy.

GEORGE Yeah.

Preoccupied with George's newly acquired merchandise, Mozambique exits.

CLEO So, Paul Newman, what's— (*Touches Anthony gently, he bolts up, and she jumps away as if she's being attacked*)

ANTHONY (*Leans against the far wall near the dumpster, where he unzips and takes a leak—the trickle of liquid trails from the wall to the curb*) Ohhh, yesss—ohhhh, this *pena es* pleasure. (*Cleo peaks discreetly at him*)

FEMALE VOICE **#5** Disgusting pig.

CLEO (*Correcting*) Disgusting *horse*.

GEORGE You scaring away my business, man. People are crossing the street. (*Hears Anthony moaning in pleasure*) What you doing, fucking the wall?

ANTHONY (*Zipping up*) To piss *es* da best action *yo tengo* in *mucho años*, long, long years.

Jesus, a strapping Latino in his thirties, enters running.

JESUS (*Hyperventilating*) Hey! Holy shit! Look who's here! (*Stops and nervously looks behind him as if to make sure he isn't being pursued, Anthony exits*)

GEORGE So where you rushin' to, buddy?

JESUS The Martinique over on 32nd.

GEORGE Well, I don't want to keep you.

CLEO Who's your friend?

GEORGE He's got to go.

JESUS I ain't in no rush. (*To George*) Where the fuck did you go? FUCK! You know what happened to me last night at the shelter—

DEALER (*Passing through quickly*) Nickel bag, sess, nickel bag, sess . . .

JESUS They got my money last night. (*Angrily*) They stole my fucking shit!

DEALER Sess, nickel bag . . .

JESUS (*Angrily watching Dealer*) Probably was some fucking drughead. (*To Dealer*) HEY! MOVE IT, FUCKHEAD!

DEALER Fuck you, asshole! (*Exits, chanting*) Nickel bag, sess . . .

JESUS (*Referring to Dealer*) That guy's gotta be loaded.

GEORGE Everybody but us.

JESUS So where was you last night? (*Moves against the wall where Anthony was sleeping, Anthony returns*)

GEORGE Why?

ANTHONY Yo, you stand in *mi* bed, man.

JESUS *No es tu cuarto, maricon.*

Jesus continues standing awhile, forcing Anthony to wait. Finally he steps off the cardboard. Anthony lies back down and curls up.

JESUS (*To George*) Last night we were supposed to sell comps together outside the Palladium, remember?

GEORGE I don't remember nothing.

JESUS Well we were. I got all those comps. Anyways, I could only sell six. But I got to the shelter early, and you said—

GEORGE (*Returns to the crowd, begging*) Spare any change?

FEMALE VOICE #6 Oh, look, you were trying to find a car radio. There's one on the sidewalk.

FEMALE VOICE #7 Don't buy things off the street.

FEMALE VOICE #6 It looks okay.

FEMALE VOICE #7 Who knows where they stole it or what diseases they carry.

GEORGE (*To female designates, jokingly*) She's right. And not just people, but things got the AIDS too. Money's got the AIDS. You should give it to me, 'cause I'm wearing a condom.

FEMALE VOICE #6 Why don't you pull your condom over your head.

CLEO (*Inspecting her arm*) How'd you know if you got AIDS?

GEORGE *(To the females)* Fuckin' ho's! Spare any change? Spare any change? Spare any change?

JESUS I got fucking ripped off last night! Someone fucking took my money. And I stuck it right up here. *(Points under his groin)*

MALE VOICE #3 Tucholsky was not a part of the Frankfurt School, you idiot. That was Benjamin, Adorno, and—

GEORGE *(To the designtates)* I adorno a frankfurter, and with your spare change—

MALE VOICE #3 I threw out all my spare change this morning.

JESUS Goddamn it, man, you fucking listen to me!

GEORGE Hey, I'm fuckin' broke. Please!

JESUS I just haven't talked to anyone all day and I feel all bottled up, see. So I just wanted to tell you what happened. *(Looks across the street)* Check out the tits over there. *(Yelling)* Hey, sweetheart!

GEORGE *(Calling over to her)* Oh, baby, be very gentle 'cause you're holding my little pigeon heart in your dainty hands. But you know that, don't you? Ignore me if you must, but please be delicate with my beating heart.

JESUS *(Frantically joining in)* Let's take a chance, let's dance romance, we can hold hands, and feel the bulge in my pants. *(To George)* Why do they dress like that and then get mad when you—

CLEO I won't get mad if you wanna—

JESUS *(Nervously biting a hangnail and frantically searching through his pockets)* SHIT, FUCKING SHIT! *(Starts kicking and punching the dumpster)*

CLEO Whatever is your problem?

JESUS They took my fucking clippers!

CLEO *(To George quietly)* Lend him yours. *(George smiles nervously)*

JESUS *(Not hearing Cleo)* My fucking mother gave them to me. They were soldered to her crucifix.

CLEO Why?

JESUS 'Cause my name's Jesus! They're all I got from her, man. Someone stole them from me at the shelter last night.

CLEO *(Nervous)* Sorry to hear it.

JESUS She gave me the clippers and her wedding ring, but I pawned that years ago. Look here. *(Pulls up his shirt and shows Cleo a scar)* See that, I used to wear my Jesus clippers on a chain, and one day this motherfucker, he goes *boom*, hits me across the chest with a bat. Those clippers stuck into my chest like in wet cement. I ain't going to tell you where that guy is now, I'll just say he ain't with us.

Man #2 enters and leisurely skims through the porn magazines.

GEORGE Cheap, cheap, real cheap, cheap, real cheap. You gonna buy one?

MAN #2 *(Inspecting the pages closely)* I'm thinking about it.

GEORGE Why don't you just take it out and whack off right here while you're at it?

MAN #2 All right. How much?

GEORGE Whatever you think it's worth.

MAN #2 I'll give you a dollar for *(Reads titles) Pregnant Lesbos, Knocked Up and Milky,* and *Lactating Lassies.*

GEORGE A dollar?! Why don't you just fuck my ass while you're at it?

MAN #2 *(Takes a bill out of his wallet)* A dollar-fifty then.

CLEO Take it. Not many folks are fucked up enough to want 'em.

GEORGE *(To Man #2)* Okay, you can stop praying 'cause they were just answered. *(Grabs the bill out of Man #2's hand)* A twenty? What are you, showing it off?

CLEO Oh! Let me see it!

MAN #2 *(Starts collecting the magazines)* I don't have anything smaller.

GEORGE Why don't you just take them all?

MAN #2 You kidding? It'll be hard enough hiding just one of these from my wife.

GEORGE I'll get you change.

MAN #2 *(Grabs it back)* Yeah, and I'll never see you again. I've been conned that way before.

GEORGE Well, all my cash is tied up in other people's pockets. You can get change in the token booth down there.

MAN #2 All right.

Psycho enters. He's dirty, his clothes are tattered and filthy, he's not wearing shoes, he's cursing, staring at the ground, gesticulating wildly.

PSYCHO SHE WANTS IT! She forkin' wants, and next thing she's goin' right for my cock—right for my forkin' dick—she went quick for my dick!

JESUS Bullshit!

PSYCHO Forkin' shit, forkin' shit—I'll kill you—I'll rip your forkin' arms off and beat you with 'em. I'll strangle you with your guts—I'll suck your forkin' eyes out.

JESUS Shut up, you fucking nut! *(Shoves Psycho)*

PSYCHO I'll kill you—I'll tear you in two—I'll kill you times two. And the kid! So help me, I will.

JESUS *(Laughs)* Shut up, you nut case! *(Shoves him again)*

PSYCHO *(Punching the air wildly)* YOU MOTHERFUCKER! I'LL— *(Quiets down but continues rambling)*

MAN #3 *(Enters, well-dressed with a clipboard, approaches Psycho)* Excuse me, are you a registered Democrat?

PSYCHO *(Leaps forward, scaring Man #3)* I'll kill you! *(Man #3 passes around him and exits)*

GEORGE *(Looking down the street)* Where's that guy with the fucking change?

CLEO *(Also looking down the street)* Maybe he met a lactating lassy lesbian.

JESUS I made six bucks hustling comps in front of the Palladium. When I left the fucking shelter this morning—

GEORGE Where, the Armory?

JESUS *(Yelling)* No, Third and 3rd! You asshole! You were supposed to meet me at Third and 3rd! Remember? Supposed to sell comps with me and then go there.

MAN #3 (*Soliciting people*) A few votes can make all the difference.

MALE VOICE #4 I'm not registered.

MAN #3 (*Moves to the next designate*) Pardon me, are you a registered Democrat?

MALE VOICE #5 Leave me alone.

MAN #3 How about you? Ma'am, are you registered in Manhattan?

FEMALE VOICE #8 No, I'm married!

CLEO (*To Man #3*) Can I make a difference, honey? (*Man #3 talks quietly to her, looking at his clipboard*)

GEORGE Where's that fuck with my change?!

JESUS (*To George*) He's gone. You should've just snatched that twenty and ran.

MAN #3 (*To Cleo*) Once you get an apartment in Manhattan you can register to vote. (*Cleo listens, clearly enamored*)

GEORGE (*To Man #3*) Give me some change and I'll vote for anyone you want.

MAN #3 (*Gives him a quarter, joking*) Vote Democrat.

JESUS Need any more voters? (*Man #3 shakes his head*) Spare any more change?

MAN #3 (*Joking*) No, but I can change a spare. (*Starts working the crowd again*) Are you a registered Democrat?

JESUS Hey! (*Grabs Man #3's arm, looks both ways, speaks in a threatening whisper*) You can and *will* spare more change. (*Man #3 gives Jesus a quarter and quickly exits*) Fucking quarter, I had six bucks last night!

GEORGE I told you you'd get ripped off there. (*Back to the crowd*) Spare any change? Spare any change?

CLEO Who would dare rip off a big he-man like you?

JESUS I don't know, but I swear I'll fucking find him and kill him! (*Punches the dumpster*)

CLEO Look at you. You're all tense. Let me rub my baby. (*Starts massaging Jesus's back*)

JESUS Even in prison I didn't get ripped off. See what I'm saying?

CLEO All those meaty muscles are just one big knot. Who would dare fool with a man like you?

GEORGE (*To the crowd while Cleo and Jesus are talking*) Spare any change? God bless you. Spare any change?

JESUS You know, I put the stuff right in here in the lion's den. (*Points to his groin*) I didn't think any human being would ever put their hands down there.

CLEO Can I pet the king of the jungle? (*Lowers her hands down Jesus's back*)

JESUS (*Turns around to face Cleo*) You know, I've fucked a lot uglier things than you.

CLEO How enchanting.

JESUS You don't wanna hear any of that "stars in my eyes" bullshit. (*Gets closer and whispers into Cleo's ear*) I know exactly what you want. You're getting all tingly, aren't you?

CLEO My nipples are turning blue.

JESUS That's the Styrofoam, not me.

CLEO Silicone.

JESUS Whatever. (*Steps over sleeping Anthony and goes to the dumpster, which he pushes forward a bit*) Hey, come here a minute. (*Cleo giggles coquettishly and shakes her head no, Jesus keeps beckoning*)

GEORGE (*Continuously begging*) Spare any change? Spare any change, please? (*Man #4 walks by eating a pretzel, George looks on hungrily*) Spare any pretzel? Spare any change? God bless you, have a nice day. (*Sees something up the block, calls over to Cleo*) Watch my store a minute. (*Exits*)

JESUS (*Looking at Cleo sincerely*) Seriously, I got something important to show you.

CLEO You do? (*Approaches*)

JESUS Yeah, what I want to tell you, girl, is— (*Romantically*) I really want those wet lips of red velvet sucking on my man muscle.

CLEO I bet you say that to all the most beautiful girls.

JESUS (*Sincerely*) Just you, I swear it. (*Crosses his heart*)

GEORGE *(Returns eating the pretzel that Man #4 had been eating, sees Jesus leading Cleo behind the dumpster)* Hey! That's a guy, man.

JESUS *(To George)* Leave me alone!

CLEO That bitch's just jealous.

JESUS Come on, honey, meet the amazing Hulk. *(Unzips as Cleo slides down along the wall)*

GEORGE Yuck! Can't you do that somewhere else, man?

JESUS *(To George)* You never served hard time.

GEORGE Well, you're free now.

CLEO *(To Jesus)* Don't worry, I won't bite you. *(Removes her dentures)*

JESUS Aw shit! Put your teeth back in your mouth. He's right, you're a fucking mess. And I'm on the outside.

GEORGE For now, anyways.

Cleopatra quietly puts her dentures back in her mouth, gets up, and returns to her store. She fixes her hair and face with a comb and a pocket mirror.

CLEO Little Georgy's jealous 'cause he had me last night.

JESUS Where'd you sleep last night?

GEORGE In a hallway and then on the benches over at Madison Square. *(To the puppets)* Spare any change? Spare any change? Please, sir, I'm hungry.

MALE VOICE #6 Sorry, but it'll kill your incentive.

GEORGE I'll kill your fuckin' incentive! You fuckin' faghole. Incentive!

JESUS Tonight I'm sleeping on the number 1 train.

DEALER *(Walks through and stands with the others)* Smoke, sess, nickel bag, sess . . .

JESUS *(Muttering to George)* Look who's back. I bet whoever the fuck took my money bought shit off'a him. *(To Dealer)* Hey, I want to buy.

DEALER What the fuck you want?

JESUS Sorry 'bout before, man.

DEALER Whatchu want?

JESUS A pound of sess right now is what I want.

DEALER Let's see some cash.

JESUS What you got on you right now?

DEALER Fuck off.

JESUS *(Sternly)* Hey, I'm asking you what you got.

DEALER And I'm telling you to fuck off.

JESUS And I thought I fucking told you to stay away! *(Shoves him against the dumpster and then grabs him)*

DEALER Get the fuck off me.

JESUS *(Shoves)* Stay the FUCK off this block! Didn't I say that?

DEALER Hey, I'll fucking blow you away.

JESUS *(Shoves Dealer against the dumpster again and pushes while speaking)* Cocksucker! Don't you ever talk to me like that. I ain't one of your whiteboy addicts.

As Dealer starts to run off, Jesus pulls a bag of joints out of his pocket without Dealer knowing it. Mozambique enters pushing a shopping cart filled with bottles and cans. Dealer shoves past her, exiting.

JESUS Pisses me off, man. You're trying to earn an honest buck and this scumbag's losing your business!

CLEO We got our own little police force here.

GEORGE Between this police force and the crime, I'll take the crime.

MOZAMBIQUE What's that asshole running from?

CLEO Don't ask.

MOZAMBIQUE *(To George)* How you doing, man? Make any money?

JESUS Who the fuck are you? His pimp?

MOZAMBIQUE Who are you? His john?

GEORGE *(To Jesus)* Hey, she's a friend. *(To Mozambique)* I sold one fuckin' thing. *(Mozambique goes over to Cleo and stays with her, keeping an eye on Jesus)*

JESUS Lend me a couple, huh?

GEORGE You see I'm begging.

JESUS *(Pissed)* I got rid of that dealer for you, didn't I?

GEORGE I don't care about no dealer. Hey, I'm fuckin' broke.

JESUS *(Remembers)* My old lady'll have something.

CLEO You're married?

JESUS She's living with some guy, but we— *(Loses interest in what he's saying)* I'm gone. *(Exits)*

MOZAMBIQUE *(Muttering)* Man, major waterbug crawled up that man's ass.

GEORGE Jesus is doing okay for someone out of his mind. I met him when I first came to the city and now I can't shake him. He's like a pit bull looking for a home.

MOZAMBIQUE Be careful. Pit bulls turn on their owners. *(Pauses)* So how much you make?

GEORGE Fuckin' buck.

MOZAMBIQUE So you broke even.

GEORGE *(Referring to the shopping cart)* Where the fuck did you get that?

MOZAMBIQUE What do you care? I had it, stashed it.

Businessman #4 walks by, finishing a can of soda through a straw. He puts it into Mozambique's shopping cart wordlessly. She takes it out and throws it at him.

MOZAMBIQUE What the fuck do I look like, a garbage disposal?

BUSINESSMAN #4 *(Exiting)* I was trying to be helpful.

MOZAMBIQUE I don't need none of your honky-ass charity! Dump on you and say they're doing you a favor, that's sweet.

CLEO Calm down, honey.

MOZAMBIQUE *(Yelling offstage)* Hey, motherfucker, Zach got arrested 'caus'a you!

MONTE *(Offstage)* Fuck you! Ain't my fault if he was too slow!

MOZAMBIQUE It's like they own the world. Never see a cop move them along.

CLEO They got the money, honey.

MOZAMBIQUE You want to make some real money? There he is. *(Points offstage)*

GEORGE Who?

MOZAMBIQUE Bad-in-the-plaid-ass motherfucker.

CLEO He was the reason the cops came by earlier.

MOZAMBIQUE *(Yelling to Monte)* He's sitting in a jail 'caus'a yo ass.

CLEO About two hours ago he transformed a ten into a hundred bucks in the turn of a card.

GEORGE You're kidding!

MOZAMBIQUE And a free man into a prisoner.

CLEO That's three-card Monte Hall.

MOZAMBIQUE I done that a couple times with Zach. He worked the cards, I placed the bets.

GEORGE Never saw no woman do it.

MOZAMBIQUE Sure, folks trust a lady.

GEORGE Here's a donation toward your future. *(Puts his wine bottle in her shopping cart)*

MOZAMBIQUE *(Reading the bottle)* No deposit, no return. Sounds more like your future.

GEORGE *(Extending an open palm to a passerby)* Maybe. They sure ain't giving it away anymore. *(Yawns)* Boy, am I tired.

CLEO They used to give more. Before begging became a pastime. *(Staring at the passing puppets for a while)*

GEORGE Look at 'em. At him and her and—

CLEO And him—

GEORGE They all look alike after a while.

MOZAMBIQUE Don't they, though? Look at this one coming up, this one here.

CLEO He's ugly.

GEORGE But she's pretty. Coming up behind him.

MOZAMBIQUE I used to have a set of breasts like that, before they dropped.

CLEO God, I wish I did. *(Pauses)* Soon you're just looking at the parts.

GEORGE Yeah, big tits and tight asses.

MOZAMBIQUE And that dude's tiny nose. And this guy's flappy ears.

CLEO Her hair is just right.

GEORGE *(Ignoring her)* This one's eyes are too wide apart and—

CLEO She has that "in look." You know, that "in look" look?

MOZAMBIQUE Don't know where you been, but her "in look" is out now, darling.

GEORGE *(Pointing)* That guy looks like this clown *(Pointing to a different passerby)* twenty years later. And that guy looks like a girl—

CLEO *(Tenderly)* Maybe he *is* a girl.

MOZAMBIQUE Over there's someone who looks like Ernie at the shelter, and what's the name of the other guy?

GEORGE *(Ignoring her)* People used to look more different. Now people look more alike. Take away the hair and dress, and girls look like guys.

CLEO And the guys start looking like the girls—that's what I've been saying all along.

GEORGE They all just look alike.

MOZAMBIQUE I think Ernie wears a cowboy hat.

GEORGE *(Murmuring)* Seen 'em all before. What do they call that way up on the Northern Pole, when everything is so white that your eyes get all buzzed up?

CLEO Snow blind.

GEORGE *(Rubbing his eyes)* Think I'm going crowd blind.

CLEO They don't see *you* neither.

GEORGE Well, I always see them. Like they's blurring me out, making me dizzy. See 'em awake, see 'em asleep—they rubbing me out.

MOZAMBIQUE Who wears the sailor's cap?

GEORGE Ernie wears the fuckin' sailor's cap and Cyril wears the cowboy hat. *(Referring to the crowd)* I wish they looked more different. Whoever made them got no 'magination.

MOZAMBIQUE But the guy who was on last night wasn't wearing no hat.

GEORGE *(Irritated)* So Cyril wasn't wearing a hat last night. I guess he didn't know it was a fuckin' fashion show. Now change the fuckin' subject!

MOZAMBIQUE Why are you such a liar?

GEORGE What?

MOZAMBIQUE You lied about how much you have, and now you lie about this. Why do you lie? Whatchu gain by it? (*George silently walks a few steps away from them*) You think you got something over me?

CLEO (*Softly*) What'd he do? He lied about the shelter?

MOZAMBIQUE Yeah, but this is what confuses me. People only lie when they got something to get from you; to rip you off or something. What's he trying to get from me? That's what I'm trying to figure out.

GEORGE Nothing! I just don't like being questioned. I got no reason to lie to you. I got nothing at all to gain by it. Hey, if you want, you can believe that I was at the shelter. Go ahead. Shit, I *wish* I was in the shelter.

MOZAMBIQUE 'Cause you *was* at the shelter.

GEORGE Fine.

MOZAMBIQUE Fine, you was there.

MALE VOICE #7 So they call this blend of fabric *synthetic mohair*. Feel.

MALE VOICE #8 Smooth. And it fits like a glove. How much did it run you?

MALE VOICE #7 If you've got to ask, don't.

GEORGE (*Approaching them*) Hey, I don't want to ask, but can you spare any change?

MALE VOICE #8 Young man, I wish I was simply broke. I'm running my business fifty thousand dollars in the red. You—I envy you.

GEORGE You look a lot less broke than me. Come on, you can spare something.

MALE VOICE #7 What are you people, a franchise? There's one of you on every corner.

GEORGE Sure, I'm french fries.

MALE VOICE #8 Well, merge with another franchise, will you? McDonald's up the block has a *Now Hiring* sign in the window.

GEORGE Hey, I'd go there but look at me. I *want* a job. If I could just get enough for a shave and a headcut—

MALE VOICE #7 I gave my quota to the guy begging down the block. Now please go split it with him, will you?

MALE VOICE #8 Who gives birth to these people?

GEORGE HEY! Mister, come here. *(Grabbing his genitals)* I got a job for you. You can suck on my Big Mac. *(To Cleo)* I'd like to see that cocksucker work at McDonald's.

CLEO Why don't you go work at McDonald's? Free food.

GEORGE Dumpster shit, fuck that. I worked like a motherfucker for two weeks at a Burger King in Baltimore. Lickin' some bitch's ass for minimum wage. Man, that bitch got me mad.

MOZAMBIQUE Is that where you're from, honey, Baltimore?

GEORGE More fuckin' questions. What are you, a cop? *(Puts his hands behind his back)* Arrest me.

MOZAMBIQUE What is your problem, boy? I'm just making small talk.

CLEO Aren't you allowed to eat all you want?

GEORGE Oh yeah, you can eat all the skanky food you want. But then they get to treat you like a slave. Uh-uh, no more.

CLEO *(Picks up the dildo)* I'm starving on my freedom.

GEORGE I never ever got my fuckin' freedom, never!

CLEO *(Teasing)* Well, you ought to go back to your old master and have him give it to you.

MOZAMBIQUE *(Amused)* Turn yourself in and get your freedom, honey child.

GEORGE To who? Where's my freedom?

MOZAMBIQUE Didn't you see *Roots*? Hey, your name's not Chicken George, is it?

GEORGE No, Kunta! Asshole. *(Resumes begging)* Spare any change?

MOZAMBIQUE He just looks so much like my Willy boy.

CLEO You better hope it isn't him.

MOZAMBIQUE I'd give anything just to find out if his name is really Willy. I haven't seen my boy in years.

CLEO Hey, Willy? (*George doesn't respond*) Names are what the police use to snag you.

GEORGE (*Limping quickly alongside a puppet*) Spare any change? Vietnam Vet with Asian Orange poisoning and the V.A. won't help me any. (*Pulls up the leg of his pants, pointing at a rash*) See?

MALE VOICE #9 Here, young man, I might have a little something for you.

MALE VOICE #10 Don't give him any money, Dad! He can work.

MALE VOICE #9 The man's a veteran. It's only a little change.

MALE VOICE #10 That's not the point. The city's turning into Calcutta. Begging is pandemic.

GEORGE Pan-fuckhead. (*Resumes begging*) Spare any change? Spare any change?

CLEO (*To George*) Hey, Willy, I mean—what's your name again?

GEORGE (*Ignoring Cleo*) Spare any change?

MOZAMBIQUE (*To Cleo*) His name's "Spare Any Change."

Cleo and Mozambique watch George begging awhile.

GEORGE What's your fuckin' name?

MOZAMBIQUE I'm Mozambique.

CLEO And I told you mines.

GEORGE Two bullshit names.

MOZAMBIQUE I was born with the name Lucy—Lucy Johnson.

CLEO (*Muttering*) I ain't telling mines.

GEORGE Still sounds bullshit.

MOZAMBIQUE What's your problem? Think we're gonna turn you in?

GEORGE I'm just not putting my name out. (*To the crowd*) Spare any change?

CLEO He's a trembling little leaf.

GEORGE Fuck you, faggot.

MOZAMBIQUE *(To Cleo)* I am really suspicious about this guy. *(To George)* You lies to me about money. You lies to me about the shelter. I gives you a nice deal on my store, and you ain't even telling me your name.

GEORGE All right! All right. If I tell you, will you get off my back?

MOZAMBIQUE Yeah.

GEORGE And you promise not to be spreading it around?

MOZAMBIQUE Who will I tell?

CLEO Cross my heart.

GEORGE My fucking name's George.

MOZAMBIQUE What about your last name?

GEORGE Now you're asking too much. And you know that, don't you? Yeah, you do.

CLEO That's what we was asking, boy.

MOZAMBIQUE See, why you got to be that way? What's the big deal? Just tell us your name! Don't be such a scared little faggot.

GEORGE All right! Regan. Name's Regan.

MOZAMBIQUE *(Angrily)* Then don't tell us your fucking name.

GEORGE I'm serious!

CLEO And I'm Gorbachev.

GEORGE Hey, I ain't proud of it. My fucking name's Regan.

MOZAMBIQUE I think he's serious.

GEORGE It's fuckin' spelled differently. It's R-E-G-A-N.

CLEO Reagan? Can I be your bush?

MOZAMBIQUE Not 'less your thing's detachable.

CLEO *(Picks up the dildo and demonstrates with it)* No, but there's this magical operation where they take the penis and slice it open, like a banana split, and sew these parts back—

GEORGE *(Grabs the dildo and puts it back down on his store)* That is fuckin' disgusting! How can you do that to yourself? God gave you a big strong body and look what you did to it.

CLEO Well, I'm sorry, but I didn't pick it. And I don't want to be *in* it. (*Dreamily*) One day I'll wake up on that operating table and some handsome boy wonder of a surgeon will be singing into my ear. (*Sings*) Girl, you're a woman now—

MOZAMBIQUE Hey, do they give it to you in a bag or what?

CLEO What?

MOZAMBIQUE You know, your thingy, when they chop it off.

CLEO Why are you so fascinated?

GEORGE Probably be like burning off a wart.

CLEO A wart! (*Points to the dildo*) That thing would turn green with envy.

GEORGE (*To the crowd*) Spare any change? Spare any change? I'm so tired.

TEENAGE BOY VOICE #3 Oh shit, looky there, a fucking dildo, dude.

TEENAGE BOY VOICE #4 Buy it for Mother's Day. (*Laughs*)

TEENAGE BOY VOICE #3 Fuck you!

CLEO (*Softly rubbing George's back*) I'm having the operation for you, Mister Reagan. So you can look me in the eyes while you're doing me.

TEENAGE BOY VOICE #4 Looky there, dude, 10 o'clock. (*Lowers his volume*) Big faggot coming on to little fag.

GEORGE (*To the teenagers*) Fuck you! I ain't no faggot. (*Breaks away*) Quit (*Shoves Cleo*) fagging (*Shoves*) on (*Shoves*) me.

CLEO Hey! Stop it.

MOZAMBIQUE (*Pulls George off*) Leave her be. (*Cleopatra takes a Japanese fan from her store and fans herself nervously*)

GEORGE I didn't hurt him. Couldn't if I tried. You ought to be pulling carriages in Central Park or something.

CLEO So you can ride me? No thanks.

MOZAMBIQUE Every he/she I've ever met who had the guts to take it to the street was a mean fighter. He hits you, you slap him back.

CLEO I just never had the fighting spirit.

WALKING PEDDLER (*Enters with an army rifle under a sheet*) Rifle, cheap. Rifle, real cheap . . .

GEORGE *(Walking with him)* Rifle! How much?

WALKING PEDDLER Forty-seven bucks. As is.

GEORGE You got bullets?

WALKING PEDDLER No, but you can get them easy. Cheap rifle . . . *(About to exit)*

GEORGE Wait a second, I got something here. *(Picks up a few porn magazines)* How 'bout a trade? *(Walking Peddler exits)*

MOZAMBIQUE You gonna be okay? *(Cleo nods yes)* Don't you be talking to him while I'm gone.

CLEO Where you going?

MOZAMBIQUE Can line at Sloan's starts at 1 o'clock.

CLEO Isn't there a Food Emporium on Sixth that has one of them machines on the street?

MOZAMBIQUE Not anymore.

CLEO Oh wait! I almost forgot, I have a gift for you. Happy birthday.

MOZAMBIQUE But it's not my birthday.

CLEO Doesn't matter. I love giving gifts. Here. *(Gives her a veil)* It's a silk veil. *(Puts it over her mouth)* I thought that since you usually wear your hair in a bundle, you could pin it up. You'd look just like Queen Victoria. Where's that pretty clasp? *(Looks through her belongings)*

MOZAMBIQUE You're such a sweetheart, girl.

CLEO Well, alone with bruiser here, I might be dead by the time you get back, so at least you'll have something to remember me by. *(Finds the clasp)* Here it is. *(Shows it to George)* Isn't it beautiful?

GEORGE Horse-ugly faggot.

CLEO Make nice.

GEORGE I'll make my foot up your fuckin' ass.

MOZAMBIQUE *(To George)* Just try it! *(Cleo fixes the clasp in Mozambique's hair)* I don't understand you at all, Cleo. I get bullied all the time and there's nothing I can do about it, but you're born a big strong man.

CLEO Maybe on the outside, but I really always was who I am.

MOZAMBIQUE Always?

CLEO Far back as I can remember. My mommy let me wear her clothes, and her boyfriend used to just flood me with compliments. "Aren't you the prettiest little girl, Claudia?" Claude turned into Claudia and that turned into Cleopatra. God, I was a happy child. Most people are sad. It'd take so little to make this girl happy. If I could just develop my figure a bit more.

MOZAMBIQUE When I still had a figure I was always worried about being raped and shit. And I was slapped around by more guys than I want to remember.

CLEO You think I haven't been? *(Finishes with Mozambique's hair)* There! Very becoming. *(George returns, listening)*

MOZAMBIQUE Wish I could swap places with you. Big strong arms. Go wherever I want, when I want. Have folks fear me, feel relieved if I'm just nice to them. Being a pretty woman makes you a number-one target, and that's about all.

CLEO That says more about men than women—loveable monsters that they are.

GEORGE *(To Mozambique)* Then why y'all girls all go strutting it around, miniskirting every which way?

MOZAMBIQUE I don't go miniskirting, hon.

GEORGE *(Pointing across the street downstage)* Well, that girl does, and that one.

CLEO *(Looking)* Which one?

GEORGE *(Yelling)* Hey! Titty girl! Luscious legs!

FEMALE VOICE #9 Fuck you!

GEORGE *(To Cleo)* That one.

CLEO *(Quietly)* I got better legs than that.

MOZAMBIQUE They're just trying to make *(Sings)* the best a, best a, best a, a bad situation . . . *(Hums it a bit)*

CLEO That's not why girls dress like that.

GEORGE Yeah, *you* know.

MOZAMBIQUE Why do they, then?

CLEO *(Looking off distantly)* Haven't you ever enjoyed just being looked at? Being cuddled and—and fussed over and held, and wanted and . . . loved?

A car screeches to a halt. Miles Gallo, a plainclothes cop with a walkie-talkie in his back pocket, rushes in and starts stomping on Zach's car radio. Cleo screams in surprise. Cleo and George are hastily trying to salvage some of the choice items in their stores. George has difficulty carrying his load.

GALLO You mothafuckas just don't learn!

MOZAMBIQUE Put it here. *(Referring to her shopping cart)*

CLEO *(Still packing)* Not done packing.

MOZAMBIQUE You'll lose it all.

As Gallo continues stomping on the radio, Cleo piles most of her things on the shopping cart.

MOZAMBIQUE *(To the cop)* I think you killed it, officer.

COP #2 *(Enters, speaks to Mozambique as Cleo exits with her cart)* I fuckin' tole you people! *(Jabbing sleeping Anthony awake with his club)* And you ain't listening. I ain't telling you again—stay the fuck off this fuckin' block!

MOZAMBIQUE *(Murmuring)* Asshole.

COP #2 *(To Mozambique)* Hey fat-ass! I got your boyfriend earlier, didn't I? *(She doesn't reply)* He's looking kind of lonely in lockup, *capisce? (To sleeping Anthony)* Move it. *(Mozambique, Cleo, and George exit)*

ANTHONY *Sí*, sir.

Anthony slowly takes a couple steps. The cops exit. Anthony lies back down. Fade to black.

ACT TWO

Same set, about an hour later. Anthony is alone, yelling at some woman just offstage. We hear her dog barking at him. There is a pile of dog shit by his cardboard bed.

ANTHONY *Mira!* Hey, *señorita,* that's your doggy's shit, you know. Clean up dis shit, you *comprende?*

FEMALE VOICE **#10** Go back where you came from.

ANTHONY I was born in Nuevo York, mudafucka.

PSYCHO *(Storms in, raging)* OXSUCKER! MOTH GUCKING FUNT, SHUNT, MUDAFONT . . .

ANTHONY *(To Psycho as he's exiting, pointing to Female Voice #10, off-stage)* Go gets her! *(George enters, Anthony points to the dog shit)* Her doggie—shit *aquí, mira! (Points offstage to the woman)*

GEORGE Hey, lady, they's a fuckin' law!

FEMALE VOICE **#10** There's a law against loitering too! *(George uses a garment Cleo or Mozambique was forced to abandon to pick up and toss the dog shit at her; she screams, suggesting a direct hit)* You fucking bastard! *(George and Anthony laugh)* I'm getting the cops!

GEORGE Just returning what you dropped. *(Sees Jesus offstage)* Shit! Here comes another mad fuckin' dog.

Anthony finds a bra and other abandoned clothes on the sidewalk. He uses them as a pillow and goes to sleep behind the dumpster.

JESUS Fucking cunt! *(Enters from offstage)* That fucking cunt! Fucking cunt, man!

GEORGE Hush up, man.

JESUS What? Fuck you, man. I ain't scared of none of 'em. *(Directed to the crowd)* Fucking cunt! Fucking cunt! Fucking cunt, man!

GEORGE So what happened?

JESUS My wife happened. Bitch wouldn't even lend me a fucking cent. Says I owe her!

GEORGE She probably has a new husband.

JESUS No, he dumped her too. I tried to be nice.

GEORGE So what happened?

JESUS She wouldn't let me in the fucking house. *(Murmuring)* Even the fucking kids were lined up against the door.

GEORGE You got kids?

JESUS No, I got laid. She got kids.

A young, well-dressed couple enter. She's swinging a small purse on long loose strings and smoking a cigarette from a long-stem holder. He's also smoking. Cleo enters, trailing behind them, holding her bundle with one hand, and in the other, a strapless sequin gown up against her body, while talking to the woman.

CLEO Just look at this, dear, it shimmers, it shines—it's alive. Just tell me it isn't you.

WOMAN **#3** It really isn't.

MAN **#5** Thanks anyway.

GEORGE Spare a ciggy?

Man #5 opens a silver cigarette case. George puts one in his mouth and takes several more for later. Man #5 pulls out a lighter. Cleo puts her bundle down and searches through it for something.

CLEO I have just the thing for those drooping argyles—sock suspenders. (*Man #5 declines and the ritzy couple exit, Cleo inhales deeply*) Smell that? Sophistication.

JESUS (*Sniffs*) Is that his cologne?

CLEO Oh yeah. If money grew from trees, that would be its fragrance.

JESUS Money, why didn't you say so. Later. (*Exits in the same direction as the couple*)

GEORGE (*Muttering*) And don't come back.

CLEO (*Picks up the wrecked car radio*) Look at what that Gallo cocksucker did to poor Zach's car radio.

GEORGE (*Holding up some clothes on the street*) This shit yours?

CLEO (*Shrieking*) My Diana Ross-at-twilight ensemble! (*Pulls the clothes out of the gutter*) Destroyed forever!

GEORGE Here, I found this stuff. (*Returns the clothes he picked up*)

CLEO (*Fixes the displays of her store*) Bless you, George. Why must people be so hard, Georgia? Why must people be so cruel? (*Sings*) Easy to be hard, easy to be cruel. (*Talks*) Why do people have no feelings, why do they ignore their friends? (*Sings*) It's easy to be hard, Georgia, easy to ignore. (*Stops singing*) This was my spring collection too. Now I'll never get my operation.

GEORGE Operation? How 'bout just a meal.

CLEO You wouldn't understand this, Georgy-porgy, but being a man physically hurts me.

GEORGE I know a way you can make money easy. If you're a real lady.

CLEO I already did the catwalk in Paris.

GEORGE How 'bout the West Side highway walk?

CLEO What fashion venue's over there?

GEORGE Washington Street around the meat market. Twenty bucks a pop, easy.

CLEO (*Innocently*) What services can I parlay there, pray tell?

GEORGE Come on, you done it before. Do it in some doorway. Spit it out. You're an Andrew Jackson richer.

CLEO Spare me your crass connotations.

GEORGE Shit! You were about to give Jesus a blowjob right there in broad daylight.

CLEO Please, I was just flirting with the boy.

GEORGE Come on, ain't no big deal. Boys and girls are doing it right now.

CLEO What are you, a pimp? Or just unhappy to see me?

GEORGE I'm just telling you how to make quick money.

CLEO (Sexually) Teach me how, hot buns.

GEORGE Get out of my face, fuckin' freak.

CLEO Tell you one thing, 'cause you might not know it and you should. You're a freak too. Just like me. You're here just like everyone else 'cause you got to be.

GEORGE Hey, I don't got to be nowhere.

CLEO You might look okay on the outside. But in here— (Points to his head) you're a little negroid—from a solar ghetto.

GEORGE Don't say that shit!

CLEO Oh, we can jerk it out but we can't lap it up, can we?

WALKING PEDDLER (Riding through on a ten-speed bike) Bike for sale, bike for sale . . .

GEORGE Don't fuck with me. I ain't here for the same reason as all your poor black asses.

CLEO You're not? What are you, some big undercover reporter?

GEORGE None of your fuckin' business. (To the crowd) Change? Change?

CLEO You look a little tan for Ted Koppel. Believe me, I know why you're out here. You go to some crappy little McDonald's or something. Go through the interview, controlling every sylla-ble. Can't tell him what we really are. Someone hires you for no good reason. You got to wear those embarrassing off-the-rack, starch-smelling uniforms with the degrading little cap and name tag. Feeling sweaty, itchy all over. People are look-ing at you funny. You're not fooling no one. *I'm not worthless*, you're thinking, *I'm not nothing*. But you sure feel it. So you don't say a fucking word. Don't give nothing away. Maybe they'll think you're just quiet, laugh when they laugh. Blend. Stay away from everyone else. But every time something fucks up or if someone farts or, God forbid, anyone steals something—

GEORGE —Or if you're alone with one of them. Like that bitch manager who didn't know when to shut up. But I knew she was afraid to be alone with me, like I was some rapist nigger.

CLEO They do you real nice, don't they? "How you doing, Claude? Need any help, Claude?" Why are they so fucking nice to you? It's like you're a retard.

GEORGE Yeah! That's right. She was always hanging over me. Always eyeballing me. And she was fuckin' blacker than I was!

CLEO (*Lightens up*) Some folks get a little buzz, just a little more power, and think they're God. They might even think they're making us better, so they push and push. "You're doing that wrong! You're late! You got a spot on your shirt—"

GEORGE (*Explodes*) Shut up! SHUT THE FUCK UP! (*Shoves Cleo up against the dumpster, Anthony awakens from her shreiking*)What the fuck do you know? Don't you ever—EVER—

CLEO WHAT?! (*Terrified*) What'd I say?

GEORGE Don't you never question me!

ANTHONY (*Rises wobbly*) Hey, hey. No hit *Señora* Liz Taylor, eh?

GEORGE Mind your own fuckin' business!

ANTHONY No *problema*. (*Gets between Cleo and George*) Take it easily.

GEORGE (*Yelling over Anthony's shoulders at Cleo*) You're a man! And no operation can change that!

CLEO (*Behind Anthony, murmuring*) Better be glad I ain't a man.

GEORGE Why's that? (*Shoves Anthony aside*) You gonna hit me? (*Slaps her*) Come on then. You got height and weight on me. Come on! (*Squares off, Cleo starts crying*) Take a fuckin' swing at me. HIT ME OR I'LL HIT YOU! (*Grabs Cleo's hands and hits himself with them*) HIT ME!! (*Cleo finally slaps George's chest*)

MOZAMBIQUE Hey! *(Enters, shoving her empty shopping cart into George)* Leave her the fuck alone!

GEORGE See, you don't know, 'cause I was helpin' him. Learnin' him to stick up for himself and fight—

CLEO *(Behind Mozambique)* He really scared me.

MOZAMBIQUE It's okay now.

CLEO And broke my nail. *(Shows)*

GEORGE I didn't fuckin' touch you. Man, you are a serious waste of time. Watch my shit. *(Exits)*

MOZAMBIQUE *(To Cleo)* I warned you not to go talking to that boy no more, didn't I?

WALKING PEDDLER *(Passing on foot quickly through the scene)* Lighters, one buck. Lighters, one buck. Lighters, one buck . . .

CLEO *(Hugs Mozambique)* He scared me bad.

MOZAMBIQUE There, there. He's all smoke, no fire.

CLEO *(Regains her composure)* Did you return all those cans?

MOZAMBIQUE Four dollars in nickels, I got them changed. *(Jingles a pocketful of coins)*

CLEO That whole shopping cart only came to four bucks?

MOZAMBIQUE Yeah, but I spent almost all of it. Guess what I got?

CLEO Let it be a handgun.

MOZAMBIQUE No, a sandwich and a deck of cards. I'm gonna do it! I did it before. If the cops are coming anyways, I might as well try for some real money.

CLEO Do it, girl! I saw the Mexican boy throw some boxes in here earlier. *(Mozambique retrieves several boxes from the dumpster)*

GEORGE *(Enters, hearing sirens, he looks around)* Just an ambulance.

MOZAMBIQUE *(Pointing offstage)* That an unmarked car?

CLEO No.

MOZAMBIQUE They've been driving unmarked lately. No sign of the pigman?

GEORGE He's eating donuts somewhere.

CLEO All day I been feeling awful about Zach being arrested. If he didn't argue with Gallo he woulda lost his stuff but he wouldn'ta gotten arrested.

MOZAMBIQUE *(Pulling the aces out of the deck)* It ain't your fault.

CLEO But Zach was halfway packed when they pulled up. I still had all my stuff out. I swear, I don't know why they didn't take me.

MOZAMBIQUE You got to learn when to leave your things and save yourself. That Gallo fucker had it in for Zach for a while.

GEORGE Why?

MOZAMBIQUE Zach says he saw him kissing a girl once. I think it was his wife. I guess he feels like now that old Zach knows his wife, he's gonna rape her. Cops don't want us peaking inside their lives.

CLEO They can arrest me if they want, but I could never leave my things.

GEORGE Did Zach say what she looked like?

MOZAMBIQUE Excuse me, I don't recall talking to you.

GEORGE Why you pissed?

MOZAMBIQUE *(Pointing to Cleo)* She is my friend. You fuck with my friend, you fuck with me, understand?

GEORGE Hey!

MOZAMBIQUE *(Approaches angrily, George backs away)* Don't you "hey" me, 'cause I will seriously fuck you up, you understand?

GEORGE *(To Cleo)* Hey, tell her! I was telling you to hit *me*. You're a man, and you got to stand up for yourself.

MOZAMBIQUE Who the fuck are you, her father?

CLEO *(To Mozambique)* He was beating on me.

GEORGE Was not. And if you don't learn to stand up for yourself, people are going to beat on you all your life. *(Jesus enters)* I was trying to teach you that. Don't lie.

MOZAMBIQUE Just like you was lying about being at the shelter, huh?

GEORGE I wasn't at no shelter! *(To Cleo)* Hey, forgive me if I scared you. All right? Maybe I was being fly.

CLEO Just don't fuck with me again.

GEORGE All right.

JESUS Did I miss some action here? What'd you two get into, a cat-
   fight?

GEORGE No.

JESUS *(Hands some items to Cleo)* What's this worth?

CLEO Long-stem cigarette holder, circa 1920. Looks familiar. A cigarette case, silver plated.

JESUS Want 'em for a buck?

CLEO The only buck I have is George. *(Smiles at George)*

JESUS George, you got a buck, come on.

GEORGE Wish I did.

JESUS What you got in there? *(Pats one of George's pockets)* I'll take
   whatever you got. *(George pulls out his pocket, showing it empty)*

CLEO I'll check him if you want. *(Pats George's back pocket gently)*

GEORGE *(Tensely)* Stay the fuck away from me, Claude.

JESUS *(To Cleo)* Claude? That's your name? Claudehopper?

CLEO At least my name ain't Reagan, the little Burger King from
   Baltimore.

MOZAMBIQUE *(To George and Cleo)* Hey, cut it out now, I ain't
   fooling.

GEORGE Better shut up before I have to slap that little horse mouth
   of yours.

CLEO Slap my horse mouth?! *(Inspecting her nails)* Golly, my hooves
   are getting jagged again. You don't have any nail clippers? Do
   you Haysuz?

JESUS Tole you. Someone fucking stole them.

CLEO A good manicure, yes sir. That's what I need to look like a big
   brawny man, which is what I am, right, Georgey? Big macho
   man. *(George looks at Cleo angrily)* Oh, we're all hushed up
   now, aren't we, dear?

GEORGE G'on, just keep on fuckin' with me.

MOZAMBIQUE Hey, the both of yous!

CLEO But my nails, they ain't manlike at all. They long and sleek.
   George, don't you want to help make me a man? *(George
   starts packing up his store.)*

JESUS What you doing?

GEORGE I don't need this faggot. I'm going to sell up that block. Fuck y'all later. *(Jesus walks offstage for a moment)*

CLEO Thank God!

MOZAMBIQUE Come on, Willy, just relax.

GEORGE *(Still packing)* I ain't no Willy, who's Willy?

CLEO You remind her of her son Willy.

MOZAMBIQUE There's no cause to run off.

CLEO Hey, we're even-steven, Sweet Georgia Brown. You can stop packing. I know that bulge in your pocket means you're just glad to see me.

JESUS *(Returns)* Hey, I thought you were broke. What's that in your pocket? *(Pats George's pocket)*

GEORGE *(Slaps Cleo, who screams)* You asked for that.

MOZAMBIQUE *(Hits George)* Now you gots to go! And I mean *now*!

JESUS *(Amused)* Let's get a bottle. How much you got?

GEORGE Nothing, man! *(Still packing)* I don't know why I ever wasted my time with fools.

Jesus shoves his hand in George's back pocket. George holds Jesus's hand in the pocket, not wanting him to see the contents.

GEORGE Let the fuck go.

JESUS Shit! I caught me a fish.

CLEO *(Coming to George's aide)* Come on, Jesus, I got something to show you behind the dumpster.

JESUS Okay, okay. Let me just take my hand out of— *(Pulls his crucifix clippers out of George's pocket)* Holy shit!

GEORGE *(To Cleo)* You muthafucka!

Jesus throws George to the ground and starts punching him wildly. Finally, Jesus pins him down and pulls out his knife.

GEORGE Helllp!

MOZAMBIQUE *(Grabs Jesus's arm and snatches the knife out of his hand)* No fucking way!

JESUS *(Still sitting on top of George)* Give me my fucking shank, bitch, or I'll do you too!

MOZAMBIQUE Just chill!

GEORGE I swear, I found the clippers on the street! I was gonna show you.

JESUS Bullshit! You stole it at the shelter. Tell me you didn't rip me off! Think I'm fucking dumb?

MOZAMBIQUE You really going to off this asshole for four bucks?

JESUS It was six.

CLEO Oh God, I'm sorry, George.

JESUS No one rips me off! Give me my fucking blade.

MOZAMBIQUE He didn't kill you, and I ain't letting you kill him.

JESUS I'll fucking kill him with my bare hands. *(Starts strangling George)*

CLEO *(Hitting Jesus on the back)* Stop it! Stop it!

JESUS Fuck you! *(Still strangling George, who is gasping for breath)*

MOZAMBIQUE *(Pushes Cleo out of the way and puts the knife to Jesus's throat)* Stop it, I ain't fooling now. Don't think I never used one before.

JESUS *(Stops)* I'm gonna kill you, lady.

MOZAMBIQUE Just listen. Let him make you your money back and then you can kick his ass, and let it go at that.

CLEO It's fair.

MOZAMBIQUE *(Still holding the knife to Jesus's throat)* You don't have no choice.

JESUS Soon as I let him up, he's gone.

GEORGE *(Frantically)* No way! I'll sell my shit, I'll make the money, I already got two bucks here. *(Jesus grabs it out of his hand)* I can beg. I'll fuckin' mug someone. I'll get it, man.

JESUS *(Lets him up)* You're dead. Just a matter of time.

WALKING PEDDLER *(Passing through, holding disposable lighters)* Bic Butanes, a buck, Bic, a buck, Bics, a buck . . .

MOZAMBIQUE *(Searching her pockets)* Here, I got four bucks some-where. *(Pulls out a bunch of nickels)* What's left of my can money.

JESUS *(Slaps the change out of her hand)* It's not the fucking money. The bitch fucked me!

MOZAMBIQUE That kid's not worth throwing away your life over.

JESUS *(Sarcastically)* You really care about me, don't you?

CLEO Look, you got him, man. You can hold him till you're satisfied.

JESUS *(Kicks George hard in the leg, Geroge cries out in pain)* Let's see you run now. You're right, he's all mine. Can't kill him here anyways. *(George hops around with difficulty)* Go ahead, run, give me a reason to fuck you up.

GEORGE *(Jumps at Cleo)* You're fuckin' dead! I'm going to kill you!

JESUS *(Mozambique intercedes, Jesus grabs George by the back of his shirt and laughs)* This guy's mean as a pit bull. I oughta put him on a leash.

MOZAMBIQUE Just cool it.

GEORGE I'm dead 'cause of that bitch!

MOZAMBIQUE *You* fucked up, not her. You shouldn'ta gone ripping off your friends at the shelter.

GEORGE And he shouldn't go fuck around with another man's life!

CLEO You slapped me.

GEORGE And I apologized too, didn't I?

JESUS *(Long pause)* All right, enough games, bitch! *(Shoves George toward the crowd)*

MOZAMBIQUE Come on, man, if he gives you back your six, say you'll let him go. Then I'll give you some cash toward his debt.

CLEO Me too.

JESUS *(Long pause)* All right, but fuck six. I want twenty. Twenty and an ass-kicking.

GEORGE *(To Mozambique)* Thank you.

MOZAMBIQUE Okay.

JESUS Must feel good, all these people working to save your ass. I want to see you beg for my money, bitch.

GEORGE (*To the crowd, with added despair*) Please, man, it's my fuckin' life here. Please, just a nickel, I ain't foolin'! I beg you.

MOZAMBIQUE Here goes nothing. (*Sets up the boxes from the dumpster and awkwardly starts playing three-card monte*) Find the red, get ahead, find the black, stay way back.

JESUS (*Amused*) Shit, you need a pigeon to do that right. Someone to make bets.

MOZAMBIQUE I know! (*To Cleo*) Come on, girl, be my mark.

CLEO I can't. I freeze up when doing shit like that.

MOZAMBIQUE Shit, Cleo—

JESUS Look, lady, you need someone to watch for the cops and you move like— Shit, just let me deal. (*To Cleo*) You watch for police. (*Takes out some money*) I got something.

MOZAMBIQUE Whatchu got?

JESUS Two bucks from asshole here.

MOZAMBIQUE Shit, that ain't enough. No one takes bets that low.

JESUS Just fold the bills over and say they're two tens. I'll deal.

MOZAMBIQUE No way, *you* bet. They my cards. I'm just a little rusty. (*Slowly practices*) How much did we say?

JESUS He's a bargain at twenty.

MOZAMBIQUE You'll owe me, boy.

GEORGE I swear I'll pay. (*Begs desperately to the crowd*) If you can spare any change, it means my life—

MOZAMBIQUE (*Referring to the cards*) Just put it down on whatever card I touch, understand?

JESUS (*Amused*) I've done more of this than you'll ever know, lady. Just play.

MOZAMBIQUE (*Exchanging cards, speaking loudly*) Find the black, make it back! Find the red— (*Drops a card*)

JESUS You kidding?

MOZAMBIQUE I'm just loosening up. (*Loudly, while dealing*) Come on, I got it here, for whoever's near. (*Drops another card*)

JESUS (*Turns a card over*) Fuck! You kidding, right?

MOZAMBIQUE Shit!

CLEO *(To Mozambique)* Just take it easy. Relax, girl.

MOZAMBIQUE You win four and you're looking for more. *(Drops another card)*

JESUS Fuck this, you're gonna be the first person who loses money playing this game. Let's go, punk. *(Pushes George)*

GEORGE No, please!

MOZAMBIQUE Come on, give me a chance.

JESUS The only way I'm staying is if I do the dealing. You can place the bets.

CLEO Let him have it, honey. Men are better at stealing money.

MOZAMBIQUE All right. *(Lets Jesus get behind the boxes)*

JESUS *(Bends the cards down the spine professionally and deals smoothly)* If we get someone, you know how to cheat on me.

MOZAMBIQUE It's all cheating, ain't it?

JESUS *(Sighs)* You see me turning asking her *(Referring to Cleo)* about some shit, you take a peak at the unturned card. *(Demonstrates)* See what I'm saying? Make 'em think that you got a winner. You bet on the wrong card, understand?

MOZAMBIQUE I got you.

JESUS *(Loudly, while shuffling the aces)* What is that—fifty you won off me?!

MOZAMBIQUE *(Betting)* Just put the cards down. I'm on a streak.

JESUS *(Shuffling)* Lady, ain't your husband and kids going hungry? Don't you got to go?

MOZAMBIQUE Feeding time is right here! Leave when I'm good and done with you. *(Continues betting)* Deal!

Two teenage boys dressed in heavy metal gear pass slowly, playing a ghetto blaster. Along with Cleo and George, they watch the card game awhile.

JESUS *(To Cleo)* You looking out for cops? 'Cause the last cop wasn't in uniform. *(As he is talking to Cleo, Mozambique peaks at a downturned card, Teenage Boy #1 sees her do this but doesn't glimpse at the card)*

CLEO Yeah. I'm looking, just relax.

JESUS I get grabbed, you gonna get hurt.

CLEO I'm watching, I'm watching! (*Looking up and down the block*)

MOZAMBIQUE (*Slams a folded dollar down*) I'm putting twenty on this.

TEENAGE BOY #1 Hold on! Me too! (*Struggling to pull out money*)

JESUS (*Waits for Teenage Boy #1 to put down the twenty and turns over the card*) Turn it over, red rover. (*She does*) It's a sin, but I win. (*Takes the twenty from Teenage Boy #1 and the folded bill from Mozambique, George jumps up and down, then stops, repressing his joy*)

MOZAMBIQUE SHIT! How'd—

TEENAGE BOY #1 Fuck! (*To Mozambique*) What happened? (*Mozambique shrugs*)

JESUS Put it down, see it round. (*Deals again*)

MOZAMBIQUE (*Excitedly puts another folded dollar on a card*) This one! (*Flips it over*)

JESUS Wrong card. (*With two cards still concealed, Jesus flips one over and then exchanges them slowly back and forth*) Pick one. Win two!

TEENAGE BOY #1 (*To Teenage Boy #2*) It's that one, man!

JESUS Just show me twenty and it's yours.

TEENAGE BOY #1 Lend me your twenty!

TEENAGE BOY #2 No way! You already lost your money.

JESUS Just show me your twenty, you got forty.

TEENAGE BOY #1 I saw it, man. Forty!

GEORGE Just show it.

JESUS I'm not taking any money from you, son, I just need to see that you got it.

MOZAMBIQUE (*To Teenage Boy #1*) He just got to see it. Show it to him and you get forty bucks.

WALKING PEDDLER (*Enters with a refrigerator box*) Want to buy a free living room?

TEENAGE BOY #1 I got a rec room in Poughkeepsie, thanks.

WALKING PEDDLER (*To Jesus*) Rec room?

JESUS Can't you see we're busy here, asshole?

CLEO He needs one. *(Points at Anthony)*

Walking Peddler wakes Anthony up, then Anthony pays him with Cleo's bra that he was using as a pillow. Walking Peddler gives him the large box and exits. Anthony curls back up in the box.

JESUS Hey, if you ain't betting, move on and give someone else a chance.

TEENAGE BOY #2 *(To Teenage Boy #1)* You better fucking be right!

TEENAGE BOY #1 You'll get forty and I'll get my money back.
(Teenage Boy #2 holds up the twenty, Jesus turns over the card)

JESUS You lose, fools!

DEALER *(Dashes up to Jesus with a pistol, trembling)* Give me my fuckin' shit—NOW!

Dealer steps even closer to Jesus and conceals the gun. Cleo turns to George and mouths the word "run." George shakes his head.

JESUS Everybody stay cool! *(Slowly reaches into his pocket and pulls out a bag of joints and hands it to Dealer)* It's cool, see. No harm done. *(Dealer keeps his pistol pointed at Jesus)*

TEENAGE BOY #2 *(To Dealer)* Man, we don't know this dude. We got to go. *(Keeping their twenty, they move away slowly and then rush off)*

JESUS I would've paid if you waited your ass a minute.

DEALER *(Grabs the money Jesus is holding and smashes him across his head with the pistol)* I ever see your ass again, I'll fuckin' kill you. *(Runs off)*

GEORGE *(To Jesus, who is bent over holding his head)* You all right?

JESUS No, I feel like this. *(Punches George in the chest)* You owe me forty now!

GEORGE Me?

CLEO *(Murmuring)* Told you to go.

JESUS *(Smacks George again)* You got something in common with that *maricon*! You both took my money. 'Cept you're fucking worse, 'cause I was good to you.

GEORGE You just got twenty. That was the deal.

JESUS What really pisses me off is you musta stuck your faggot hands in my underwear to get—

GEORGE No way, man! It musta come loose, 'cause I came in late and saw you asleep. I tried to wake you up. See, I saw the money on the edge of your bed and I knew someone was gonna snatch it. So I took it just to hold onto it for you.

JESUS And the crucifix.

GEORGE Yeah.

JESUS Bullshit! *(Hits him again)* So tell me something, asshole. The six dollars that'll cost you your life, what'd you do with it?

GEORGE I just wanted to get out of here.

JESUS *(To the others)* A six-dollar trip, wow!

MOZAMBIQUE Don't fucking lie to the man. You bought a bottle with that money.

GEORGE That's the only place I can go for six bucks.

JESUS There's the morgue. *(Punches the dumpster)* FUCK!

MOZAMBIQUE *(Pathetically attempting to play a three-card monte)* Hey, come on. We still got a deal. *(Shouts out)* There's more where that came from, folks!

JESUS That drug-dealing motherfucker took my money. Can't monte without money.

MOZAMBIQUE Well, I'm sure gonna try. *(Loudly)* Keep your eyes on the red. Show me the red for free. Come on. Show and tell me. *(Tries, but she clearly lacks the dexterity)*

CLEO Honey, this just ain't a woman's game.

JESUS *(Shoves George in front of the crowd, knocking him into them)* Keep fucking begging!

GEORGE Pardon me, man—

MALE VOICE #11 Watch where you're going!

GEORGE *(To the crowd)* Spare any change? Please help me! *(Shifts from frustration to rage, singling out individuals)* Fuck this! I didn't make you ugly, I didn't make you dumb, I didn't fuck up your life. Y'all better than me, so you fuckin' owe me something!

JESUS *(Jumps up)* Hey! Don't do it like that. Do it right. Or I'll fucking kill you!

GEORGE Right's not working.

JESUS You beg them right. 'Cause I will fucking kill you. *(Grabs George's neck and squeezes it)*

GEORGE Okay! *(Breaks free and closes his eyes)* Spare any change? Have a good day. Spare any change? Thanks anyways . . .

A junkie slowly stumbles up, blocking George's path, and starts nodding out.

JESUS *(Goes right up to the ear of the addict and screams)* HEY!! Die somewhere else.

JUNKIE *(Fading as he talks)* I have a right as an American citizen . . . to stand wherever I fuckin' want. It says in the Constitution of the United States that I— *(Nods out)*

JESUS Here's your fucking rights as an American. *(Grabs him and runs him offstage, we hear a car screeching)* Back to work, asshole.

GEORGE Spare any change? Have a good day. Spare any change? Have a good day. Spare any change? Have a good day. Spare any change? Have a good day? *(As he speaks faster, the pace of the puppets increases)* Spare any day? Have any change.

JESUS *(Angrily)* Keep it up. Go on, test me, you think I'm fooling. *(George resumes begging properly)*

CLEO *(To Mozambique)* Do you know what I miss more than anything else? My TV. Me and my mom—we watched TV for fifteen years and didn't do nothing else. Tell you something too, I loved every minute of it. 'Cause if we ever got bored—

MOZAMBIQUE Just change the channel.

CLEO Yeah, but TV just got too good. Sucked Ma right in. More she watched, more she just faded. And we'd never turn it off. Fall asleep in front of it. Wake up and just keep watching it. Eat and crap at commercials. Then she took sick and that greasy-ass hotel manager ambulanced her away. He was always trying to get us to lower the volume. She passed right on into TV land. And I got tossed out. Clicked off and unplugged. Remember the Friday-night line-up a couple years ago—

MOZAMBIQUE I had them fucking Jersey boys, didn't I? The second boy lost his second twenty. If that dealer didn't come we woulda—

CLEO Just like that old man this morning. It's harder and harder finding fools who aren't wise to three-card monte. You should go to the shells. That's the latest rage, you know.

Man #6 walks through reading a newspaper, holding a half-eaten sandwich, which he tosses into the open dumpster. George retrieves it and starts eating.

JESUS HEY! (*Grabs the sandwich from George*)

GEORGE Come on. I'm starving here.

JESUS (*Smacks George, then gobbles the remainder down*) Ought to kill you and eat you. Beg, asshole. Beg! Beg!

MAN #6 (*Inspects George's store*) How much for this? (*Points at the dildo*)

GEORGE That's—

JESUS That's mine—ten bucks.

MAN #6 Forget it.

GEORGE How 'bout four. (*Man #6 hesitates*) What's four bucks? 'Bout three tokens, two bags of cans. Pocket full of pennies, right?

MAN #6 Let me think about it. (*Goes to Cleo's store, picks up a key on a long brass chain*)

CLEO That was the pass key at the old Cherokee Hotel on 24th Street. Remember the old Cherokee? (*Sings a mock–Native*

American chant, tapping her hand over her mouth; Man #6 shakes his head no) Mary Astor used to stay there whenever she was in town. Oh! And this was Tallulah Bankhead's cigarette lighter. *(Picks it up and lights it)*

MAN **#6** *(Doubtful)* Sure.

CLEO *(Hands him the lighter and points)* Read that inscription.

MAN **#6** *(Reads aloud)* "Dear Tally, I'll never forget our wondrous night of love and bubbles—" I can't read the rest of it.

CLEO The rest was too personal—I had to scratch it out.

MAN **#6** *(Chuckles)* Okay, how much is it?

CLEO It was seventeen-fifty, but today's Miss Bankhead's birthday so it's on sale for a buck.

MAN **#6** Take two. *(Gives Cleo two dollars)*

GEORGE *(Waving the dildo)* Two bucks. Just two.

MAN **#6** It's not the money. Please take that thing away from my face. *(Exits)*

CLEO *(Gives the two dollars to Jesus)* To the George Regan relief fund. *(George starts exiting)*

JESUS *(Grabs George)* Where the fuck you going?!

GEORGE I kept my side of the deal! That dealer stole your money and you already beat the hell out of me. I'm done: two from him, the two I gave you before, two bucks for the sandwich. I'm all paid up, six bucks. That's what I took.

JESUS You don't get it. In fact, it ain't even about payback. Now I just *own* you, see. You're my own private little nigger.

GEORGE Fuck you.

JESUS Think I'm kidding? *(Steps close)* Leave and I'll kill you. And you wouldn't be my first, neither. *(George looks away hopelessly)*

CLEO *(To George softly)* If'n I really was a strong man, I'd— Well, this is why I hate what I am. Not so much 'cause I don't look like how I feel, but because I look so big and strong, and I just ain't. And everyone's just disappointed in me. I'm sorry for what I did and for what I am.

JESUS *(To Cleo, amused)* My bitch can't talk to anyone now. She's making Daddy some money. Tricks time. *(Shoves George back to the crowd)*

GEORGE Spare any change?

Suddenly a car screeches to a halt. Jesus and George rush off. Mozambique deliberately drops Jesus's knife on George's store so she won't be caught with it. The two plainclothes cops from earlier reenter. Cleo tries to hastily pack up her store.

MOZAMBIQUE *(To Cleo)* Leave it! Leave it!

GALLO Fucking pigeons. Loud noise they fly away. Turn around, they're back on the ground.

COP #2 *(Looks at Mozambique, then at George's store)* And after I warned you?

MOZAMBIQUE I's just minding my own business.

COP #2 This ain't your shit?

GALLO *(To Cleo)* What are you doing, hon?

CLEO I'm sorry, officer, I'm done for good. Won't see me here ever again. *(Collects her things)* Never, ever, never.

COP #2 *(Picks up the dildo)* Probably lose this thing inside you, huh?

MOZAMBIQUE *(Muttering)* Fucking son of a—

GALLO What'd she say?

MOZAMBIQUE I didn't say nothing.

COP #2 Come on, you won't need to use that no more. Your boyfriend wants to see you. *(Handcuffs Mozambique)*

MOZAMBIQUE Officer, please, I swear to almighty God. They's ain't mines, man.

CLEO I can vouch for her. That ain't hers.

Cop #2 pushes Mozambique offstage toward the unmarked car.

MOZAMBIQUE *(To Cleo)* Take care of yourself.

GALLO *(Amused, to Cop #2)* This one can vouch for that one. *(To Cleo)* And what earthling can vouch for you?

Cleo's almost entirely packed as Gallo casually stomps on the remaining items of her store.

CLEO Please, officer, those are my personal effects. I do have rights!

GALLO They ain't no one's no more. *(Picks up some of her clothes and tears them apart)*

CLEO Please, they're my life! I don't got nothing else but my mom's clothes—

GALLO *(Claps his hands)* Fly away, bird.

CLEO Officer, you don't understand, I—

GALLO You want to join big bad Mama?

CLEO No, but these are mines and—

GALLO You people pull this crap out of the garbage or you steal it. Let's see some ID.

CLEO I don't have any.

GALLO Then you're coming downtown.

CLEO Wait, I have this, my hospital ID card. *(Gallo looks at it)* But, but—

GALLO Claude, what'll happen to your butt after four days in lockup? Now take a walk, Big Bird, or you're going into a big cage. *(Cleo starts to walk away, but Gallo grabs the belongings out of her hands)*

CLEO *(Screams)* No! Those are my things!

GALLO Let go or you're under arrest.

CLEO *(Fitfully)* Where am I suppose to go? Those are my things!

Gallo tears up the rest of Cleo's clothes as George reenters with Jesus close behind. While Gallo is busy, Jesus snatches his knife off the ground.

GALLO Claude, I'm giving you a break here. Go home, like every-one else.

CLEO But I don't have a home.

COP **#2** Get a fucking job, like everyone else.

CLEO But I don't—I'm not like anyone else!

George starts to walk away. Jesus grabs him, holding him around the neck like a buddy.

JESUS Hang cool! It's all right, man, we'll work it out. *(Grabs George's arm, George resists, struggling to stay near the cops)*

GALLO GET THE FUCK OUT OF HERE!

CLEO What will I . . . *(Starts to exit, crying)*

GALLO This is not funny. We tell you to leave and ten minutes later you're back. This is the third time today. I got every shopkeeper on the street complaining that people steal their merchandise and clients. Any of you assholes here again, you're going downtown. *(Sees Anthony, still asleep inside the refrigerator box)* Oh, looky here at what Santa left us. *(Stomps on the side of the box)*

ANTHONY Hey! Stop! Fuck! Stop! *Maricon.*

GALLO Afternoon wake-up call. *(Anthony crawls out, coughing and holding his gut)* Want to sleep? Go to a hotel. MOVE IT!

Anthony limps away, exits. Jesus whispers into George's ear intimately, George struggles to get away.

GEORGE I ain't no fuckin' slave. *(Breaks free, runs to the cops)* Arrest me. I raped a Burger King manager in Baltimore.

JESUS Me too, I shot President Kennedy. *(Gallo looks at them in amused disbelief)*

GEORGE That was my store, not hers. *(Pointing toward Mozambique offstage)*

JESUS How do you get into the Police Academy? I want to become a cop.

GALLO *(Losing all patience)* FUCKING WALK! NOW! I'LL ARREST THE BOTH OF YOU!

GEORGE I ain't foolin', I did it.

JESUS He's *poquito loco*. I'll take him, officer.

GEORGE No, he's going to kill me!

JESUS *(Joking)* Yeah, I'm a convicted murderer.

GEORGE Keep the fuck away from me. *(While Jesus laughs, they struggle, finally George runs off)*

JESUS Wait up, pal. Hold on a sec—

Jesus exits. Gallo exits. All we see is the revolving crowd. We hear sirens commence and then fade. After a moment, George races back into the scene.

GEORGE I paid you. Leave me the fuck alone.

JESUS *(Enters, pursuing George)* You don't get it, I own your ass!

GEORGE Fuck you, man! I played this shit long enough. What the fuck you gonna do? *(Jesus hits him)* Beat me up, then. But you ain't going to kill me on the street for six bucks.

JESUS *(Amused)* I'm not? How come?

GEORGE You ain't that stupid.

JESUS Oh shit! You don't think I got the guts. You think this is all jive, don't you?

GEORGE I'm just saying you ain't stupid.

JESUS And that I don't have the guts. Say it!

GEORGE Look, I ain't even somebody, I'm done. I'm rubbed out. So you can't kill me, 'cause I'm not nothing. *(Raises his hands and begins to walk away)*

Jesus throws George against the wall next to the dumpster. He pulls out his knife and stabs George repeatedly in the stomach. George screams, but Jesus puts his hand over George's mouth.

JESUS Muthafucka! *Now* whose got the guts?!

GEORGE No! Help—hel—

MALE VOICE #12 What's going on here?

JESUS (*Turns, waving the bloody knife*) Come here and find out, you
    fuck.
MALE VOICE **#12** Calm down, man. It ain't my business, man.

*George tries to crawl away. Jesus shoves him behind the dumpster and
keeps stabbing him, out of view. Finally, covered in blood, Jesus runs off.
Anthony enters. George's legs still kick behind the dumpster. He tries to
lift himself up and speak, but falls back down behind the dumpster and
dies.*

ANTHONY (*Looking behind the dumpster*) Ambulancia! Ambulancia!
    Pronto, pronto!
FEMALE VOICE **#11** What's happened?
MALE VOICE **#13** What's going on there? My God, look at all the
    blood. Did he do it?
ANTHONY Not me, no. (*Nervously exits*)

*The crowd carousel stops and a din of frantic voices drown out any par-
ticular one. In the distance we hear sirens. Fade to black.*

Also available from Akashic Books

SUICIDE CASANOVA
by Arthur Nersesian
368 pages, trade paperback, $15.95

"Sick, depraved, and heartbreaking—in other words, a great read, a great book. *Suicide Casanova* is erotic noir and Nersesian's hard-boiled prose comes at you like a jailhouse confession."
—Jonathan Ames, author of *The Extra Man*

"Nersesian has written a scathingly original page-turner, hilarious, tragic, and shocking—this may be his most brilliant novel yet."
—Kate Christensen, author of *In the Drink*

"A tight, gripping, erotic thriller."
—*Philadelphia City Paper*

MANHATTAN LOVERBOY
by Arthur Nersesian
203 pages, a trade paperback original, $13.95

"Best Book for the Beach, Summer 2000."
—*Jane Magazine*

"Best Indie Novel of 2000."
—*Montreal Mirror*

"Part Lewis Carroll, part Franz Kafka, Nersesian leads us down a maze of false leads and dead ends . . . told with wit and compassion, drawing the reader into a world of paranoia and coincidence while illuminating questions of free will and destiny. Highly recommended."
—*Library Journal*

THE FUCK-UP
by Arthur Nersesian
274 pages, a trade paperback original, $20
*Original Akashic Books edition with chapter illustrations, available only through direct mail order or www.akashicbooks.com

"The charm and grit of Nersesian's voice is immediately enveloping, as the down-and-out but oddly up narrator of his terrific novel, *The Fuck-Up*, slinks through Alphabet City and guttural utterances of love."
—*Village Voice*